The Talmud states, "If a man claims he searched but did not find, do not believe him." Why? Because the essence of discovery is the search itself.

—Reb Menachem Mendel of Kotsk

Do not try to walk in the footsteps of the sages. Rather, seek what they sought.

—Basho

1

...

Rather than possess what I desire, I prefer to desire what I possess.

—Rebbe Pinchas of Koretz

Every worthwhile sin begins with thrill and trepidation, arm in arm, wary fraternal twins.

They'd arrived at Elisha's favorite part of the holiday service, when the *kohanim*, the priestly descendants of Aaron, bless the flock. He had always savored the drama of this ancient ritual, imagining himself among the throng in the Temple yard dressed in a white tunic like the Israelites he'd seen in illustrated Bibles. The other daydreamers in the small Chassidic synagogue snapped to attention as well. The private conversations scattered across the room ceased in midsentence, each talker promising to reconvene his remarks the moment the rite was over. The congregation rose in unison.

Because it is forbidden to gaze upon the priests during the benediction, the married men drew their prayer shawls over their faces, while the unshawled, not-yet-married lowered their black hats over their bent foreheads. Out on the street, the children paused their holiday game of flinging filberts against the *shul* wall and rushed inside to nestle under their fathers' outstretched *talisim*, the fringed prayer shawls now converted into private tents preventing those underneath

I

from looking out and everyone else from looking in. Elisha watched as his younger brother and his youngest sister crouched under his father's makeshift canopy, giggling and jockeying for position, his sister especially eager, knowing that in a year or two she'd be banished from the men's section during services. Even at a distance of a few feet, Elisha could smell the manly, musky scent of his father's *talis*, its coarse wool yellowed with age, the silver trim shimmering in the fluorescent light. His father gestured playfully for Elisha to join his siblings. He wished he could. For there, sheltered underneath that wool awning, his cheek flush against his father's flowing beard, Elisha felt safer than anywhere in the universe.

But he was a young man now, nearly seventeen. And so he stood apart and bowed his head like the others.

"*Kohanim,*" the cantor bellowed, summoning the priests to attention.

"*Yevorekhakha,*" they blessed in unison.

Elisha decided to peek. He'd had the urge before, a flare of mischievous curiosity that to his later relief evaporated at the last moment. But this time was different. This time he'd go through with it. It would take no more than a stretch of the neck, a glimpse so quick, so furtive, even God might miss it. Elisha scanned the room. Every shoulder was arched downward, all eyes shut or staring at the ground. Only his grandfather, the rebbe, the spiritual leader of the congregation, stood erect, one hand stiffly at his side, the other flush against the Eastern Wall.

Elisha looked up toward the ark. A row of six priests stood shoeless, their arms extended in front of their chests, the middle and ring fingers of each hand spread apart forming a V. Elisha recognized the pair of red socks. They belonged to Solly Roitman, a fractious eighteen-year-old twice arrested for shoplifting but who nevertheless qualified to bless the others by dint of his priestly lineage. Elisha noted with relief that the priests could not see him looking at them, for their vision, too, was blocked by prayer shawls draped across their faces. In this ceremony only voices connect the blessers with the blessed.

A fleeting glimpse, a fleeting eternal moment. What he'd observed didn't matter; that he'd observed mattered momentously. A shudder sprinted down his spine. True, this was a minor infraction, a trifle really, but he was a Chassid, was he not? A Jew who embraced the yoke of the Torah and every iota of its laws? Why then this itch to transgress? How deep did it run? Elisha brought his hand up to his *payis*, the sidecurls adorning his cheeks, reassuring himself his face hadn't mutated into the face of a sinner.

In his periphery, Elisha detected a head move. He turned to see his uncle Shaya staring straight at him. Catching Elisha's eyes, his uncle smiled and nodded, a slow, telling nod, then, calm and unhurried, turned to observe the priests.

Elisha answered the final amen, extended holiday greetings to his father and grandfather, and made his way to join the after-prayers chatter on the street. Knots of women were displaying their holiday finery and, with equally feigned nonchalance, their soon-marriageable daughters. Men huddled in threes and fours, some trading news of the latest business ventures in Boro Park, their blossoming Brooklyn Jewish enclave, others offering President Nixon advice on how to outsmart Ho Chi Minh. The adult conversations were regularly interrupted by the whoops of pre-bar mitzvah boys pitching Spaldeen balls against the stoop of the building next door. Elisha stopped to eavesdrop on a debate between two rabbis on the current blazing issue in Jewish law: the permissibility of artificial insemination. A few shy yeshiva students clustered close by, confused and fascinated by the subject's unspoken premises.

But for Elisha's friends gathered across the street, the reigning topic was neither global affairs nor Jewish law but the previous night's opening World Series game. Their somber appearance meant Zanvel's report could not be good. Zanvel—even the children called him by his first name—was the synagogue's inexplicable source for baseball scores on holidays when turning on a radio was forbidden; how he came by his impeccable information was an enduring mystery, another conundrum of those select European Chassidim who arrived to America's shores with prepackaged maps of its ways and means.

Zanvel welcomed Elisha with a hard slap on the back. "Nu, boychik, so what do you have to say? Your Mets, these new bums of ours, lost four to one." Zanvel reported the dismal details between rolling wheezes and a timpanist thumping on his chest. "I guess you'll have to pray harder," he said, wagging his finger at each of the boys.

They chortled in response, dismissing the profanity of petitioning the Lord of the Universe to assist their beloved baseball team, but knowing they'd indeed sneak in hurried appeals for the great cause. After all, this was a year for miracles—two months earlier men had walked on the moon. Elisha and his friends lifted the brims of their hats and set about devising the ideal lineup for the next day's game. No one noticed Uncle Shaya walking toward them.

"Elisha," Uncle Shaya roared, though addressing them all. "I have a riddle for you about stealing looks at the priests during the blessing."

"Please, don't," Elisha implored silently. "Don't humiliate me…turn my feeble mischief into a piece of comedy." He bit on his lower lip, not knowing what to expect. His uncle was never predictable.

"Now think carefully," Uncle Shaya said, his voice, like his body, capacious and demanding. "Suppose the first time you peek at the priests, your right eye goes blind. And the second time you glance at them, you lose sight in your left eye. What happens the third time you peek?"

"Oh, c'mon, that's too easy," Elisha answered immediately, astonished no one else noticed the obvious trick.

"Well?"

"You can't look a third time 'cause you're already blind."

Elisha exhaled, relieved. His uncle was teasing, but reassuring him, too: their transgression would remain their private secret.

"True, that *was* too simple," Uncle Shaya agreed. "But I'll get you next time. Catch you when you least expect it."

"Or I'll catch you," Elisha said with a modest laugh.

"And maybe you will," Uncle Shaya said, beginning, then stifling a grin. He said nothing for a moment or two, his thoughts elsewhere, before focusing again on his nephew. "Ah, yes, I was to ask if you could babysit for us tomorrow night."

Elisha was delighted. He could use the money and the few hours of privacy. But mostly he was eager to return to the marvelous discovery he'd stumbled upon the last time he babysat at his uncle's house.

As was everyone in Elisha's extended and extensive family, Uncle Shaya was a scion of Chassidic rebbes. But even as a child, Elisha sensed Uncle Shaya was unlike the others. How else explain his family's bewildered sighs when Uncle Shaya left the room? Only Elisha's father greeted his brother-in-law with transparent glee. The two would emerge from his father's study hours later, leaving behind a sandstorm of dust above the piles of rabbinical tomes that blanketed every available surface. They'd discharge each other with the backs of their hands, one clucking, "Ah, you can't follow a simple line of commentary," the other responding, "And you confuse an argument with an oozing from the belly," the mutual admiration apparent on both their faces.

In addition to being an uncle by marriage, Uncle Shaya was also related to Elisha through multiple strands of ancestors. From the earliest years of Chassidism's founding in the mid-eighteenth century, the grandchildren of the movement's leaders wed only other Chassidic bluebloods forming a Mobius maze of intersecting links; Elisha's own parents were twice second cousins and third cousins four times over. Elisha tried to pay attention when his cousins sat at the Sabbath table and untangled their twisted pedigree, but soon wearied of the countless intricacies; knowing the names of the major Chassidic dynasties from whom he descended would have to do. Uncle Shaya rarely joined these excavations either, preferring to sequester himself in the living room with a page of Talmud.

He was no less devoted to the pages of secular writings. In his teeming attaché case, a recent novel or book of history always shared space with a sacred text. It was his wardrobe, however, that emphatically proclaimed his dual life. Shifting sartorial choices were commonplace in the immediate postwar years of Chassidic reinvention in America—Elisha's immigrant family, loosened links in their golden chain of tradition, oscillated between the dark religious uniforms of their pre-Holocaust youth and the bright styles of the New World; but when the pendulum came to rest decades later, only a few remained with their modern dress.

Uncle Shaya, on the other hand, simultaneously maintained both looks and outlooks. On the Sabbath and holidays, he wore a *bekeshe*, the black silk robe of the Chassidim; on weekdays he dressed in fashionable suits from Brooks Brothers, his shirts crisp, monogrammed affairs, the ties designer labeled, and his shoes Bally only, "because," he explained, "I stand on my feet all day whatever the day." He trimmed his beard for protean effect, serving both as an element of pious garb and as a rakish tint to his au courant attire. You couldn't help but wonder if he felt comfortable in both guises, or neither.

"Good timing," Aunt Malka said to the appearance of Elisha in the mirror. "Uncle Shaya's in the car reading." She didn't turn around but continued to adjust her *sheitl*, the wig worn by all Chassidic women after marriage. "He's been out there for ten minutes. No patience, that man."

Elisha took a few steps into the living room, eager for his aunt to leave as well.

"See how easy it is to be a blond," Aunt Malka said, without enthusiasm.

"It suits you well." Elisha couldn't decide if this was true. He wondered what his own mother looked like under her wig; he hadn't seen her natural hair since he was a child.

"You should have an easy night," Aunt Malka said, still positioning her hairpiece, "Lei'la is fast asleep. And Yankel any minute now."

"It'll be fine," he said.

"The wedding's in Williamsburg," his aunt said, finally buttoning her coat. "A young Chassidic woman I work with. I call her a woman? She turned eighteen two weeks ago. Crazy if you ask me, but that's how it is these days. Like back in Europe. A charming girl, though. And very religious. I'm sure there will be a mammoth *mechitzha*, a ten foot wall of flowers separating the men and women."

Elisha agreed. "The rules get stricter by the minute, don't they?" To avoid further discussion of the matter, he busied himself with an orange from the full fruit bowl.

Five minutes after his aunt waved good night, Elisha tiptoed to the back of the house, confirmed the children were asleep, and then hurried to the living room. He stood in front of the breakfront covering three quarters of the wall, a mainstay fixture in every Boro Park home. On display were the requisite silver candelabra, engraved Kiddush cups, and a turret spice box. A mélange of crystal miniatures crowded a silver tray.

The top shelf featured a gold-framed wedding photograph bracketed by pictures from the old country. Elisha took them down for a closer look. One was of Aunt Malka, a beaming teenager with auburn hair flowing down her back, flanked by her older brother, Elisha's father, and their three younger siblings. He studied the three younger children, two girls with identical chestnut eyes and the boy between them with small, grim eyes and thick sidelocks. The two girls, the aunts Elisha would never know, perished in Auschwitz; the boy was murdered elsewhere—there was some awful, never fully revealed story associated with his death. Elisha's younger brother Avrumy—Avruhum

9

Yitzchak—was named for this child and Aunt Malka's Lei'la, for one of the girls, Leah Shprintza. Chassidic newborns received two or three names in memory of their dead kin, but there were hardly enough to commemorate all the murdered souls. Elisha took peculiar solace in being named after dead adults rather than dead infants: Elisha, for his father's father who'd managed to escape to the Russian side of Poland only to be sent to Samarkand where he died in a typhus epidemic, and Shimon, his middle name, after his mother's aged grandfather who died in the Lodz ghetto.

Elisha turned to the second photograph. Uncle Shaya was the fourth in a row of six children, easily recognizable by the keen, narrow eyes, and the heavy eyelids drooping at the outer corners. The boy is clearly unhappy sitting for this family portrait and tilts his head to the side, away from the camera. Directly behind him, severe and suspicious, his mother grips the child's neck, trying to turn him to face forward.

Elisha returned the photographs to the shelf and surveyed the books that flanked the breakfront. On one side were the indispensable sacred texts, the Pentateuch with commentaries, a sixteen-volume set of the Talmud and the Code of Maimonides. On the other side, in this divided universe, stood the secular books: *Marjorie Morningstar, Dr. Zhivago, Gone with the Wind, Only in America, The Rise and Fall of the Third Reich,* and an adventure saga, *Kon Tiki,* the only one of these books he'd read.

Elisha figured he'd waited long enough, had demonstrated sufficient restraint, and began rummaging behind a row of journals on the lowest shelf. He soon found what he sought: the book he'd carefully replaced there three weeks earlier. He brushed his hand over the austere brown cover and peculiar title: *Tropic of Cancer*. The subtitle, *Unexpurgated Edition*, declared this was not a textbook on the northern latitudes.

A seventeen-year-old boy's body has its inventory of curiosities and in these bewitching pages Elisha found redress. Awaiting him was no mere stolen glance at the rifled pages of *Playboy* at the corner candy store, no hurried fantasies provoked by the crudely drawn graffiti at the 50th Street subway station or more vividly by the Italian girls from New Utrecht High School who were gloriously oblivious to the strictures of female modesty. Here, down the seedy side streets of Miller's Paris, he'd meet the vagrants and whores who boozed and sexed unabashed and undiluted. It was all so unfathomable, all so wonderfully impermissible. Elisha stretched out on the carpet; his imagination fired beyond imagination. Who knew one could also read with one's skin?

He didn't hear Uncle Shaya enter the room.

"Interesting book, isn't it?" His uncle flashed the same conspiratorial grin as he had that morning in shul.

Elisha, flustered, rose quickly to his feet. "I didn't hear you come in."

Uncle Shaya squinted at him with one eye.

Elisha said, "I was browsing through your collection and found…"

"Yes?"

"It's…uh…rather explicit." Elisha was certain he was blushing, his attempt at indifference futile.

"Explicit? But you need to see beyond that."

Uncle Shaya took the book from Elisha's twitching fingers and held it in the air. "Most people, including Aunt Malka with her social-work degree and all, only notice the sex, nothing wrong with that either, mind you. Ah, labels. Mental straightjacket is what they are."

Elisha shrugged, unsure what to say.

"A dirty book, they call it," Uncle Shaya said, angling his bulky frame into the cubic easy chair across from where Elisha stood. "The holy Baal Shem Tov often reminded his students, 'Even a holy body is still a body.'" He rifled through the book's pages, a sentence here and there catching his attention. "These characters are so visceral, aren't they?"

Uncle Shaya spoke English with a distinctive Eastern European accent, not that Elisha knew what *visceral* meant, even had his uncle not pronounced it *wisceral,* but his intonation was eerily similar to Elisha's favorite teacher going on about Hawthorne.

With a single deft move, Uncle Shaya removed a Pall Mall from the left pocket of his jacket and a gold lighter from the lower right pocket of his vest, all the while talking, warming to his lecture. Did Elisha know anything about the expatriate American writers in Paris? Had he read Hemingway? Dostoevsky at least? "Young man, rely on your teachers and you'll learn nothing."

"Actually, my English teacher has us reading American short stories and—"

"Yes, yes, good," Uncle Shaya said, absentmindedly brushing his hand against the sober tweedy fabric of his chair, an emphatic foil to the adjoining chintz couch protected in transparent plastic. This was clearly his chair, his choice. He crossed his legs, fixed his gaze on some object in distant space, and drew the final drags from the butt of his cigarette.

"Time to go," he announced with a start as if waking from a decade-long slumber. "Return I must to a table of dull men telling dull stories about their dull lives. I came back here because I forgot my checkbook, a good excuse to escape for a while but which, now that I think of it, I've almost forgotten again. But the point is, Elisha, you can read anything. Never mind what they say. Anything. Everything. How else can a person live more than one life?" He handed the Miller book back to Elisha. "Unfortunately, I don't suppose I could lend you this."

"I suppose not," Elisha said. He knew exactly where he'd hide the book.

Uncle Shaya registered his nephew's disappointment. "Sorry," he said, "but you know we'd both get into trouble."

When he reached the door, Uncle Shaya swiveled on his heels. "One more thing. We—and by *we*, I mean especially us Jews—forget life isn't only lived in one's head."

"I'll bear it in mind. And in body as well," Elisha said, garnering a hearty chuckle from his uncle.

Enticement crumbles on the shoals of permission. Henry Miller was now literature. Was this a promotion or demotion? Elisha returned the book to its secluded home behind the row of *Physical Reviews* and five offsets of "On a Harmonically Pulsating Source Panel Method for Subsonic Flow" by Dr. Shaya Rabinowitz.

In Elisha's Eastern-European Jewish tribe, brilliance spreads a forgiving cloak on many sins. While other talents win points—a faculty for drawing, say, or oratory, certainly business acumen—nothing, not even an aptitude for piety, is on par with mental prowess. Chess produces prodigies and accompanying esteem (Elisha could name a half-dozen people who claimed to have drawn a game with the Orthodox grandmaster Samuel Reshevsky); music has its geniuses (Heifetz, albeit assimilated, was nobility in Elisha's mother's hierarchy of veneration); so, too, do math and the sciences (untainted and admirably rigorous); and, of course, Talmud, the royalty of both cerebration and sacred learning. Uncle Shaya's combined expertise in Torah and astrophysics was a throwback to the legendary Torah scholar/scientist of the Middle Ages, a breed that had expired in modern times. But this was America, where all sorts of hybrids were in formation.

And so Elisha, born and raised in burgeoning Brooklyn, USA, asked his uncle Shaya, born and raised in the hamlet of Zmigrod, Poland, to teach him about America. Reveal its gifts, unfold the possibilities. Elisha was an eager student, and his uncle feasted on the challenge.

It would not be easy. The city (as everyone from the boroughs referred to Manhattan) had been forbidding territory to Elisha, as foreign as Bucharest or Istanbul. On those rare trips there—an annual childhood pilgrimage to the Barnum and Bailey Circus during the Passover school break, a consultation with an orthodontist, an excursion to the diamond center on 47th Street—he'd marvel at the assortment of people scrambling along the crowded streets, self-conscious of his own contribution to the pageant, a startled boy with sidecurls tucked behind his ears wearing an oversized black hat even during a summer sizzle.

He cut an even more bizarre figure now: a gangly, young Chassid transfixed by a Cezanne fruit dish at the Museum of Modern Art, the fugitive junior rabbi in the balcony at the Philharmonic enraptured by the Mozart concerto. How did he appear, he wondered, this unlikely fellow trolling the shelves of East Side bookstores, eyeing the baubles of Madison Avenue with his new books clasped under his arm? But Elisha ignored the curious gapes. He was, after all, but another passing patch in New York's crazy quilt, another odd sighting in this metropolis of anonymity where no one was a stranger because everyone was.

On occasion, he managed to inveigle one of his more puckish friends to join him on one of these expeditions, but most often he preferred to go alone. He'd eagerly report to his uncle after each sortie, and his uncle responded with a fresh assignment. There were limits, of course. Uncle Shaya wished he could send his nephew to see a film by Fellini or Bergmann, "But recommending a movie would be crossing a line with your father. I'm not sure he trusts me to remain within bounds. He does trust you."

"I know that," said Elisha, but for the first time the thought crossed his mind that perhaps it was a trust he didn't deserve.

One adventure had Elisha attend a lecture on religion at Columbia University. This was the first time he'd visited a college campus and Elisha was struck by the majesty, almost a sacredness, of the imposing buildings engraved with the names of history's great thinkers. More surprisingly, the students seemed earnest and thoughtful, not at all resembling the "frivolous sex/drug-crazed youth" he'd been warned about in yeshiva. Nevertheless, said Elisha to his uncle, the experience had been unsettling.

"Not too many Chassidim around, I bet."

It wasn't that. It was the lecture itself that made him uncomfortable. He'd never heard the Bible explained with references to ancient Sumerian myths and linguistic evidence from the Ugaritic, Syriac, and other Semitic languages. He was lost. But what perturbed him most was the question and answer period, people showing off, standing up to make their own little speeches. Not at all like yeshiva.

"What about you?"

"I didn't say anything."

"No, I mean college."

"Me? Go to college?

"Why not?"

"It's an idea, I guess," Elisha said, reflecting.

"You'd do well."

"Maybe. I finish high school this year and then, of course, I'll study Torah full-time for a year or two. But afterward? You never know."

"Your father would be open to the idea."

"You think?"

"I think."

2

.....

For the one who believes in the Creator's goodness, there are no questions; for the one who does not believe, there are no answers.

—Rebbe Yaakov of Radzine

The rains rolled in this autumnal night in a monsoon rage. Even the hearty few who dared venture out onto the New York streets, their arms tight against their chests and backs curved like question marks, soon yielded to the tempest and scurried underneath overhanging doorways and battered scaffolds. Rats joined cats to shelter below the car hoods. A nasty night for all.

Elisha pushed up his sleeve and looked at his watch. It was past eleven. The sign above the teller's booth at the City College subway station was unequivocal: FLOODING. CLOSED. The man at the window shook his head, forestalling any appeal. Try the bus to 125th Street, he advised.

Elisha surveyed the deserted avenue, the protruding spoke of his tattered umbrella nearly poking him in the eye. Not a vehicle in sight. He lifted his collar and began the twelve-block journey down Broadway, Harlem's grand boulevard turned dark and nebulous in the egalitarian downpour.

For a year and a half after high school, Elisha had been the paradigmatic yeshiva student. He sat in the study hall ten hours a day, honing his skill at Talmudic analysis. He'd arrive early for daily prayers, meticulously fulfilling the religious commands of the hour and season. His teachers had no doubt that with his talent and pedigree, Elisha was destined for a role of rabbinic leadership in the community.

But they did not see him in the late night, in the privacy of his room, where other possibilities were proposed. Elisha had not stopped thinking of the restless New York precincts he'd walked before, still eager to taste their contemporary offerings. When the hour turned late and his door closed, he fed his curiosity. He read quickly and he read often: Burroughs and Bellow, Hesse and Hemingway, biographies of medieval Jewish thinkers and biographies of his own century's statesmen and villains. An unheralded interest in cosmology and the Big Bang controversy lasted for months while the box set of great violin concerti played in the background until the Victrola collapsed from exhaustion. And one stirring evening, Elisha sat in the back row of the Film Forum for a screening of Fellini's recently released *Roma*.

He'd begun college the previous winter term, enrolling for two classes two nights a week, a slow wade into unfamiliar waters. All these intellectual expeditions to the secular would help prepare him for the university's disciplines but not for its freedoms. He'd be a stranger in a very strange land. He sat in the back of the classroom, attentive but quiet, self-conscious of his black velvet yarmulke and sidecurls neatly combed around his ears. He roamed through the college catalogue, wishing he could explore half the courses listed, and registered for three nights, three classes for the fall semester. And earlier that week in his anthropology class, he resolved to come out of his dark-garbed shadows. He had questions to ask about the distant cultures he'd studied, thoughts to share about why they were not so distant after all. In his briefcase, this wet evening, he carried two unassigned books on the rituals of sub-Saharan tribes.

This was the second time that week he'd come home from college at midnight, an ungodly hour for a godly yeshiva boy. Once again, he'd been sifting through anthropology books in the college library and the hours had slithered away without so much as a touch on his shoulder.

The girl was there too. She sat on the same chair at the same table as the last time, scrawling in her notebook, unconsciously brushing away the strands of long sandy-blond hair that licked the page. Elisha had positioned himself behind a space along the bookshelves where he could view her without obstruction. But his reconnaissance had come to an abrupt halt when, bending too low, his head crashed against a shelf and his hat spun to an open area on the floor.

"You okay?" the girl asked, as he rushed to retrieve the black fedora.

"I'm f-fine," he stammered. "My hat b-b-bumped into—"

"Yes, it's dangerous getting intimate with those books." Her smile revealed a deep dimple in one cheek.

Elisha blanched, certain she'd observed him observing her.

She pointed to the dusky bay window. "'It was a dark and stormy night.'"

"Yes, it's raining hard," he'd replied stupidly, discomforted by the odd inflection in her voice (and only now realizing she must have been quoting something or other). Elisha had grabbed his hat and retreated into the stacks like a servant caught mingling with the guests in the parlor. When he'd emerged twenty minutes later, the girl was gone. His reaction surprised him—a disappointment tinged with a sweet elation he'd never felt before.

Elisha was thinking of the girl as he trudged down Broadway, thinking how she resembled the woman in the Pepsi poster at the subway station, only prettier, with softer skin and more intelligent eyes. He didn't notice the two black men walking toward him. One swigged a bottle from a wet bag and passed it to the other who somehow managed to take a chug without letting go of the piece of plastic over their heads. Elisha buried his face into his coat like a child who believes he becomes invisible by shrouding his eyes.

Back home they'd warned him about the dangers of this jungle where no white person not bent on suicide dare trespass. "True City College was once 'the poor man's Harvard,'" they lamented, "a haven for smart Jewish kids excluded from the Ivy leagues. But these days? What sane young person chooses to go there? Especially a young man dressed like a Chassid."

The two men were now ten yards away and walking directly in Elisha's path. He felt for his wallet.

"What you doin' out here?" said one of them as they blocked his way. He was older than Elisha had expected, well into his middle-age. "Don't you think ain't nobody should be walkin' round in weather like this?"

"Neither should we be," said the younger man. "But what's this rabbi doing here on these streets?"

A good question, Elisha thought. The question lots of people he knew were asking.

The older man moved in toward Elisha. "I didn't hear your answer, Mr. Rabbi."

"I said, yes, I agree. I shouldn't be walking around here."

Elisha tightened his grip on the umbrella. He'd been confronted physically before. School yard invasions by young Italian hordes from neighboring Bensonhurst were an annual rite of summer in Boro Park. The largest of the marauders would push his body against the tiniest of the Yeshiva boys: "You troo playin' here aren't you Jewboy?" and the cowered Jewboys would truckle home, minus their court, basketball, and a bicycle or two. But the dread wringing Elisha's intestines was something new. He swallowed hard to stifle the vomit inching up his throat.

The younger of the two men circled behind Elisha. "Torrential rains this evening," he said, mimicking the clipped delivery of a radio weatherman. "Don't you agree,

Snow White? But this ain't no white snow. We are having ourselves a black blizzard."

"A black blizzard," the older man repeated and laughed hard. He withdrew the bottle from the bag and offered it to Elisha. "You're shivering," he said. "This'll warm up your inners."

Elisha declined politely. They let him walk on.

But he ran, nonetheless, finding refuge in the nearest storefront. In the window display, mannequins were decked in tie-dyed shirts and rainbow striped pants, the conspicuous uniform of his conspicuous generation. Could he even masquerade in these clothes? Between the wet streaks on the glass, he discerned the soaked collar of his white shirt peeking out from his black suit. He inspected the sidecurls twined over his ears. Hadn't this become a masquerade, too? He knew what he must do. He knew what he would do. It is inevitable, he told himself, to calm the tremor erupting in his chest. He shut his eyes and felt the gale lash his face.

He'd assured his father college would not change him, but it had. The submerged doubts of his high school years were now unrelenting. These past months he peppered his father with questions about religious belief and the authenticity of Jewish tradition and, as always, his father gave him wide berth for his interrogations, a freedom of inquiry his teachers would never have allowed. But even his father had his limits, and Elisha was careful to couch his challenges within those borders. And it was on those borders that Elisha increasingly found himself standing.

The next shabbos in shul, Elisha looked at the one question that puzzled him most: his uncle Shaya. What did his uncle truly believe? How could he speak with such ardor about Holy Scripture and, a paragraph later, hold forth with equal zeal about literature and science? He'd heard his uncle rail against the uncritical pronouncements of these zealous Jews around them, but there he was, draped this Sabbath morning as every Sabbath morning in his king-size talis, praying with the fervor of a saintly Chassid? Elisha watched his uncle sway his shoulders side to side as he sang along with the cantor. His uncle was an enigma all right, and solving that enigma was, Elisha sensed, somehow connected to solving his own future.

"Your uncle fascinates you, doesn't he?" said Reb Sender to Elisha. "You keep looking in his direction."

Reb Sender was a Talmudic scholar who'd been a member of a rabbinic court before the war and wore a longish, rectangular beard that ended in a perfectly straight horizontal line. But he preferred talking to people than to God, and so he sat at Elisha's table in the rear of the shteibl, the Chassidic one-room shul. For gathered at that table were the schmoozers, the untamable, irreverent characters who always knew more than anyone about everything. Elisha had grown up listening to them argue constantly with the world and each other about religion, politics, and the stock market and learned to shift his moods along with them as each week they retold their tales of human corruption and human compassion. Elisha's father periodically asked him to move to more decorous surroundings, but like a stray cat who knows where its abdomen is best tickled, Elisha always found his way back to his home base.

"Your uncle has an *eizene kop*, no question," Reb Sender said, using the Yiddish metallurgic idiom of steel to describe a luminous mind. "But listen to me. How he lives is not for everyone. Jews in America think they can live in two worlds. In the long run, it can't be done."

"It's worth a try," Elisha said.

"I've got news for you, young man," Reb Sender replied, applying his own avuncular squeeze of Elisha's neck. "The next world? Paradise? Maybe you'll achieve it, maybe not. That depends on you. But this world? Forget it. You'll never fully enjoy it."

"Why not? What's wrong with me?"

Reb Sender squeezed Elisha's bicep this time. "You're a grandchild of Chassidic rebbes from both your father's and mother's side, an heir of the Holy Masters of Chernobyl, Belz, Ger, and Ropczyc. For you, there'll always be too much guilt."

The names of these dynasties had always loomed like majestic empires to Elisha, though they traced to East European villages with populations smaller than a Brooklyn apartment house. Being a descendant of these foremost Chassidic rabbis was his pride, but also his burden.

His hand still gripping Elisha's arm, Reb Sender said, "Believe you me, it's not worth the effort."

Elisha offered a halfhearted, polite nod. But what did these men know, these tired men with their patches of scars from the other side of the ocean, from the other side of history? The streets of their youth were gated and locked, but this is America, where the avenues are everyone's playground. Here we run the bases with yarmulkes on our heads.

Elisha looked over again to his Uncle Shaya. He sat along the Eastern Wall with the shteibl's elite, the affluent, the learned, and the pedigreed. Elisha's father sat at that table as well, welcomed too for his scholarship and genealogy, certainly not his wealth.

"I know, I know," Reb Sender said. "Your uncle takes all those fancy shmancy flights to Washington, meets with fancy shmancy scientists and government hotshots, but, let me tell you, even in those expensive shoes he still walks the dusty roads of the shtetl. That's home for him. You can't really escape it. None of us can."

None of us? The words still jangled in Elisha's ears at the end of services when he noticed his father beckoning him to his table. The rapt attention of the men gathered near him was a sure sign his father had begun to tell them a tale. His father carried a trove of Chassidic legends in his pocket the way others carried sticks of gum, always ready to dispense a story or anecdote as the occasion demanded; Elisha was usually his most eager audience.

"Come join us," his father called to Elisha.

Elisha took a few further hesitant steps in his father's direction, but remained standing several feet away from the others.

Elisha's father gathered his beard in his fist, shook his head in disappointment, and turned to the others. "This anecdote comes from the earliest years of Chassidism." He shot another look at Elisha. "It's about the importance of passion. Warm passion versus cold reason."

As you all know, from its inception, most Torah scholars were deeply disturbed by the Baal Shem Tov and his new Chassidic movement especially when it began to find such popular reception across Russia and Eastern Europe. They deemed its success a serious challenge to Jewish tradition.

The rabbis were especially troubled when Chassidim insisted it wasn't only Torah scholars who deserve veneration, for even the simplest Jew could attain the loftiest spiritual heights. They were discomforted by Chassidism's attention to storytelling, to music and dancing, the emphasis on joy rather than fear as the best way to serve God. They belittled the role of the Chassidic rebbe, the tzaddik who leads his followers on their spiritual journey. And they were upset, too, with the new siddur, the Chassidic prayer book that incorporated the mysticism of Kabbalah into the traditional service.

Well, it seems one of these prayer books found its way into the study hall where Rabbi David Saul Katznelenbogen and Rabbi Yaakov Yosef of Polania were meeting. The two Talmudic giant scholars of their generation were also among the most vehement enemies of Chassidism. When Rabbi Yaakov Yosef noticed the sinful prayer book he flung it to the floor.

"Heresy!" he cried in a fury.

Rabbi Katznelenbogen, on the other hand, rushed to pick up the siddur. "Nevertheless," he said, "the text contains sacred words and must not remain on the ground."

When they conveyed this episode to the Baal Shem Tov, he said, "The rabbi who picked up the siddur? Him I have no hope for. He is a captive of rules. He will never become a Chassid. But the other rabbi? The one who hurled the siddur in a rage? That one has fervor. That man has the soul of a Chassid."

Sometime later, so the legend goes, the Baal Shem Tov came to speak in the town of Sharograd where Rabbi Yaakov Yosef was the presiding rabbi. The crowd was mesmerized by the Baal Shem Tov's storytelling and failed to notice they were late for services. Outraged, Rabbi Yaakov Yosef rushed to confront the upstart. But he, too, was captivated by the tzaddik's storytelling and remained listening. Soon thereafter, Rabbi Yaakov Yosef, renowned as much for his ardor as his great scholarship, became, as we all know, the Baal Shem Tov's foremost disciple.

Elisha could feel his father's eyes on him as he walked out alone to the street. He recalled a remark his father had once quoted from Reb Dov Ber of Lubavitch: "You need to be wise to tell a story well, but you need to be even wiser to hear a story well." He knew his father had intended the tale for him, but it was becoming increasingly difficult to hear his father's stories well when other, competing stories demanded his attention.

3

.....

No man can simultaneously serve two different desires.

—Tzvi Elimelech of Dynav

"What's that you got in there, *mon ami*?" the girl on the window ledge called to Elisha.

A flutter of excitement rushed through him again just as it did the past few times they'd greeted each other in the library.

At first he'd managed only acknowledging smiles, but the last time a paragraph's worth of sentences. She'd told him she liked working in that section of the library, surrounded by descriptions of different human lives. It reminded her, she said, not to celebrate her own choices too quickly. He felt the same, he had said, and told her about the book he was reading. And later he'd review every word of their exchange: how banal he must have sounded, how uncomfortable he must have seemed.

"Yes, it's me," she said and picked up the case beside her. "Show me yours, and I'll show you mine."

"A clarinet," Elisha said, ignorant of the commonplace connotation. "I'm a beginner, a real beginner. I've just begun lessons a few months ago. And you have—"

"A flute. I flaunt the inner flautist. I am the flute girl at the Greek symposium. The maiden of the upper registers. And I never asked you your name."

"My name?"

"You do have one."

"It's Elisha."

"Elisha," she repeated. "That's a new one."

"I've had it all my life."

"Mine is Katrina, by the way, in case you meant to ask."

"Sorry."

"It's okay. Katrina Nelson. Sometimes I think I should change it to something a bit more exotic like yours."

She sat with her legs tucked beneath a billowing, chartreuse skirt, her T-shirt emblazoned with a drawing of Mickey Mouse and Minnie Mouse in passionate embrace. Her pink sneakers were laced with iridescent green shoelaces. Elisha sneaked glances at her marine-blue eyes before turning his gaze to the sides, to the floor, to the window behind her, then back to her face.

"Tell me about those curls behind your ears," Katrina said, easing herself up against the back wall. "If you don't mind me being so brazen."

"The earlocks are a religious thing."

"Earlocks?" Katrina burst into laughter. "I'm sorry. But I must tell you, that is a truly funny image."

"I suppose it is," Elisha agreed.

"They're kind of cool though. Sorta like spit curls."

"Spit curls isn't much better than earlocks."

"No," Katrina agreed, "come to think of it. Disgusting, actually."

"They're also called sidelocks," Elisha said. "And I've heard them referred to as sidecurls."

"What do you call them?"

Elisha hesitated. Why this discussion about his attire? "*Payis*. It's a Hebrew word."

"And the reason for them?"

"The word means corner. There's a Biblical prohibition in Leviticus against cutting the edges of the beard, cutting the hair on the side of the face. Something like that...I'm translating."

"Oh, you're Jewish," Katrina exclaimed in mock astonishment.

A shaft of twilight sifted through the glass beads that trickled through Katrina's hair like birthday streamers, bestowing an otherworldly glimmer on her skin. Elisha watched the contours of her mouth form words in her full lips; she didn't so much speak sentences as cast them into the stratosphere, where they floated like low flying kites.

She told him that she'd parachuted a year earlier to the hallways of CCNY from Racine, Wisconsin, a place on earth that sounded to Elisha as exotic as the Indonesian cliffs and the Peloponnesian villages he'd been reading about in his class. Elisha had never studied a woman's face this closely before and longed to lean nearer still, but the intermittent shadows that passed over her cheeks reminded him they were not alone.

Katrina said, "You don't have to stand, you know. You look like a nervous commuter waiting for a train. Plus you're wasting precious shoe sole. Come sit next to me."

But Elisha remained standing while she told him about *Anna Karenina*, the book she was reading when he walked by.

She was a comparative literature major, to the chagrin of others who had different expectations for her. Elisha said he, too, intended to switch from engineering to a more conceptual subject, one that dealt with human lives. She pointed to her flute—what did Elisha think of Vivaldi? She was working on one of his flute compositions. Elisha was unfamiliar with the composer, but someone had introduced him recently to John Coltrane. Had she heard his music? Their conversation drifted to their high school education which, they agreed, was largely a waste of time. He asked her what she thought of her current classes. What she thought about New York. The war in Vietnam. One question followed another. But what he really wanted to ask was whether they could continue talking like this forever. He was astonished and proud at how at ease he felt.

Elisha could recollect only two previous conversations with girls outside his family. One lasted no more than ten minutes, on the subway with Solly and two girls from Midwood High School, both in orange shorts and orange halters, on their way to Bay 3 in Brighton. Solly did almost all the talking, tossing leering asides about his adept breaststroke. Elisha was relieved when the train reached his stop.

His other exchange was briefer though more memorable. She was the daughter of his parents' friends, an extraordinarily tall girl, with curly red hair, freckles, and braces, her face framed by purple glasses, and whose name he never managed to summon, Suri or Shoshi, or Shana.

Because Elisha's yeshiva shared a bus stop with a girls' yeshiva, the schools' administrators scheduled arrivals and departures to ensure pants never mingled with skirts. But one afternoon, Elisha left school early and the two family friends exchanged chitchat. A voice boomed behind him.

"Is that your sister?"

Elisha whirled around. Rabbi Eiderov, the assistant principal, was poking the tip of his umbrella into the ground, a cudgel he carried even on sunny days. The rabbi had been thoroughly secular until his early twenties when, for reasons obscure though rumored to involve a drug problem, he'd discovered his grandparents' Judaism, became observant, then ultra-observant, then Chassidic, and, ultimately, ultra-Chassidic, an obsessive trajectory propelling him to greater piety than even the Heavenly Host Himself.

"I asked you a question," Rabbi Eiderov said, continuing to jackhammer the umbrella into the sidewalk. He walked up to Elisha and scrunched his eyebrows, causing islands of black dots to converge around his bulbous nose.

"Is…that…your…sister?" he repeated, enunciating each syllable as though reading out an arrest warrant.

"No," Elisha recoiled. The old Puerto Rican woman waiting with them picked up her bag and took a few fearful steps backward; the two Italian ladies came closer in for a better view. The tall girl had quickly vanished like a cloud of breath on a winter's day.

"You degrade the yeshiva," Rabbi Eiderov shouted, oblivious to the astonished bystanders or not caring what they thought. "And you, a Chassidische young man, degrade yourself. Talking to girls. In public."

"Is talking in private better?" Elisha said, as a bus pulled up.

"Chutzpah, too?" the Rabbi squeaked at his back. "You'd better change your attitude, young man."

He'd certainly changed his attitude, thought Elisha, a half smile crossing his face as he imagined how Rabbi Eiderov would react to him now, standing in a college hallway, enthralled by a non-Jewish girl wearing pink sneakers sitting on a ledge.

"What's flitting across your mind, young man?" Katrina asked. "Do share the joke with the rest of the class."

"Sorry. Old memories. Strange juxtapositions."

"Well, speaking of old memories, tell me more about these dark clothes you wear. This world you're from."

Elisha flinched. He didn't want to be tugged back home.

"I don't mean to pry," Katrina said. "But I see these men on the subway in their black coats and black hats and black glasses—do they all wear glasses?—their noses always in their books, and they have those curls on their sides like you do."

"They're called—we're called—Chassidim."

"Well, I see dem, too—but who are they?"

Elisha laughed, catching the twinkle in her eyes. "They are who they are."

"And the language they—"

"Yiddish."

"Do you speak it?"

"It's my mother tongue. My father's, too, going back centuries. Thirty years ago, back in the 1930s, Yiddish was the first language of more than twelve million people." Elisha repeated the number, twelve million, and winced.

"The Holocaust," Katrina said, quietly.

"Wiped out."

"How many speak it now?"

"I don't know. Some Jews in Russia. In Argentina, Belgium, a few other places. But mostly Chassidim here and in Israel. In a couple of decades, though, it'll only be Chassidim who'll keep Yiddish alive."

"That's unfortunate."

"It is. I love that language."

"Tell me about them," Katrina said. "The Chassidim."

Elisha shook his head. "It's a long story. Maybe some other time."

"The short version, then. Please. I'm curious about them…about you." She looked for Elisha's eyes; her own, sympathetic and intent.

"Really, it's too complicated." He looked away, embarrassed but gladdened by her attention. He slowly turned to face her. She was waiting. "All right," he said. "Here's the condensed history."

He told her how the Jews had flourished in Poland when they first migrated there in the fourteenth century and how fortunes sank over the decades that followed, a downward spiral culminating in the devastating pogrom of 1619 when Bogdan Chmielnicki and his Cossacks massacred more than a hundred thousand Jews. Desperate and forlorn, the Jews crowned a crop of false messiahs who promised salvation from their woes, most prominent among them, Shabtai Tzvi who later converted to Islam, and Jacob Frank who eventually became a Catholic.

"Apparently," Elisha said, "the big attraction of this Jacob Frank was his communal orgies."

"That'll bring 'em in," Katrina said. "Though not us WASPs. Too many thank-you cards to write."

"I don't get it." Elisha said.

"Never mind. Sorry about the interruption. Go on. You haven't gotten to the Chassidim yet. And will you please sit down? I feel like I'm in a lecture hall."

Elisha sat beside her.

He had to acknowledge his delight in sharing his tradition's history with this young woman with remarkable eyes. He picked up his chronicle with the founder of Chassidism, Israel Baal Shem Tov, the Master of the Good Name, sometimes called the Besht. He was born around the year 1700 in Podolia in the Carpathian Mountains. An orphan, he first worked as an assistant teacher to children when he wasn't off in the woods contemplating nature and the Divine, but also spent his days among the poor and the unlearned. The Besht integrated Kabbalistic wisdom into his own teachings. Had Katrina ever heard of Kabbalah?

She hadn't.

"Explaining this won't be easy," he said. "The basic idea is that goodness is everywhere, trapped even in the marrow of evil, and it's mankind's task to free the sparks of holiness and restore the world to its original light, the light of creation."

"I'm losing you here," Katrina said. "But keep going. I love this."

"Well, even most Chassidim don't study the Kabbalah in detail. Anyway, the Besht was also accused of being a false messiah, but rather than subvert Judaism, he gave it new life."

"And the black coats and the fur hats?" said Katrina. "What's all that about?"

"Hold on. You need some more background." There was so much to tell—what would she want to know? He informed her of the mystical devotions of the early Chassidic masters and their followers, their emphasis on joy and faith. He lifted his clarinet case. "Music's essential, too. Chassidim say, 'Tears open gates, but music breaks down walls.'"

Speaking quickly, making sure her interest did not lapse, he told her about the importance of storytelling, how Chassidim considered it a form of prayer. He quoted the Rebbe of Breslov: "A story can put you to sleep. But a story can also wake you up."

"I like that," said Katrina. "But I'm still waiting to hear about the black clothing."

Elisha held up his hand. He was getting to that. "The movement swept across Eastern Europe, and by the twentieth century, there were more than a million Chassidim. You know, it's the unchanging fashion, those fur hats, the black kaftans, the head coverings,"—Elisha pointed to the black felt yarmulke on his head and the black hat resting at his side—"that keeps people within the tradition." He twitched involuntarily, and stopped talking for a moment. "But not all agree," he added.

"And your family has been Chassidim for a long time?"

"From the beginning. We belong to the leading dynasties."

"So you're a prince." Katrina bowed her head.

"Of sorts, I guess. Though I don't think this ledge is the throne my royal family had in mind."

"Tell me, tell me, tell me. What was it like growing up like you did?"

Elisha said, "I've talked enough, don't you think?"

"Are you kidding?" said Katrina. "This is all so unusual. So are you, Elisha."

"Yes, I'm unusual," Elisha said, disappointment, excitement, fear, pleasure, and guilt, all competing for his attention.

Katrina sat up straight and clasped her hands on her lap. "I meant that positively."

"But I know nothing about you," Elisha said. "Except that you come from a distant galaxy somewhere in the middle of America, that you play the flute, read Tolstoy, and detest Nixon."

"I'll tell you about me some other time. More than you want to know." A solemnity had suddenly crept into her voice. "But not today. Today we learn about you." She took hold of Elisha's elbow.

Elisha withdrew his arm immediately.

"The leprosy's cured," Katrina said, taken aback by his reaction. "I promise. Look." She wiggled her fingers in front of his face.

"We're prohibited from touching women," Elisha explained, shifting his eyes toward the ground.

"Speaking of unusual! Are you serious?"

"Those are the rules," Elisha said.

"So let me get this straight. Men can't touch women. How about a doctor—let's make this juicier—a gynecologist and his female patient?"

"Doctors are different. With few exceptions, health trumps all prohibitions."

"Okay, a policeman. A cop arresting a women bank robber. Do they have to wear gloves?" Katrina pressed on with litigious glee. "Or say the woman is dead? The man is a mortician and he has to clean her up very carefully because, I don't know, she's a sooty, homeless female person who'd had a fatal heart attack while looting crockery from a dumpster."

Elisha laughed. "A mortician? Used crockery from a dumpster? You do have a strange mind." He explained that, technically, contact was only forbidden if it was intimate or could lead to intimacy.

"And holding on to your arm is personal?" Katrina said. "'Cause, my dear prince, if you consider that intimate, you're in for some very pleasant surprises. Though I must tell you," she continued, still grinning, "this part of Chassidism doesn't seem so enticing."

"Tell me about it," Elisha said.

They talked for minutes or an hour, an hour or minutes, Elisha couldn't say, didn't care, regaling Katrina on her ledge-throne with his discoveries about the marriage rituals of the Itury Forest Pygmies careening into enthusiastic descriptions of his motley relatives; she, in turn, beguiled him with her analysis of Tolstoy and even more with her eyes, on which he so comfortably indulged.

"So tell me a Chassidic story," Katrina said.

"What, now?" Elisha glanced at his watch. Ten thirty.

"I didn't realize how late it was," he said. "It takes me a good hour and a half to get home. And I have to be up at six."

"Lifting weights?"

"I wish. Trying to unload weights off my shoulders is more like it No, it's morning services at 6:30. I don't sleep much."

He told her perhaps it was genetic. One of his rebbe ancestors famously explained how he managed with only two hours of sleep a night: "Some people read quickly, some eat quickly, I sleep quickly."

Katrina said, "Well, I sleep very slowly. Why rush a pleasure?"

"Talking to you has been a pleasure, and"—he gestured to his watch—"not rushed either."

"It's been enlightening," Katrina said. "I'll be looking for you in the library. You owe me a story." She looked into his eyes and smiled and ran her fingers down his arm. This time he didn't move it away.

4

.....

A father gives more of himself to his son than the son to the father. It was always like this. Adam had no father.

—the Rebbe of Ostrovich

The next evening, Elisha walked into the bathroom, locked the door, and stood in front of the mirror. The scissors quivered in his hand. Are we ready, ladies and gentleman, for the revised Elisha? Was he?

He pursed his lips and exhaled a long column of air. In a moment. As soon as his wrist stopped trembling.

With his finger behind his right ear, Elisha flipped his payis onto his face. Then the same with the left ear. The payis draped his cheeks, reaching his chin, the sacred frames of the Jewish face. A tear drifted down to his chin, its trajectory parallel to the sidecurls grasping his temples. He stroked the thatch of hair as he would the head of an innocent child and put the scissors back on the ledge. Another minute to say good-bye to who he was.

This isn't drastic, he calmed himself. Shearing off one's payis isn't eating shrimp, not in the same league as lighting a fire on the Sabbath. Even most orthodox Jews don't wear payis and, anyway, can't one always grow them back? Sure, he had his questions, but his core beliefs were solid as bedrock. He still could call himself a Chassid, with or without these adornments. And no, no, no, this has nothing to do with the girl on the ledge, the delicious tingle he felt thinking of her. But he could not be the spokesperson for a world he no longer wished to defend. He'd free himself of this harness that proclaimed he would not turn right or left, when, in fact, he wanted to turn in every direction.

Elisha checked the bolt on the door, picked up the scissors and snipped off the bottom edge of his right *payeh*. Another long exhale and he amputated the entire lock of hair. He stared at his reflection for a full minute, one payeh still gripping his face, daring him.

"Forgive me, Tateh," Elisha whispered. He cut off the second sidecurl. "This is about my life, not yours."

Elisha made his way down the corridor to his father's office, the Talmud in his hand as heavy as when he tried to lift it as a four-year-old. He turned the doorknob and saw his father at his desk reading. Elisha waited.

"My God!" his father said, aghast.

Elisha remained standing, voiceless.

"So you did this, after all," his father said.

Elisha walked into the room, his head still lowered.

"I thought we'd talked about this," said his father. "Weeks ago. You said it was a passing notion."

"Apparently, the notion stayed put."

"But why?"

"I had to, Tateh."

"Had to? There is no such thing as had to. You chose to."

"All right then. I chose to."

"I must say I'm not really surprised. But right before the holy days of Rosh Hashanah?"

"I thought about that, believe me. But I'm not ashamed. Not for me, not for God either."

His father covered his mouth but the anguish was still visible in his narrowed eyes. "Tell me," he said, slowly, parsing his words. "Is this the beginning of something or the end?"

"The end. Only the payis."

Elisha finally looked up to meet his father's gaze. "I didn't mean to hurt you."

"This isn't about me," his father said.

"No, it's not. And I'm still who I was."

"About that I'm not so sure. And I'm not sure you believe that either."

"But I am. In what matters," Elisha said, more to himself than to his father.

Elisha sat down across his father's desk and turned to the page they were to study, feeling his father's mahogany eyes still drilling toward him. How startling this must be for him, Elisha thought: after all these generations, ten, twenty, perhaps all the way back to King David, and it is *his* son that cuts off his payis.

Elisha raised his head in time to see a crinkle form around the edges of his father's eyelids, his lips parting in the genesis of a smile.

"What?" Elisha asked.

"I was just recollecting an incident in Poland."

"Poland?"

"I was a child, no more than nine or ten. We were in *cheder*, our tiny, one-room schoolhouse. Someone had gotten hold of an atlas, and we all crowded around it. What a find! We turned to a page that had a picture of Chinese boys in braids. Back then the Chinese wore braids that reached way down their backs. 'How strange they look,' we smirked and cackled, all the while twirling our payis. Suddenly—who knows why?—I stood back from the circle, realizing the oddity of it all."

"And behold you now," Elisha said, pointing to his father's full beard.

"Tradition requires commitments."

"But wasn't there a brief moment when you didn't look like this? I'm thinking of that picture of you taken when you'd just arrived in America."

At the bottom of a box in the back of a closet was the one photograph of his father beardless. He was standing on a thoroughfare in the Lower East Side, the Division Street sign visible in the corner, dapper in a double-breasted suit topped by a gray felt Homburg, an exuberant, crisp, postwar immigrant. But the smooth-faced exposure to the American sun would be short-lived, for soon a thick mantle of hair would sheath his face.

"After the war, many didn't grow their beards again," his father said. "Few thought Chassidism would ever revive. At times I felt like a custodian of a vanished people."

"The last of the Mohicans."

"What's that?" his father asked. "In any case, here we are, twenty-five years after we were almost wiped out and flourishing once more."

"Welcome to America," Elisha said. He was eager to keep the conversation away from what he'd done to himself minutes before.

"Yes, the land of opportunity," said his father, heavily. "And that's the paradox for us."

"What do you mean?"

Elisha's father looked straight ahead while he rummaged in his jacket pocket and extracted a cigarette. "All these American Jews with their fancy English names of nobility. Seymour, Bernard, Sherwin."

"Milton and Sidney," Elisha contributed, still unsure of his father's point.

"Their parents thought they'd turn their kids into real Americans. But I think they didn't understand this country. They still don't. In real America you don't have to give up who you are, you don't have to deny where you came from. You can live as you want and do just fine. Here you can be Moshe, not Morris. You can make your fortune as Hershel not only as Harold."

"That's quite a theory. So it's we Chassidim who are the real American Jews."

"But that's the problem, isn't it?" his father said. "With all this freedom it's also so easy to stop being who you are."

This was all aimed at him, after all, thought Elisha. He'd try to deflect the direction of the discussion. "Tateh, you're definitely doing your part to keep who we are going strong."

"One has responsibilities."

Elisha shook his head. "Responsibilities can't be imposed. You have a right to accept or reject them."

"Right?" replied his father. "That's all I read these days, this right, that right, everything's a right. Well, I have news for you. A person comes into the world with duties…to himself, to his family, to his community, and to his heritage. Rights or no rights."

"I don't agree," Elisha said with a brazenness that astonished both of them. "One chooses obligations."

Elisha's father bent forward and pressed his lips together so hard they went white. "Listen, Elisha," he said, his eyes riveted on his son's, "perhaps I'm being naïve, but I have faith in you. I trust *you* will always know who you are, where you came from. What I worry about are your children…if they grow up without your *imposed* background. And yes, let me assure you, appearances do matter. External features— like payis—aren't trivial. I'm also sorry the Chinese boys no longer wear braids. They've lost something important too."

Elisha's father adjusted his new reading glasses and opened the book on his desk. "But enough talk. It's time to study Torah."

Elisha unhooked the hands he'd kept folded like an admonished schoolboy, rolled up his sleeves, and opened his Talmud.

But his father wasn't quite through with his declamation. "What I'm saying, Elisha, is that this worship of rights isolates people. It undermines community. Do you understand what I'm trying to tell you?"

"I think so," Elisha said flatly. This was his father's elliptical way of expressing concern.

"All right," his father said. "Now I'm really finished with the speeches." He turned the pages of his Talmud. "Where were we holding?"

"Three lines before the next Mishnah," Elisha said, pointing to the appropriate place on the page.

His father would always be his dearest teacher. A double blessing portending double anguish. But for now the two joined in the distinctive singsong that accompanied the reading of rabbinic texts and were soon transported to the lush four cubits of Torah where nothing else mattered, not politics, not Chinese braids or payis, not even a young woman with a single dimple.

5
.....

Fear is contraction, love is diffusion.

—the Bnei Yissoscher

Katrina was in her usual seat behind a barricade of opened books, laying claim to half the library table, in a quiet niche off to one side of the room.

"Hi there," Elisha said cheerfully, sitting down across from her.

"Elisha! And in daylight!"

He had off from yeshiva on Friday afternoons, he explained, and had come up to the college for an office hour meeting with his professor and had stopped by the library for a book he needed. He doubted she believed the part about the book.

"Wait a minute," Katrina said, shaking her head, flinging the ponytail she wore that day from side to side. "Something's different. Your payeeez."

"I cut them off," Elisha said.

"But why?"

"It's complicated."

"I'm sure it is. But I bet you lost something important."

"Very complicated," Elisha repeated. He still noticed his new reflection every time he passed a mirror.

"Guess what? I've been reading up on Chassidism," Katrina said. "After we talked the other day, I thought I ought to know something about the background of my new devout acquaintance."

"Devout? Hardly. What have you been reading?"

"Martin Buber. He wrote a book of Chassidic tales. Mostly anecdotes and sayings, actually."

Elisha snickered. "Buber? What does he know?" Buber was a German philosopher—okay, Jewish too, but nonobservant—who never sweated through a page of Talmud or an afternoon in shul, never lost himself in a Chassidic dance or sat at a rebbe's table on a shabbos evening. "An authority on Chassidism? Oh, please."

"Listen to you! I never heard you rant like this. Did you ever read him?"

"No."

"I didn't think so. I don't get most of his references, either. I know my *Crime and Punishment* a lot better than I know my Bible."

"A shame, young lady. You're missing lots of nasty crime and nasty punishment in the Bible, too."

"No doubt. In any case, you promised me a Chassidic story, remember?"

Elisha sat back in his chair and raised his palms in the air. Telling Chassidic stories was what his father did and his father before him, but not quite to an audience like Katrina.

"I wouldn't know which to tell. Besides, I need to get back before sundown."

"Not that 'I have to leave' excuse again," Katrina said, insisting. "A short one. Okay?"

Goodness, she was pretty.

And why not? He had promised, after all. "Well, we have a holiday coming up," he said. "Yom Kippur, the most important day of the year for Jews. This is a story about Chassidism and Yom Kippur."

He told her it was a famous tale with dozens of versions, but this was the version he'd heard from his father. It starred one of his ancestors, the Rebbe of Leszensk. "And it's thankfully brief," he said, beginning the tale.

In a small town in the Ukraine a poor Jewish innkeeper, a widower, passed away, leaving behind a six-year-old boy. A Christian couple who'd befriended the innkeeper brought the orphan into their own home next door and together raised the boy with kindness and affection. Several years later, the couple decided the young orphan was sufficiently mature to learn about his past.

The boy was sitting on his bed when they entered his room holding a small package. They told him his father was a Jew, a fine man, but poor, and this bundle contained all of his belongings. As soon as he was alone, the child opened the package and carefully emptied the contents onto the floor: an old broken watch, a pin, a few trinkets, and a prayer book.

The boy picked up the prayer book and sniffed the timeworn pages. He held the book upside down and opened it from the wrong side. What did these odd markings mean? He'd studied Hebrew as a small child, but the letters were now indecipherable. I have no use for this, he thought, and put the book in the bag with the other items, placed the bundle on a high shelf, and went outside to play.

The boy was kicking a ball with his friends several weeks later when a wagon carrying a group of Jewish men in black jackets and black hats and a few women, too, dressed in black coats and kerchiefs, rode into the driveway. The young orphan reminded himself he was a Jew like these men milling about the inn. He approached the wagon.

"Where are you going?"

The men ignored him. The boy repeated his question.

"On a trip," an ancient Jew answered.

"Yes, but to where? And why are all of you dressed up in such finery?"

Seeing the boy's curiosity was sincere, the old Jew replied, "Tomorrow is the Jewish New Year. We are going to Leszensk to be with our rebbe, our teacher, and together with Jews from all over the region, we will pray for a good and blessed year." He waved as the wagon resumed its journey.

The young boy stood on the road, his heart beating quickly. I am one of them, he whispered to himself. I belong with them. I, too, should pray for a good year. He remained on the road watching the wagon grow smaller until it disappeared around the bend.

That evening the boy took the prayer book down from the shelf and carefully blew away the long accumulated dust. Once more he tried but couldn't decipher the unfamiliar, impenetrable script. But this was his language. He thought of the Jews and the wagon and ached to be with them.

Several days later, the wagon once again rode up to the inn, again crowded with Jews dressed in their holiday best. The youngster recognized the old man. Where were they headed this time?

"To the same place," the old Jew replied. "Tomorrow is Yom Kippur, the holiest day of the year. Tomorrow the fate of the world is decided, the destiny of every creature sealed in the book of life…or death. Why even the fish in the sea tremble on this sacred day. So we are going to Leszensk to be with our beloved rebbe to ask God for a blessed year."

"I am also a Jew!" the boy shouted, waving his arms. "Take me with you. Take me to Leszensk. Let me pray with you."

The old man gently shook his head. "You are a child; you belong at home."

But the boy was tenacious. "Please, please, I must go with you."

"You will need your parents' permission first," the old Jew said, acceding at last to the child's incessant pleas. And seeing the child's earnestness, the boy's caretakers agreed to let him travel with the Jews to Leszensk.

In a flash the lad ran toward the wagon, but as he was about to jump on, he exclaimed, "Wait! Wait! There is something I must take with me." The boy ran to his room and returned clutching his father's siddur. He sat down in a corner of the wagon, keeping a tight grip on the prayer book. He was comforted when he noticed the woman sitting across the wagon floor holding an identical book.

A shiver overtook the boy as he entered the synagogue and observed the sea of white robes draped with woolen prayer shawls on the backs of men with earnest faces. The men's bodies swayed like branches in a storm, their lips moving as if casting magical spells. Some prayed loudly and occasionally clapped their hands while others stood still like soldiers. The rebbe, too, stood erect, wrapped in a majestic, silver-edged prayer shawl that nearly reached down to his ankles.

The boy took a seat next to a withered, gray-haired man who repeatedly dabbed his eyes with a white handkerchief. Behind him, the boy could hear the undertone of prayers from the women's section. Their moans caused him to tremble.

The child was alone, helpless, and confused. He slowly opened his prayer book. A few tears ran down his cheek and wet the pages of his beloved siddur. How he wished he could recite the holy words like the other boys in the room. He listened carefully to the prayers of the people around him and to the chanting of the cantor, but the words vanished before he could repeat them. And what good was repeating other people's words? But he was unable to read a single line from the prayer book on his lap, unable to utter a single phrase of Hebrew.

The tears flowed freely as the boy, his heart aching, picked up the prayer book and held it up in front of him. He lifted his eyes toward the Heavens and called out in Polish:

"Master of the Universe. I don't know how to pray to you. I don't know how to ask for your blessing. My father left me this prayer book when he died, but I cannot read a word of it. But Almighty, you can. So dear God, here is the prayer book. You choose the words. You form the prayers I am supposed to say."

After the service, the Tzaddik of Leszensk addressed his Chassidim. His holy visage was more radiant than usual.

"I want you all to know today was not easy. At first, our prayers did not find favor at the Holy Tribunal. Our petitions were refused. I trembled for our future. But then a young boy among us cried out with a prayer that came right from the depth of his heart. His anguished words were the most beautiful expressed anywhere on this earth on this sacred day. The boy's tears reached to the very chamber of the Divine Throne. And on his account our pleas were accepted."

"That was wonderful," Katrina said. "And you told it wonderfully, too. The words sounded as though they were coming from some other place, some ancient treasure chest."

Elisha was pleased by her compliment, but it unnerved him, too. Only now, his tale completed, did he realize how immersed he'd been in the telling.

"Wait a sec," Katrina said as Elisha prepared to leave. "Before you go."

From her calico pocketbook the size of a small satchel, Katrina withdrew a thick paperback book.

"Have you ever read Kafka?"

"Didn't he write a book about a giant cockroach?"

"*Metamorphosis*. This is a collection of his short stories and fables. I'm almost finished with it, but take it. That Chassidic story you told me? It reminded me of him. Kafka's less optimistic, but there's the same respect for mystery."

She wrote her telephone number inside the flap. "Tell me what you think."

"See you in a while, crocodile," she said with a wide smile as Elisha stood up to go.

"Later, alligator," he said, pleased with his matching reply.

Elisha's extended family gathered at his house for shabbos dinner that night. His conversation with Katrina still bubbled in his head as he paid half-attention to the boisterous discussion in the living room.

The day before, the United States government agreed to allow the North Vietnamese troops to remain in South Vietnam. There was continued talk of peace at hand. But for Elisha's cousin Mayer, this was but another instance of American naïveté. Mayer had come to the States in 1958, later than most of the family, already wealthy, having made his money in the gray alleys of currency exchange in postwar Europe and ever since was ruled by a sense of his own overriding importance.

"Do you truly think the Russians and their Chinese proxies don't have a better understanding of the situation? America has no idea whom it's up against." Hencha, his immense and expensive wife, bobbed her head up and down in gestural echo.

Mayer stabbed the air with his index finger and lowered the Asian-shaped folds of his eyelids, the inheritance, presumably, of a Tartar's rampage during a pogrom. He aimed his rant at Elisha, the American native in the room.

"Hear what I'm telling you. I spent the war in the steppes of Russia where your spit froze before it hit the ground, so cold it was. Ask your father; he was there. We experienced the Russian government firsthand, don't even ask."

"True, better you shouldn't ask," Hencha chimed in.

Mayer's finger now pointed directly at Elisha. "The Russ isn't soft like you Americans with your hula hoops and cowboy television shows. We play games, while they do what must be done. No wonder their missile capabilities are far ahead of this country's."

Uncle Shaya darted a contemptuous look at Mayer and strutted to the back porch. Elisha waited impatiently for a break in Mayer's tirade and followed him.

Uncle Shaya was sitting on a deck chair inspecting the clouds. "Talk, talk. Opinions are like armpits. Everyone has a couple." He was still frowning as Elisha pulled up a chair beside him.

"Do you know why human beings were the last of God's creations?" Uncle Shaya asked. "A Chassidic rebbe answered that if humans were created first, they'd immediately start advising God on how best to complete the creation of the world, and God didn't want to be bothered with their advice."

"But what about the arms race? Mayer seems pretty convinced we'll eventually lose."

"Ah, what does he know about missile technology? What do these people know about America altogether?"

"He thinks we underestimate the Russians."

"Mayer, Hencha, they're terrified the good side will once again underestimate its enemies. They don't understand America is different."

"Speaking of America," Elisha said, itching to tell Uncle Shaya about his latest jaunt. He'd been to a place called the Bleecker Street Café where beatniks and hippies congregate. The café reminded him of their shteibl, people sitting around tables in a scruffy room, and as noisy, that's for sure, everyone talking, even during the performances.

They hadn't noticed Mayer suspended on the doorpost, his mouth a half-moon of scorn.

"I don't know what you two are talking about," Mayer said, "and I don't want to know. This week's Torah portion, I'm sure it's not." He smiled unpleasantly into his brushed moustache.

"Can we help you?" said Uncle Shaya.

"I came out here for Elisha. We're about to sit down for dinner. I'm sure his father would prefer him inside with the rest of us than out here discussing…who knows what."

They could hear Mayer grumbling as he slammed the porch door behind him.

The moment felt deliciously conspiratorial, a good time, Elisha decided, to raise the issue that'd been gnawing at him these past months.

For a while, he said, it had been squaring science and religion. But he thought he'd figured that out.

"It can be done," Uncle Shaya agreed.

"But what bothers me, what really jolts my faith?" said Elisha. "Evil. God and…this."

Elisha looked over to the indelible blue numbers tattooed on his uncle's arm. He'd learned early on not to inquire about these souvenirs from the netherworld, not to ask questions for which there are no answers. Reading those numbers was how he'd learned Europeans crossed their sevens.

Uncle Shaya said, "Your dilemma is an old hornet's nest. Thinking people have always worried about its sting."

"I know. But how does one—how do *you*—resolve the contradiction?"

"I don't."

"What do you mean?"

"What does it sound like? I mean I don't. That's the truth. I don't know the answer."

"But how then can you pray the way you do?"

"What can I tell you? You're right, it's not easy binding phylacteries around my arm every morning, reciting thanks to the Almighty for bestowing His wonderful kindness on His beloved people." Uncle Shaya's mouth tightened. "Such kindness."

Uncle Shaya was staring above Elisha's head as if speaking not to his nephew but to everyone on the planet. To himself.

"My big hurdle isn't the absence of God's sympathy. That I can deal with. It's the absence of His revenge. The Torah says God reaps justice on His enemies. Well, I'm still waiting."

"But you're not waiting," Elisha said too loudly, his impatience bubbling. "It's too late for justice." He glanced again at his uncle's arm. "The dead won't return."

"No, they won't."

"Then how can you worship, sing God's praises, if you deny His goodness?"

"I don't deny. I don't understand."

"But I see you in shul. You pray like you're standing at the foot of Mount Sinai."

Uncle Shaya shut his eyes for a few moments before continuing in a lower, confidential pitch. "There are days when I think of prayer as God—the cosmos, the Ultimate Explanation, call it what you will—listening in when I talk to myself."

"I'm sorry, but I still don't get it," Elisha said.

"Then again maybe it's no more than simple nostalgia. Or no less. Nostalgia is never simple."

Elisha stood up and looked out at the backs of the recently built houses around the corner. He was disappointed: tradition for tradition's sake was the last refuge of everyone around him. He expected more from his uncle.

"You're being inconsistent," Elisha said, almost in a shout, no longer hiding his frustration.

Uncle Shaya lifted his hand as if fending off a blow then let it fall into his lap. "What can I say? At times I think it's all theater on my part. But did you ever hear a recording of Pinchik singing *Roza d'shabbos*? Ah, the greatest piece of cantorial music ever recorded. Pinchik isn't religious. He goes by the name Pierre. I hear he even drives to shul on shabbos. But when he chants the Friday evening kabbalistic hymn, the man is pure holiness. The Baal Shem Tov himself couldn't be in closer contact with God."

Uncle Shaya closed his eyes and sang a few measures... *roza d'shabbos eehee d'shabbos*...the secret of shabbos, this is the shabbos....

Elisha listened for a few moments to his uncle humming in his chair and wondered if he, too, was destined to a life of contradictions.

6

.....

Writing is a form of prayer.

—Franz Kafka, *Diaries*

"Has anyone here heard of Jiri Langer?"

Elisha had read the book Katrina had given to him, nearly all of it in one night, and then spent the next few days devouring everything he could find in the library by and about Franz Kafka: letters, essays, and more stories. And there in the diaries, he'd come upon a startling entry: Kafka's account of his trip with his Chassidic friend Jiri Langer to Marienbad to meet Elisha's great-grandfather, the Rebbe of Belz. Who was this mysterious Chassid friend of the great Franz Kafka?

Elisha found a copy of Langer's *Nine Gates to Chassidic Mysteries* at the bottom of a pile of books in a small Lower Eastside Jewish bookstore, and stood in the aisle for the next two hours reading Langer's fables of saintly Chassidic tzaddiks, the Choizeh of Lublin, the Yismach Moshe, the Rebbes of Ger and Rhyzin, and Langer's own rebbe—the Rebbe of Belz. The book's preface, written by the author's brother, tells of Jiri's childhood in an assimilated, bourgeois Czech family and his growing fascination with mystical Judaism and subsequent travels to the distant shtetls of Galicia, Poland. Jiri returned to Prague a Chassidic disciple garbed in complete Chassidic regalia, the long black kaftan, beaver hat, and full red beard. But Jiri was a Chassid who immersed himself in literature as well as Torah. He spent his days praying and studying in shul and his evenings in cafés pondering poetry and Western belles-lettres with Prague's intelligentsia and his friend Franz Kafka to whom he'd taught the Hebrew language.

Elisha's father had never heard of him.

"He wrote Chassidic stories," Elisha said.

"Chassidic stories?" Elisha's father twisted his mouth into a scorn. "Tell me. You discovered the book in the college library? This Langer is also a mechanical engineer?"

"Please don't start."

"To tell you the truth, I never expected you'd make your living handling slide rules. Practical is not your forte, shall we say."

Elisha ignored the digression to his own life and said Langer was a disciple of the Belzer Rebbe.

"In that case, ask Mother," his father suggested.

Elisha's mother was bent over the sink and kept her back to Elisha when he entered the kitchen.

Elisha said, "I think you made your point already." She'd been distant since the day he'd severed his payis.

"What do you expect?" his mother said, turning to face her son. "I should be pleased with this new look of yours?"

"I don't expect anyone to be pleased. Not you, not Tateh."

"It upsets me. Plenty."

"We'll all get used to it."

"That's the problem."

"Do you know anything about Jiri Langer?" Elisha said, determined to change the subject.

But his mother wasn't. "You don't see why that's precisely the problem? You're getting used to this…this new you?"

"Can we please move on for a minute? He was a writer in Prague."

Elisha's mother turned her back and busied herself with the dishes. "I don't remember the details," she offered matter of factly, but did recall something about Langer and Kafka and Tante Leika visiting Zaidy and Babche when they lived in Prague.

"Kafka? Kafka visited my grandparents!"

Elisha ran the eight blocks to his grandparents' house, a classic brownstone with broken drainpipes and cracked bricks, a perfect façade for a movie director in search of pre-war frontage. The house was attached to the shteibl and Chassidim often congregated on the steps of both buildings while waiting for services to begin, their numbers augmented by petitioners waiting for a private audience with Elisha's grandfather; the aftersmell of their visits hugged the stair-wells for hours. But it was late in the evening, and no one impeded Elisha's charge up the steps into his grandparents' home.

His grandmother put her hands to her face when she saw him. "I still can't get use to seeing you like this," she said, pushing her cheeks side-to-side.

"Please, Babche. Not you too."

The inside of his grandparents' home reeked of a past even more distant than the building's exterior: peeling ceilings, creaking floors, shelves crammed with rust-brown Hebrew books piled on their sides, a Philco radio in the bedroom that hadn't worked in five years, the petrified time of broken time pieces strewn in drawers in every room.

Elisha had always felt an odd mixture of stigma and good fortune at having living grandparents—he was one of only three students in his class who did. His friend Benzion, born in a DP camp, said he was eight years old before he'd discovered that even Jewish children had grandparents. And surely it was unusual, too, for a grandchild to so easily picture his grandparents in their youth. But Elisha had only to attend to his married Chassidic cousins to see the same white turbans his grandmother wore in Europe covering their shaved skulls, the same opaque dresses that began at the neck and reached the ankles skimming the same clunky black shoes designed with orthopedic disregard of fashion.

Babche found an empty patch on the littered table, an uninhabited island in a sea of half-used teacups and Yiddish newspapers and set down a plate of honey cake. "So what did you want to ask me?" she said, hesitant, still acerbic.

"Mother says you met Kafka, the writer. In Prague."

Babche narrowed her eyes and said nothing. Did the name not register or were other memories intervening?

"He came to your house with Jiri Langer," Elisha prodded. "Did you know Langer? Also a writer."

"Jiri Langer. Of course. He was—how should one say—unusual." Babche concentrated her eyebrows and stared skyward, conjuring an image from across half a century. "He'd stop by unannounced with his band of luftmenschen, scribblers, and painters. How they all loved to talk, as if it were up to them to solve all the world's problems. There was this fellow named Max Brod who also loved to sing. I tell you, the things one remembers."

Elisha pictured his grandfather, the recently married young Chassidic rebbe, sitting at the head of the table, his bristling brows furrowed under his prodigious forehead, listening to the commotion but understanding little of their Czech, even less of their references, and then quieting the visitors with a Chassidic interpretation of the week's Bible portion.

"We lived in Prague at the end of the first World War," Babche said. In the Vinohrady section with Jews from Poland, Hungary, Romania, and Austria. Prague was like a giant train station, everyone coming and going, and that's how we ended up there, running from the turmoil in Poland. A noble city, Prague. It's the only place in the old country I wouldn't mind seeing again."

Babche stopped talking.

Elisha feared these long suspensions in conversations with adults in his family for, so often, they meant a door had opened to the private cellar of their horrors. He'd also learned to distinguish between those who spoke of their wartime experiences and those who did not: the former had remained alive by working in labor camps, concealed in attics, passing as Polish Gentiles or as exiles in places like Tashkent; the others, the wordless ones like his grandmother, endured the death camps.

Babche was tall for an Eastern European Jewess, certainly tall for a Chassidic rebbetzin, towering a full head above his grandfather. Elisha's height—"our six-footer" they called him, though in reality, a half-inch shy—was attributed to her genes. Babche had passed her seventieth birthday yet her posture was erect and proud. But now as she bent forward, Elisha could see the hardened veins in her neck and the etchings of harsh recollections circling her eyes. He wanted to sidle her away from "those years" back to the afternoon in Prague.

"You were saying. Kafka. Jiri Langer—"

"Ah yes," Babche said, relieved as well to return from the brambles of her memories. Langer, she remembered, had been raised in a home with no *Yiddishkeit*, no shabbos, no kosher, no study of the Holy Scripture, but by the time he visited them, he was already a Chassid. He'd contacted Zaidy as soon as he learned a grandson of the Belzer Rebbe was living in the city. She remembered him encouraging Zaidy to sing Chassidic tunes, especially Belzer melodies, which they'd hum together for a half hour or more. Too bad you can't ask Zaidy about all this."

But Elisha's grandfather was asleep in his room. His Parkinson's disease had worsened these past months, and conversations were now erratic and indecipherable.

Elisha said he wanted to hear about Kafka.

"I suppose Langer was exterminated in the Hitler years," his grandmother said.

Elisha said he'd died in Israel in the 1940s, of tuberculosis. He asked again about Kafka.

"*Dafka* Kafka you want to know about?" Babche contemplated Elisha. "You are my oldest grandchild. I don't understand what's happening to you. Why do you have to travel all the way to a school in Manhattan?"

"I go to college there."

"And Brooklyn College where the others go isn't good enough? You're afraid you might have an extra hour to study Torah in yeshiva?"

Elisha explained without much conviction that City was the only public college offering engineering.

"We worry about you plenty," Babche said again.

"What do you mean 'we'?"

"People. Your mother…don't ask. Even your father, who always sings your praises to everyone, even he is concerned."

"I think he understands," Elisha said weakly.

"True, he says you know your limits. But I wonder. I don't hear as well as I used to, but blind I'm not. Your clothing, the books you read, the way you mumble through grace after meals. And now your payis. Too embarrassing, is that it?"

"No, that's not it," Elisha said admitting to himself that was precisely it.

"Elisha, here in America it's easy to forget where you come from. I beg you, don't forget who your grandfathers were."

Elisha nodded halfheartedly, a half-reassuring gesture. "Perhaps it's just a phase," he said, borrowing the feeble catchphrase used by every parent whose child has stepped off the proper path.

"All right, this Kafka," Babche said, not satisfied but capitulating. "He became famous, no?"

"But only after he died. Also of tuberculosis. His three sisters were murdered in Auschwitz. But what about that afternoon with Leika?"

Babche's reminiscence invited Elisha into her small apartment in Prague, the wine-colored couch and dark wood chairs scarcely visible in the half-shadow of the dwindling shabbos afternoon light. Elisha envisaged his grandfather's silver-tipped cane leaning against a bookshelf filled with holy books just as it leaned here in Brooklyn. He imagined Kafka, Langer, and their compatriots sitting around a table with bowls of nuts and fruit and plates of honey cake, stiff in their starched collars, folding and unfolding their round, wired spectacles each with simmering dreams the next war would turn into nightmares.

Babche remembered Kafka as unkempt and wearing a shabby jacket with torn lapels. His neck was narrow like a bird, she said, and topped by very thick black hair and piercing dark eyes, and his lips were thin. She wouldn't exactly call him handsome, but he had an intelligent expression. Elisha always found it odd his Chassidic grandmother took such careful notice of people's physical features.

"Did Kafka talk much?"

"Not at first, but then, yes, he told clever jokes and clever stories. He was also one of those people who didn't eat meat. Another strange *mishagas*." Elisha's grandmother tugged on her earlobe struggling to wrench a memory from the archives of her long, scrambled life. "Ah yes, he also informed us his Hebrew name was Amschel, after a religious great-grandfather who ritually bathed in the river every day. That's how Zaidy called him: Amschel."

"What happened with Tante Leika?" Elisha asked.

"You're not going to leave me alone about this, I see," she said, getting up from her chair to open a window but returning to her seat to submit to Elisha's unrelenting prodding.

"Leika was just a girl, only seventeen, visiting from Jaroslav, where our parents lived. What can I tell you? *Zee hut farleibt im dem Kafka?* She fell for him."

"*Farleibt!* He was nearly twice her age."

This was spectacular, bizarre but wonderful—his great-aunt had a crush on Franz Kafka.

Babche used her fingertips to push her face from side to side. "Leika had always wanted to learn everything," she said. "The Bible, the Prophets, even Talmud. Secular subjects, too. She'd sneak alien books into the house— 'if Father had found out, don't ask.'" Leika also learned English on her own, mastered it so well that she taught a neighbor in exchange for violin lessons. But one afternoon their older brother Lyzer caught her practicing. A Chassidic girl playing a musical instrument? Her brother was a fanatic, his grandmother conceded, and that was the end of the violin and Leika's musical career. She wept for weeks.

Elisha only knew his great-aunt from photographs and a memory of her visit to America. He recalled her collosal orange hat and matching elbow-length gloves and how she took him aside for a talk. It was important, she insisted, that Elisha be familiar with the titles of English royalty and carefully reviewed for him the distinction between the Queen mother and Queen Dowager. But Elisha's thoughts now were on that afternoon in Prague. What ran though the mind of this Chassidic girl from Jaroslav as she sat at her sister's table across from this intense man with his fantastical ideas?

"Leika was taken by him," Babche said, interrupting Elisha's rumination. "She was young. What can I tell you?"

You can tell me everything, Elisha wanted to scream. You can tell me about my alternate family, secrets you will let die with your generation's passing. You can tell me about books hidden under beds and those who dared put them there. You can tell me about a great-uncle who slipped a Yiddishist novel inside his Talmud, about another who befriended Trotsky, about a great-aunt who relinquished her rolling pin to make *aliyah* to Palestine when the land was desert and swamp. And if no forbear of mine managed these escapades, you can tell me about those who dreamed they would. You can tell me I'm not the first in our family overcome with a restlessness that will not cease. But to begin with, you can tell about that shabbos afternoon in Prague.

"And what did Kafka think of Leika?" Elisha asked his grandmother.

"As you might imagine he enjoyed the attention of a young, pretty girl with long hair as black as tar." Leika had asked Kafka to prepare a reading list for her, and at the conclusion of the Sabbath rushed to his apartment. "I assure you, we weren't pleased when she returned with a book list three pages long and a smirk pasted on her face for days. A young girl's infatuation, I tell you."

"Did they remain in contact?"

"I can only tell you that once when I visited my parents, I cleaned Leika's room and an envelope fell out of a book. It had Kafka's Berlin return address."

Elisha's mouth opened in anticipation. He envisioned the newspaper articles heralding the unexpected literary discovery—"Kafka's Chassidic girlfriend"—telephone calls from biographers, urgent queries from curators. His grandmother yanked him back to the ground.

"There was no letter inside. Not then, not later. Leika left to study in England at some famous university. She became a professor. So tell me, what does that get you? She never married, never had a family. This is a life?"

"It's one kind of life," Elisha said.

"Living alone is not a life."

Babche stood up without warning. "But enough of this already," she said. She handed Elisha a heavy shopping bag. "On your way home, please drop this off at the warehouse."

On Thursdays, Chassidic women across New York City, Israel, and wherever else they live prepare complete shabbos meals for indigent families, the disabled, and the elderly. They provide oven-fresh braided challah bread, potato and noodle kugels, gefilte fish, chicken, broiled or roasted, chicken soup weighted with carrots and parsnips; many add herring and a bottle of wine.

Because the highest form of charity preserves the dignity of the poor, the packages are delivered to the warehouse in the evening and picked up early the next morning ensuring that the needy and their benefactors never come into contact and learn each other's identities. Elisha once heard his father explain that the Hebrew word for charity, *tzedaka*, derived from the word *tzedek*, justice. *Tzedaka* is a duty and does not depend on one's feeling of compassion. Chassidim embraced this obligation with the same religious zeal they fulfilled all other commandments. Babche had never missed dispensing a Thursday package or two, and until recently, when his brother and cousins began to assume the responsibility, Elisha had made the weekly deliveries.

"Do you hear me?" his grandmother called after him as he descended the stairs. "Enough already with this Kafka business. You have more important things to think about."

But the Kafka business would not withdraw. Nor would his thoughts about the young woman who introduced him to this mystifying Jewish Czech writer.

Elisha took a six-block detour and found a phone booth at a deserted garage on Fort Hamilton Parkway. He hesitated before he dropped the coin into the box. This was no mere glimpse at a priest during services. This was no accidental encounter in a hallway at a library table. What was he beginning here? Where did he want it to end? Why had he memorized her number?

"This is Elisha," he said slowly, trying to dampen his excitement at hearing her voice. "You lent me your book and—"

"Hey! I thought you were transformed into a bug. Did you know that happens to every fifth person who reads Kafka?"

"So that explains these weird wings."

"What did you think of his stories?"

"I'm eager to tell you."

"But not in the library. Or the hallway in school. Someplace we don't have to whisper. Okay?"

They made plans to meet later in the week in the coffee shop down the street from school.

"Soon, raccoon," she said.

"In a trice, mice." He was prepared.

Later in his room, Elisha reread Kafka's diary entry about his trip with Jiri Langer to meet the Belzer Rebbe. Kafka was unimpressed: "Langer tries to find or thinks he finds a deeper meaning in all this; I think the deeper meaning is there is none, and in my opinion this is quite enough." Kafka's disappointment with Elisha's illustrious great-grandfather was disheartening but a relief, too.

He lay down on his bed and read Kafka's litigious letter to his father, their relationship so frigid and disturbing, so unlike that between Elisha and his own father. He read another of Kafka's fables and, as always, it reminded him of a Chassidic story, teasing and pinching your cheek, the unexpected ending waiting in the wings, directing the tale's unaccountable alchemy. Did Tante Leika read Kafka's tricky inventions? Were his words the rope she lowered from her window to escape her family's own nest of fables? For of this Elisha was certain: you can't abandon one set of stories without adopting another.

What did propel her to leave the Chassidic shtetl? Her eccentricity? Curiosity? Not anger, Elisha hoped. The people he'd met who'd left the fold with resentment—a friend's uncle, a cousin's neighbor, the old man who owned the candy store down the block—were consumed by their bitterness. Anger never leaves those who leave with anger.

Elisha closed his book and stared at the ceiling. Rabbinic ancestors drifted by, each reciting a fragment of Torah, one adding a promise of good things, the other premonitions of doom. Among the sages a sullen Kafka appeared and reappeared, saying nothing but staring down hard at Elisha.

From the corner of the room, a grisly voice called to him. "Here, over here. Have a look at my scrapbook." Henry Miller was holding a book with pictures of tight-sweatered teens from New Utrecht High. With a mischievous wink, Miller turned the page to show him a photo of a lissome, freckled girl with gleaming braces and purple glasses in a white miniskirt standing alone at a bus stop. The photograph faded into a long-legged woman in a Pepsi ad, pouting and licking her moist top lip, and that picture, too, became someone else, Katrina, radiant Katrina, her hand reaching out to Elisha's cheek and keeping it there as Elisha reached down his belly to between his legs where he'd find momentary relief.

ר
.....

*The depth of a man's heart must equal that of his
mind.*

—Rebbe Simcha of Premyszal

With the darkening sky, the sobriety of Rosh Hashanah
settled into the Chassidic shul where it would remain for
the next two days.

On the High Holidays even Elisha's table of constant
talkers ceased their banter. But most austere of all were the
young men in the bloom of their piety. This was a Day
of Judgment and they remained standing throughout the
service, their faces as pale as the pages of the prayer books
in their slender hands, their shoulders and arms undulating
back and forth as they recited the liturgy. Elisha moved
his neck to keep time with them, and, he imagined, in
rhythm, too, with his other contemporaries thousands of
miles beyond, the tanned bodies in cutoff shirts at demon-
strations in Berkeley, California, and with those thousands
of miles farther still on swift boats churning the Mekong
Delta. The message of them all, the peaceniks, the soldiers,
and the penitents at his side, was oddly the same:

Dear parents, this is how it looks when we, your children,
practice what you preach. You say you value selflessness and
peace? Then come sip our wine and join our protests. Is it
the brave who fight for their country that you laud? We're

here, counting the stars above these sticky Asian rivers, praying it is not our faces that will rip with the next explosion. And you, dear elders, who beseech us to uphold our religious tradition, observe us here in your shteibl, swathed in prayer, reaching for repentance. But Elisha could march with none of his generation, not the peaceniks, not the soldiers, not the young Chassidim. The vehemence of his isolation tore through him with a shudder.

"Blood money!"

In the other corner of the shteibl Berel Roitman was pushing his way out of his chair, his fist shaking mightily. "This is who gets called to the Torah? It's a *shanda*. An outrage."

A table tottered, people scattered. Roitman's son Solly begged his father to calm down, but Roitman, in red-faced fury, continued to hurl curses in Yiddish.

"Him you honor? A man who makes his money from the *Daitschen*, those accursed Germans, may their name be obliterated?

"It's okay, calm down," people implored, waving their hands up and down as if stilling a loosed tiger.

"But he's right, you know," some at Elisha's table murmured. "It's not proper."

A chair caromed at the Eastern Wall, missing Elisha's father by inches. Elisha hurried over.

"*Nebikh,* the poor man," His father said.

"Mr. Roitman?"

"He's upset Kalman Weiss was given an aliyah to the Torah."

"And what's wrong with Mr. Weiss?"

"He just returned from Vienna. He's in the import-export business, and his main clients are Germans and Austrians."

"Roitman always seemed to me a bit unstable," Elisha said.

"He was in the camps," his father explained.

"Then I shouldn't judge."

"No one can. Weiss was in Auschwitz too."

Mr. Roitman, not done hollering, stomped out of the shul, ordering his son to follow. Solly hunched his shoulders as he stepped behind his father and kept his eyes toward the ground, but Elisha could see his tears as he passed by.

Elisha returned to his seat, more agitated than before. At the next table, Reb Moshe Zeigler was staring at him with interest.

"What's the problem?" Moshe Zeigler asked. "Why all the fidgeting?"

Reb Moshe was a tiny man, and when he sat, his body dissolved behind his smoke-colored endless beard. He was a quiet man who kept to himself, yet all listened with reverence when he did speak, for he was a gentle and learned Chassid who could recite entire Talmudic tractates from memory. Elisha once heard him tell his father that he wasn't particularly religious before the war, but now, how could he not believe in a God, a God whose designs we can't understand? How else could he make sense of the horrors of the Holocaust that included the death of his wife and son? An anti-mirror of Reb Sender.

Elisha said, "I'm not feeling up to prayer today, to atoning for my sins." In fact, he'd been contemplating whether there were other Gods who demand atonement for sins *not* committed. Elisha astounded himself with the brazenness of his remark. He persisted, nonetheless.

"You, Reb Moshe, are less guilty than anyone here. How do you manage to recite this litany of transgressions? You've committed none of them, I'm sure."

Reb Moshe raised and lowered his eyebrows a few times in quick secession. An involuntary twitch of his eyelid, familiar to Elisha, suggested he was revisiting "those years."

"Not guilty?" Reb Moshe said, taking a step toward Elisha. Behind the thick, shaded lenses, Elisha could see the pupils expand in Reb Moshe's drained eyes.

"I remember that first Rosh Hashanah service after our liberation from Auschwitz. We arrived at the section that calls for the recitation of sins: 'we have transgressed, we have betrayed, we have stolen.' The rebbe who had gathered us together perused the hollow eyes peering back at him behind the skin and bones... 'we have scoffed, we were rebellious.' Who? We who were forced to stand aside as our parents were murdered? We who witnessed our brothers and sisters dragged and beaten to death? We who were made to watch our children flung into furnaces? We have scoffed? We have rebelled?

"The rebbe closed his prayer book. He couldn't go on. He himself had lost his wife and eight children to the gas chamber.

82

"But then the Rebbe reopened his prayer book. 'We will continue,' he said. 'Perhaps there were moments, passing moments, when we gave up. When the horror was overwhelming and we wished to die. For those moments, for losing hope, we must ask forgiveness.'"

Hitler ends all discussion. Along with all others born in the years right after the war, Elisha had learned the rules of inquiry: Do not stab at broken hearts with pointed questions. Pretend along with your parents the lesions of memory are healing. And the most important lesson of all: what is unspoken reveals the hardest truths.

But Elisha refused Hitler the last word.

That night, Elisha found his father sipping tea in the kitchen. The light atop the stove bathed the room in a serene, muted blue that heightened the scent of the holiday soup and brisket. It was late and it was quiet, the best place to talk, the best time to talk.

"I want to ask you about hope," Elisha said to his father.

He'd come prepared for battle. Here was the swash-buckling young musketeer wielding the scythe of logic with which to slash through the thicket of Brooklyn metaphysics. He announced the weapons of engagement: the rigors of hard reason and that alone; appeals to soft intuition were strictly verboten. His father nodded his head warily to his emboldened son.

Elisha said he was well aware positive thinking could be self-fulfilling. Sure, believing your health will improve might help it improve. But wishes are idle…hopes can't change reality. Why encourage the cruel mirage of hope? "Why do the Chassidic Masters—why do *you*, Tateh— offer this chimera to the desperate?"

Father and son volleyed for a half hour across the philosophical court. When does longing become self-deception? Who decides? Elisha flaunted his new vocabulary, dropping his newly acquired allusions along the way like breadcrumbs in a fairy tale.

His father poured a third cup of tea. He'd had enough. "Elisha, you're fond of this style of debate. You have a flair for it. I don't know if it's a blessing or a curse."

"How can reason be a bad thing?"

"Or what you call reason. Do you realize what a life without hope is like?"

"That's not a legitimate argument," Elisha said, unrelenting. "It's sloppy. Sentimental."

"Sloppy? Sentimental? You'll learn soon enough life is sloppy and sentimental. It's not about word games."

Elisha exclaimed, "Can't we have a conversation without you suggesting I'm immature?"

"I didn't call you immature."

"I'm well aware life is more than words. I'm also old enough to know that Mr. Roitman, Moshe Zeigler's wife and children, all the others, hoped for a different outcome all the way to the crematoria."

Seeing his father's face pale, Elisha said, "I'm sorry, but I was only making the simple point that hope didn't save people in the camps, it didn't rescue Stalin's victims, not the men and women of Hiroshima nor, these days, the children in Vietnam. Why delude oneself? It's childish."

"Oy," his father moaned but then grinned. "Sentimental. Sloppy. Now childish."

"I'm just saying we need to preserve our rationality."

"I understand. You've read a bit of Spinoza or whoever and become Mr. Rational while the rest of us are, as you say, self-deceptive. You know what the problem is? You have too little respect for mystery."

"I agree."

"You do?"

"Yes. Except I don't see it as a problem. That's the difference between us. You worship mystery; I want to explain it away."

Elisha's father raised both his hands as if he were yielding to a gunman. He was at the end of their verbal tango.

"Instead of arguing, why don't I tell you a story?" he said, inviting Elisha to sit down again. "A Chassidic tale about another Mr. Rational. A story about hope, in fact. But then all Chassidic stories are about hope, aren't they?"

Elisha, too, was relieved to end the duel. His fondest childhood memories were of climbing into his father's bed on fitful nights to hear magical tales of Chassidic rebbes, relishing a special thrill when they were about his own wondrous ancestors. He'd journey on the carpet of his father's words to the enchanted place of his forefathers where a flicker of human decency and wisdom would upend the danger at the door or soothe the storm in a man's heart.

Elisha's father shut his eyes and settled back in his chair. He opened his fist sending forth another Chassidic legend into the Rosh Hashanah night, a tale tattered from retelling, but restored once more in his gentle rendering.

Hertske deserved his reputation as a young Talmudic scholar. He married, went into the lumber business, and successfully transferred the analytical skills he'd honed in yeshiva to forging complex business deals. He was pious, studious, wealthy and philanthropic, and esteemed by all in his town of Zlotchov.

Hertske was also a Chassid. Not your typical Chassid, he'd insist, for he balanced an appreciation of the mystical with a firm commitment to reason. In his younger years, he'd scorned the very notion of a "rational Chassid" as a blatant oxymoron. He was the first and loudest in lambasting the budding movement as a bunch of muddled kabbalists who willfully transgressed hallowed traditions. Their leaders, he'd shout, were no more than ignorant charlatans who preyed on the superstitions of the masses.

Arguments do not change points of view; people do. One shabbos morning, Hertske decided to visit the small

Chassidic shteibl of Reb Mekhel of Zlotchov. Hertske stood in the rear of the shul, his arms folded against his chest, and listened intently as Reb Mekhel addressed his Chassidim at the end of the service. Hertske was dazzled by the rebbe's erudite exposition of Talmud, and so began his conversion to Chassidism.

Yes, Hertske seemed to have it all: affluence, intellectual rigor, spiritual sustenance, and communal fraternity...and a wife he adored and who adored him in return. There was, however, one gaping fracture in Hertske's otherwise complete life: he was childless.

The absence of a child pained him deeply. He and his wife Pesel had visited fertility specialists across the country, but after years of dashed hopes, Hertske had come to terms with reality: God willed he have no progeny. Unable to raise children of his own, he devoted time and money to helping nurture the health and education of the community's needy children. Surrogate children could not, of course, replace the void of a childless household, but Hertske accepted the Divine judgment with equanimity.

Alas, such equanimity was not possible for Pesel. Her days were exercises in distraction, her nights torments of desperation. The festivals were worst of all. "It's the bitterness itself I've come to detest," Pesel said to Hertske, not hiding the bitter tears. She regularly beseeched the rebbe to intercede, to plead for them, to do something for Heaven's sake, only to hear his testimony that God acts in His good time.

She complained again to her husband after her most recent visit to the rebbe several weeks before the holiday of Passover. "Why is it always me who asks for his blessing? Ah yes, you, of course, won't deign to ask for an exception from the normal course of biology. Nature is nature, right?"

"Pesel, we've talked about this a hundred times," Hertske said. "You know how I cherish Reb Mekhel. He is my teacher, my mentor. But fealty to the rebbe does not mean treachery to reason. So, yes, Pesel, nature is nature, and no human being, not even a holy tzaddik like Reb Mekhel, can revoke its laws. Let's face what we must: we cannot have children. So be it."

"So be it?" Pesel shouted. "So be it?" she repeated, this time quietly but with even greater rage. "Do you have any idea what it is like for me in shul?"

"I can imagine," Hertske said softly.

"No, you can't. For me every shabbos, every holiday, is a day of mourning."

Pesel closed her eyes for a moment and continued in her low, broken voice.

"I hear a baby cry in its carriage and I want to cry, too, because I have no child to console. My sister rushes to tell me her little son Nussy has just mastered the entire aleph bais and I'm astonished how a heart can burst with so much pride and despair at the same time.

The children next to me sing their prayers and I accompany them with broken sighs. I try to concentrate on the cantor's prayers, but all I hear is the murmur of young mothers discussing the pros and cons of diapers, baby carriages, baby shoes, schools, doctors, story books, nursing tips, who is pregnant and who is not, and I want to dash from the room. Sometimes I do."

"Pesel," Hertske said, his own heart breaking at his wife's anguish. "You've got to come to terms with the destiny ordained for us. This is the only way we can truly celebrate this coming Pesach."

But this year would not be easy. Passover had always been the exception to the gloom that enveloped Pesel's holidays. On this night their home bustled with family, friends, and needy strangers joyously participating in the lavish Seder. Pesel directed the presentation of the magnificent dishes, while Hertske, robed in his spotless white *kittel*, sat in regal splendor at the head of a long table covered with choice linen, upon which was set opulent white china bracketed by sparkling silverware and glittering silver Kiddush cups. The Seder was filled with the spirited reading of the Haggadah and even more spirited singing into the wee hours of the morning.

But the wheel of fortune whirls to its own inscrutable rhythm, and with the tick of a spin, those who have become those who have not. During the past year, the market for Hertske's timber had abruptly dried up.

The banks foreclosed on his properties. In less than six months, he was bankrupt. Nevertheless, he stoically endured his deepening destitution, for this was God's will, and he would assent to whatever fate bequeathed.

Hertske helped set the Passover table as always, determined to create what festive mood he could. Gone were the gleaming goblets, the fine china, and the splendid dishes. Gone, too, and most distressful of all, were the holiday guests. But Pesach was Pesach, and a Seder must be a Seder. He prepared the pillows for his chair, arranged the matzos and Seder plate, and began the ceremony.

He poured the first glass of wine and recited the Kiddush with his usual Chassidic rapture. Lifting the matzah, he read aloud the passage describing the bread of privation and prepared the second of the mandated four cups of wine. Here the Haggadah instructs the son to ask the father the *ma'nishtana*, the Four Questions. Hertske hesitated. He looked over to Pesel who'd been observing him from the onset of the service. Each saw the tears well in the other's eyes. Hertske tried again: "…and now the son asks…"

Hertske could not go on. He collapsed in his chair, crushed by the weight of years of disappointment. "I can't continue," he sighed, rocking slowly in his seat.

"Father in heaven," he sobbed, letting the tears flow freely. "I'm sorry, but I can't continue with the Seder because I, your son, have a fifth question for you. I am now penniless. My poverty notwithstanding, I have done everything you have required for the Seder and have set as graceful a table as possible with the few coins at my disposal. But I cannot fulfill the part of the Seder that calls for the child to ask the Four Questions. Why won't you allow me to fulfill your commandment? Master of the Universe, where is the child I need to complete my Seder?"

Pesel watched in astonishment as Hertske closed the Haggadah and put on his coat. "To the rebbe," he said, answering her unspoken question. "I'll ask him my fifth question."

As this was Passover eve, the Jewish quarter of Zlotchov was deserted. The only sounds one heard wafted from dining rooms above the streets, the voices of men, women, and children reading aloud the Passover story of the redemption of the People of Israel from slavery in Egypt.

Hertske walked steadily in the dense drizzle and thought of the four sons of the Haggadah, the wise son, the wayward son, the simple son, and the son too dull to even formulate his question. "The dumbstruck son, that's me, isn't it?" he said aloud, his tears merging with the rain. "All these years, I, too, didn't know how to question. Well now, I will not only ask, I will demand." He lowered his hat and walked with renewed determination to the rebbe's home.

The Zlotchover Rebbe showed no surprise at seeing Hertske standing in his hallway. He placed his hand on Hertske's wet shoulder and ushered him into the living room where the rebbe's family and guests were seated at the Seder table.

"I have a fifth question to ask—" Hertske started to say, but the rebbe held up his hand.

"Yes, I know," the tzaddik said. "As a matter of fact your question already made an impact in heaven."

"I don't understand," Hertske said.

"Listen carefully. I'll explain what all this is about." The rebbe looked over to his assembled guests. "There's a lesson here for all of us," the rebbe said. "The great misfortune of your life, my dearest Hertske, is that you have no child. Yet you admirably met this adversity without complaint, as God's decree. But somewhere along the way, you submitted to your lot as though it was immutable, fixed forever. You confused acceptance with acquiescence…you ceased to hope. But don't you see the hubris in this?"

No, he didn't, said the look on Hertske's face.

Reb Mekhel said, "It's a conceit to think we know the ways of the world, to live life refusing to expect the unexpected. The surrender to fate is a rejection of faith."

Hertske bowed his head. "I think I understand now."

The rebbe took Hertske's hand. "And so this was your punishment: you weren't granted the child you didn't ask for. Eventually, your refusal to petition God, your ceasing to hope, led to the loss of your wealth as well. But tonight…ah, tonight at your Seder, at last, you asked the fifth question. And my dear precious Hertske, tonight your question has been answered."

Need we add that a year later the sweet cooing of a newborn son regaled the many guests who'd come to enjoy the most stately Seder ever held in the home of Hertske and Pesel.

8

.....

Imagination was given to man to compensate for what he is not; a sense of humor to console him for what he is.

—Chassidim (and others)

It was Elisha's new friend Trevor who suggested they grab a snack before the concert. "No way Satchmo shows up before nine," he'd said.

The diner he chose was *treyf*, as unkosher as the moo shu pork at Ping's next door, and to make matters worse, the square-shaped waitress ushered the two young men to a table up front, right up against a vast window. When Elisha hesitated she scraped her head exposing black roots that reached a third the way down her faux platinum hair. "Sonny," she said with practiced irritation, "it's the only table available. Take it or leave it."

Elisha calculated: if one could see out, one could see in. He gritted his teeth but sat down.

"Salad," he said to the waitress, more an order than a request. "Nothing cooked. Just the salad, please." And to Trevor: "Can I borrow your baseball cap?"

"I thought the Yankees were your tribal enemies."

"For the meal only. I'd rather not sit here wearing a yarmulke and I certainly won't wear this." He lifted the black hat he'd placed on the seat next to him. "I don't eat with my head uncovered."

"You look ridiculous," Trevor said, as Elisha tried to finesse a stylish angle for the oversized cap. Trevor C. Arthur was four inches shorter than Elisha, but his head was of pumpkin dimensions, held up by shoulders the size of a truck's grille.

Elisha said, "Actually, the whole head-covering thing is more tradition than law. In fact, Sephardic Jews—"

"Sephardic Jews? We're getting a little technical here, aren't we? Spare me."

"Spared," Elisha said. "And check this out."

He handed Trevor the record he'd been carrying. *Bitches Brew*. "It's Miles's most recent release."

"Neato."

"For you. A present. In appreciation for tonight's tickets to the Waldorf. For introducing me to jazz."

"Thanks, I'm going to love this. But you be careful," Trevor intoned with the gravity of a doctor dispensing medical advice. "This music is one voracious bug."

That was pretty much what the sales guy at J&R had said to Elisha. "It become an obsession man, suck out your brain. Happened to me, happened to others. But never seen it among your people."

Elisha agreed and with no small degree of pride. He'd bet he was the first Chassid in human history to argue the fine points of Bird, Trane, and Dizzy.

Trevor was pursuing a rebellion of his own. He was a direct descendent of President Chester Arthur and grew up in Fairfield, Vermont, a mile from the house where the former president was born. There were expectations readied for Trevor, expectations he'd disappointed. His lawyer-father and banker-grandfather were infuriated when he'd accepted a cello scholarship to a music school in New York City; Trevor hadn't yet ventured to tell them his true ambition was to play bass in a jazz band.

Elisha had met Trevor in a practice room at the Manhattan School of Music. In exchange for remaining in yeshiva extra hours on Thursday nights, Elisha had enrolled for music lessons. Years earlier, a cousin visiting from Paris had left an old Selden clarinet in their house and didn't want it back. Elisha was instantly mesmerized when the guest demonstrated the instrument's range, from doleful low notes to the good-humored higher registers. He kept the clarinet in his closet, determined to elicit more than only the few shrill peeps he'd managed before taking lessons.

"Let's get to the important matters," Trevor said. He took off the sunglasses he wore even at night to "get into character," and with elaborate studiousness folded them on the table.

"Tell me about Katrina."

"What's to tell?"

"The essential will suffice."

"What do you want to know?"

"Do you remember when I first met her in that grocery store on 116th Street? I observed the two of you in the back aisle comparing cereal boxes."

"And what, do tell, did you observe?" Elisha asked uneasily.

"How much she liked you. And you her."

"She's a friend."

"A friend? Fess up, my boy. I'm telling you, she's mighty taken by you."

"How would you know?"

"Trust me. I'm good at this." Trevor pointed at Elisha. "You, on the other hand, apparently understand nothing about women."

"Well, excuse me, Casanova here."

Trevor drummed his fingers against his palm. "Listen, the few hours we spent together in the park afterward were more than enough time for me to confirm my judgment. I pick up the harmonies. Ride the cadences. It's my training. She's adorable, by the way."

Trevor stopped drumming and clasped his hands behind his neck. "Are you getting any at least?"

Though he hadn't heard the expression before, Elisha guessed its meaning. "Orthodox Jews don't get," he said, more combative than he'd intended. "We aren't permitted to be physical with women."

"Let me understand this," Trevor said. "My man here jives with Miles but no licks for chicks?"

"Why does everyone find this so impossible to believe? That's how it is. Anyway, it's not like she and I could... you know—"

"No, I don't know. I'm telling you man, she digs you."

"And I'm telling you, the issue is moot."

"Whatever," Trevor said and excused himself to visit the bathroom.

Elisha recalled that afternoon, the three of them leaving the store with bags of soda and potato chips in their arms, skipping the entire hundred yards to picnic on the Columbia University lawn below the steps of Butler Library, the majestic building that so awed Elisha a few years earlier on his first foray to a college campus.

He and Trevor had played chess, Trevor all the while discoursing on the intersection of Freud and Marx and the coming revolution sneaking up on the distracted bourgeoisie. Katrina, as bored with the political yapping as with her Russian grammar book, concentrated on a game of catch between two young boys until bored with that, too, she announced it was time to eat. She displaced her quarry from her shopping jaunt of the day before: *melomakarona* from Greek Astoria, Irish whiskey marmalade from the Bronx, *pyrohy* from the Ukrainian Lower East Side, and "for our esteemed rabbi" direct from the Jewish Lower East Side, kosher salami from Shmulke's on Essex. Elisha marveled at how relaxed he felt lying there on the grass with his new friends.

He and Katrina spent time together now, walking the city, talking about their lives, unraveling their aspirations. What sweet astonishing hours. How exhilarating that he could feel such exhilaration. But what he'd said to Trevor was the truth, wasn't it? The impossibility of him and Katrina. Elisha nibbled on his salad and stared out into the city dusk. Some things must be as they are.

"There is no must be."
It was his father's voice.
"There is only choose to be."
From where?
Elisha looked up the street. His father was walking toward him.

In Midtown? At this hour? But his father taught a class on Maimonides on Tuesday nights, the shul so packed the men spill into the vacant women's section. Elisha looked again through the window. Two figures in black frocks with bursts of white shirts were heading briskly in the direction of the diner; one, his father's size and gait, the same distinctive slope to the right, the other familiar, too—a teacher from the yeshiva? A relative he'd met at a wedding?

The men were a full block and a half away, but like a gazelle scenting a leopard shifting in the grass, Elisha could detect a fellow Chassid when still a speck in the distance. At a block away he could judge by the tilt of the person's hat and cut of his coat to which Chassidic sect he belonged;

any nearer and Elisha could tell you what the person would be doing this Saturday night.

They were coming closer. Elisha's jaw locked. But Tateh, look at my plate. No meat, no fish, not even a piece of cheese, only a tomato and a few radishes. These green sprigs are called watercress.

Don't panic, Elisha instructed himself, panicking.

"What's the matter?" Trevor asked, returning to his seat.

"Nothing's the matter."

"Oh yeah? You're pulling my cap down to your eyeballs, squiggling like a worm on a hook, peeping out the window like you were expecting an enemy squadron to attack. You're making me dizzy."

"Nothing, it's nothing."

Elisha forced himself to look out again toward the darkening street. The Chassidim were halfway down the block pointing toward the diner. No, he didn't recognize either one of the two, but they certainly might recognize him. He gripped the table's edge so hard the blood fled from his knuckles.

Why does this restaurant need such a humongous window, he thought. It's like eating on the street.

Elisha's heartbeat surged: Staccato. Bebop. Again, from somewhere, his father's disembodied lament: "Nice, Elisha, so now you eat in *treyf* restaurants…wearing baseball caps… with friends named Trevor…skipping classes to go to jazz shows…very nice."

Elisha could see them clearly now. One, more tall than not, his beard more gray than not, the other much shorter, his beard ash-colored as well but streaked with yellow. What did they want of him?

From the corner of his eye he watched as the shorter Chassid entered the diner. The man's stride was incongruous, the top half of his body bent forward from the hips while his feet remained ramrod straight, a carriage that reminded Elisha of a favorite toy soldier. The Chassid headed straight to the counter, but failing to get anyone's attention, turned and strode to the first table in the room. Elisha's table.

"Hexcuse me?" the Chassid asked in a familiar Yiddish-inflected English. The Chassid cast a glance at Trevor then back to Elisha.

Elisha picked nervously on the tip of his calloused elbow. Was the man one of his grandfather's Chassidim? A collector who made the rounds for some charity? Elisha was certain the man recognized him.

"We're from out-a-town," the Chassid said, motioning to his associate pacing on the street. "Can you tell me maybe, how I can find the train?"

"Pardon me?"

"The subway? You know maybe where it is?"

"The subway," Elisha repeated, his voice cracking.

"To Brooklyn."

"Where in—"

"Boro Park. It's in Brooklyn."

Elisha considered giving him directions in Yiddish, but instead answered in accent-less English. He was glad the temptation to reveal his background had passed.

"And it goes to Boro Park this train? In Brooklyn?"

"Yes, yes, to Boro Park, straight to Boro Park. Believe me."

Elisha watched as the two men followed his directions, and his heartbeat slowed from gallop to trot.

"You all right?" Trevor asked. "You seemed weirded out there."

"It's complicated."

"Did you notice the guy's posture?"

"Yeah. A presupposing preposterous posture." Katrina had used the phrase in one of her tongue-twister creations and Elisha tried to mimic the way she rolled the words.

Trevor said, "He's one of your people, isn't he?"

"I'm one of his people, yes."

The original Waldorf-Astoria stood on what is now the grounds of the Empire State Building. William Astor built the hotel there in 1893 to nettle his aunt who lived next door and with whom Astor was feuding. "And did you also know," Elisha said, carrying on with his tour guide intonation, "this was the first grand hotel with electricity and private bathrooms? The first to abolish a Ladies' Entrance?" Elisha spouted the hotel history to assert his local, big city stripes but didn't manage to disguise his awe of the surrounding splendor. He combed his shoe against the lobby's plush carpet and eyed the gowns and tuxedos traipsing in and out of ballrooms.

"You envious?" he asked Trevor before Trevor could ask him.

"Of this shrine to money? You kidding? I'm here only for the music."

Elisha rubbed his hand against the arm of a teak wood ottoman. "But you've got to admit the place has elegance."

Trevor faked a spit. "Elegance? What we should do is sneak in here late some night and put up one of those 'End the War Now' posters. It'd look terrific on that wall next to the painting of those spiffed-up hunters and their dogs lolling in a meadow."

A group of young people had encamped on couches in the lobby, porcelain-skinned girls festooned in pink and lilac dresses with hair ribboned in matching colors accessorized with young men in striped ties and white sports coats. Elisha could hear them tittering about his black hat and accepted a staring contest from the rowdiest among them, a pug-nosed fellow with hair just a shade more yellow than albino. Elisha relented when Trevor called his attention to the fifteen-foot gilded mirrors on the opposite wall.

"Better still," Trevor said, "we should put the posters right on the mirrors."

Elisha said, "Those mirrors bring to mind a comment of the Chassidic master, the Rebbe of Berdichev."

"Here we go. Another of your Chassid stories?"

"Not a story. A relevant insight. The rebbe once asked a miser if he knew the difference between a window and a mirror. He brought the man to the window. 'You see,' the rebbe explained, 'when one looks through an ordinary glass pane, one sees other people, but when one looks into a mirror, one sees only himself. And do you know why? Because the glass of the mirror is lined with silver. So, too, when some line their pockets with silver, they no longer see other people.'"

Trevor hadn't listened to a word. He was sitting on a sofa, his chin on his fist.

"What's the matter?" Elisha guessed from Trevor's grimace the news was not good.

"Goddamned draft board."

"I thought so. You've heard from them?"

"I tried not to think about it tonight. But, yes, the bastards didn't forget me after all."

Three years earlier, on December 1, 1969, all American males born between 1944 and 1950 were pacing their rooms, their hands halfway obscuring their faces if they stood in front of a television set or partially blocking their ears if they were getting the news from the radio. The Selective Service was holding its national draft lottery, and the birthdays called during the next minutes determined who would live and who might not. A New York congressman from the House Armed Services Committee had the honor of drawing the first of the 366 blue capsules from a large glass jar. Number one—September 14. Trevor's birthday followed soon thereafter: number 31; Elisha's not for a while, but not late enough: May 9, number 197. A middling danger.

"You'll figure something out," Elisha said.

"I should have gotten a deferment like you. Enrolled in clergy school."

"Rabbi Trevor Arthur," Elisha said. "Dances off the tongue."

Elisha lightly massaged his friend's shoulder. "Cheer up. Most of the troops have already left and you heard Kissinger's speech about how a peace treaty is in the works. I'm telling you, you can count on spending your wee morning hours sawing your bass in mangy clubs cursing the feeble tips of the drunk customers."

Trevor angled a smirk toward Elisha. "Kissinger. Sure. Now I can relax." But he agreed to forget about the future for now. It was time for Mr. Louis Armstrong.

On the way into the Empire Room, Elisha mentioned he'd also read the Waldorf-Astoria was the first hotel to introduce room service. He hadn't the foggiest notion what that meant.

Between sets, Elisha undertook his own tour of the hotel. One hand installed in his pants pocket, pretending to belong, he drifted from banquet hall to meeting hall and into the dim light of the second floor lounge.

At the far end of the room, Uncle Shaya had his arm around a woman.

This was no mirage. No invented voices, no phantasmagoric faces. There was no mistaking the shock of black hair, the sharp patrician nose underscoring the emphatic drooping eyes. A half bottle of wine shared table space with two empty glasses. The woman was of indeterminate age and indeterminate origin, but not young and not American. Her head lay comfortably on his uncle's broad shoulder, her long dark hair suspended over his back, and her bronze-colored arm slung lazily at his side, the repose in perfect harmony with a Ben Webster tune caressing the room. Her eyes were closed; his stared straight ahead. Elisha wanted to turn away. Too late. Uncle Shaya observed Elisha observing him and smiled, unhurried and unafraid.

9

.....

Money lost, nothing lost; courage lost, everything lost.

—Rebbe Simcha Bunim

The *shteibl* was crammed this Saturday; the holiday of Chanukah would begin the next night. Chassidim had arrived from Europe and Israel to be with Elisha's grandfather for the lighting of the first candle, and over the next day, many more would arrive from the precincts of Williamsburg, Kew Gardens, and small cities in New Jersey where, to the stupefaction of the local populations, Chassidim were driving stakes deep into the ground of the New World. But this year their rebbe's brocade chair was empty.

Few were surprised; whispers of Elisha's grandfather's debilitating health had crossed the ocean. Here, in the rebbe's own shul, the whispers had become full-throated. These past few days, they said, the rebbe had taken a major turn for the worse. Parkinson's was like that, don't you know, slow decline, plateaus, more slow decline, and then a telling lurch of infirmity. Senility often accompanies this awful disease, too, so they heard—even if the rebbe had the strength, his memory was now too sporadic to risk reciting the Chanukah blessing in public. Some said that some said there was talk of a tumor in the brain.

But no one spoke of illness in Elisha's own family. Why tempt the fates with gloomy declarations? Bad news demanded delicacy, euphemisms of euphemisms: "Zaidy is having some difficulties, but the doctors say the slowing down is natural and to be expected." Only the baleful sighs at the end of every conversation hinted at the gravity of his grandfather's condition.

"Your father will perform the blessing tomorrow," the men at his table said to Elisha. "It's no small thing. For you, too, you understand."

Elisha understood. His grandfather's mantle would migrate to his father's shoulders where, though not yet in name, it would remain; and in the ricochet of gossip across Chassidic tables in shteibls everywhere the changing of the guard would be noted along with Elisha's elevation from grandson to eldest son. "The son also rises," he said to no one in particular.

Elisha looked across the room to Uncle Shaya seated in his usual place against the wall. He pictured the woman's head resting on his uncle's shoulder, the strands of her hair entwined with the fringes of his uncle's prayer shawl, then to chase away the image, shook his head hard, almost violently, the juxtaposition too painful. Here it was again, the latest version of the same old puzzle: which was his uncle's secret identity—Uncle Shaya in the rear of a hotel lounge or Uncle Shaya in his seat against the shul wall?

Elisha slouched back into his seat and into the warm banter of his tablemates.

Next to him sat Bumshe Borowitz who, every shabbos morning, had some new life lesson to teach the table. Though a fifth cousin, Bumshe was welcomed into the clan's hive, for after the war who could be choosy with kin? He was even shorter than the rest of Elisha's Lilliputian relatives, five feet in his elevator shoes, making it easy to count the craters that potted his bald skull.

Elisha fondly remembered the day in his childhood during those first summers in their Catskill Mountain bungalow colony when he had been Bumshe's teacher. Bumshe had recently arrived to the United States and asked for instruction on the rules of baseball, this strange American sport. In their first softball game Bumshe had somehow managed to single and, like an immutable Buddha, planted himself on the stone they used for a base. Elisha, next up, hit a ground ball and yelled for him to run to second. "Nosiree," Bumshe shouted back, "you young thief, American *ganif*, trying to fool me. This is my base, and I'm not budging."

This morning Bumshe was expounding on his theory that all human faces resembled different animals. He turned to Elisha and said, "I even know people who look like fish. Maybe it's evolution, shmevolution. I'm not saying why, I'm just saying how it is."

He pointed to Chaskel Laufer the American, and instructed Elisha to notice the narrow neck, the eyes almost on the sides of his head—"a horse, no question, am I not right?"

He was right.

"Good. Now you try it."

Elisha surveyed the playful, soulful men around him. He looked at Mendel Shwab, Gargantuan Shwab, twice the size of anyone else in the shul with his broad forehead and piggish cylinder nose, an expert diamond cutter it was said. Next to him sat Mr. Spitzer with his two giant mutton-chop sideburns that reminded Elisha of a Davy Crockett character on the back of his Sugar Smacks cereal box who once again that morning tried to interest Elisha in a career in the corrugated box business. But Elisha settled on Fuleck sitting at the corner of his table. An eagle, he decided. The permanent frown, the tiny black eyes converging on his aquiline beak and even a twitter in his high-pitched voice. Fuleck Friedman glided into shul later than anyone and immediately joined the conversation, peppering the discussion with shameless off-color jokes. He was one of Elisha's favorite talkers and definitely an eagle.

Elisha was considering Zanvel's zoological counterpart when a commotion erupted at the other end of the shul.

Reb Muttel Pinter had fainted. A crush of experts gathered around the old Chassid, vintage-aged since anyone could remember.

Give him air.

Give him water.

Sit him up.

No, better he should be lying down.

Not on the bench! You crazy? Keep him on the floor.

Face up, face up! What's the matter with you?

What face up? Face down is better. That way gravity helps.

What do you know?

And what makes you such an expert? You're no doctor.

My son-in-law's a dentist. He's had experiences.

Elisha noticed the light of a police car flickering in the shul's window.

He ran outside. "Someone has fainted inside," he explained breathlessly to the policeman, but before he could even ask for an emergency call to be placed, the officer said he knew all about the prohibition against using the phone on the Sabbath and was connecting to the ambulance service.

Elisha turned to see his father bounding up the stairs of his grandparent's house. Scampering after him, he tracked his father's urgent voice to the kitchen: he was on the phone providing directions in Yiddish to someone from *Hatzolah*, the new emergency service instituted by Satmar Chassidim in Williamsburg and replicated in Chassidic communities everywhere.

According to Jewish law, the requirement to save a life supersedes all prohibitions—public idol worship, murder, and sexual transgressions such as incest are the sole exceptions. Chassidim preferred not to rely on the slow response of hospital emergency services and had begun training in CPR and manning their own ambulances. You could find

Hatzolah's emergency number affixed to the telephone of every Orthodox home throughout the city.

"But is a man fainting dire enough to desecrate the Sabbath?" Elisha asked, as soon as his father hung up the phone. "He's conscious again."

His father replied, "That's why I rushed here to make the call myself. I worried others would ask the same question you did and we'd be mired all afternoon in an endless legal debate."

"Well, it's not obvious his condition does qualify."

"So, Elisha, all of a sudden you're concerned with the technicalities of the law? Let me ask you then, why don't we recite a blessing before we give charity? After all, *tzedaka* is a mitzvah, too, and we always recite a benediction before we fulfill a commandment."

"Good question, But what's the connection?"

"The tzaddik, the Bnei Yissoscher, answered that you must provide sustenance immediately to a person who is hungry, and who knows what will happen to him or her by the time you complete your blessing? Don't you think delay is even worse when someone's life might be at stake?"

On the way back to the shul, they watched as two Chassidic young men gently placed Mr. Pinter on a stretcher and carried him into the waiting Hatzolah ambulance.

And fifteen minutes after services were over two men in medic uniforms poked their heads into the empty synagogue. "Happens all the time," one of them complained.

"We get a call, we show up, and no one is around. What's with these people?"

All afternoon Elisha darted looks at the clock. When Katrina first asked him about the "bizarre restrictions" of his Sabbath and why he was incommunicado for an entire night and day, Elisha acknowledged the frustrations, but assured her they were worth it. There was much to be said for devoting one day a week to dining with your family, conversing with friends, attending services, studying Torah with others, taking a siesta, going for walks, followed, of course, by more eating. Business is strictly verboten; even handling money is forbidden.

No one cheats, he vouched to Katrina; not on the major prohibitions, anyway. Elisha had read in his psychology textbook that the compulsion of the addict was too strong to overcome by a simple decision of will, yet all around him were people who smoked two packs of cigarettes a day but went cold turkey from sundown Friday until Saturday night; the moment three stars appeared in the sky signaling the end of the Sabbath, they would dash to light up their first smoke of the week.

"What about sex?" Katrina asked. "Is sex permissible on the Holy Sabbath?"

Elisha looked for at least the outline of a grin but saw none.

"What?" she said. "It's an appropriate question."

"It is," said Elisha, pleased she'd asked. "Sex and holiness go well together in Judaism. They're in bed with one another, you might say. In fact, according to Kabbalah, it is a special merit for a couple to have sex on Friday night." He produced the missing grin and added, "Married couples, that is."

He described to her more details of the Chassidic Sabbath and why he agreed with the adage, "it isn't the Jews who keep the Sabbath but the Sabbath that keeps the Jews." "The tradition definitely got this one right."

But that afternoon he was glad the days were winding down into the winter's solstice and this shabbos afternoon was among the year's shortest. In a few hours, he'd be on the subway to the city with Katrina's address clenched in his fist.

When she'd first asked him to visit her new digs on the East Side, he declined. It was inappropriate for him to visit a young woman who lived alone, he told her; and why risk even more temptation, he told himself. But his reluctance softened to ambivalence as she charmed him with playful incentives. She'd teach him how to perform a fake card shuffle, she said. She'd show him the secret to juggling three balls while chewing on a piece of celery. She'd demonstrate the best way to crack an egg, "and there is a best way." If he liked, she'd deliver a mini-lecture on the theme of hope and despair in nineteenth-century Russian literature.

"Stop by. I promise not to bite."

When Elisha balked, she smiled and said, "Okay, I promise I will bite."

Elisha was impatient. Three hours to go.

He tried to concentrate on his reading assignment on the Thai Lahu tribe of the golden triangle, but the pages were clouded by apparitions of Bumshe, Mr. Spitzer, Laufer, and Fuleck with their animal features prominent, along with other Chassidim in their long silk jackets and fur hats enjoying their shabbos constitutionals along the mountain roads of Thailand. He admitted defeat, closed his book, and set up a chess board on the dining room table. Elisha had taken up the game again after Trevor had brought him to a chess club in the Village several weeks earlier. For the next hour Elisha played a few matches with his brother Avrumy, a predictably ungracious loser, then busied himself in finding a response to the queen's gambit, Trevor's favorite opening. He didn't notice his father standing across the table, patting his hands on his chest.

"Are you okay, Tateh?"

His father studied the chessboard. "I remember the first time you checkmated me," he said. "You must have been fourteen. I wasn't happy losing, but I was even happier with your winning."

"What's the matter?" Elisha said, responding to his father's dour expression.

"You're aware tomorrow Zaidy won't be lighting the menorah?

"So I gather." But Elisha sensed something else was on his father's mind.

"I'll have to substitute."

"Pinch hit, they call it."

"Yes, pinch hit. Let's pray Zaidy has a speedy recovery. Being a rebbe isn't easy."

Elisha's father sat down and took piece of paper from his pocket and held it between his fingers. "Being a parent isn't easy either."

"What's that supposed to mean?" So this was the matter.

His father said, "The Ropcyzster Rebbe, my favorite Chassidic ancestor, once remarked 'It's easier to be a prophet than a rebbe.' A prophet, he pointed out, need only view the future, but the leader of a community must see the present. That's often much more difficult."

"Because?"

"Because you don't have the advantage of distance. Up close, you can miss the big picture."

Was this about parenting? About his father and him? Elisha thought it prudent not to ask. "I guess being a rebbe is a lot like being a therapist," he said, anchoring the discussion in safer waters.

Elisha could now make out the paper in his father's hand. It was a receipt.

"Believe me," his father said, "being a therapist would be easier. Until recently, people called on me mostly for legal rulings. A woman is in a dispute with her brother over an inheritance. A man wants me to decide whether he can take a trip on a Friday morning and risk violating the Sabbath if the plane's delayed. A rabbi sends me a letter asking me to support a proclamation against autopsies in Israel and another rabbi stops me on the street, indignant with my ruling about the kosher status of swordfish. That's my job, to interpret the law. But now they mostly come about personal matters."

"I bet that's a lot more interesting," Elisha said. He eyeballed his father's hand, certain the piece of paper had something to do with him.

"Let me assure you, people don't rush to my office to tell me how wonderful their lives are. They come bearing *tsuris*, one problem after another."

"Zo, Dr. Freud."

Elisha's father fluttered his index finger in the air. "These psychologists have a luxury I don't. They don't have to give advice. They leave it up to their patients to make their own decisions. God forbid a therapist should make a moral judgment, tell people what they do is wrong."

Was this a lesson on how to be a rebbe? Or something more immediate—a lesson on how to be a son?

His father continued, "But people do want to hear what's right and wrong. Just yesterday, a young woman arrived in a frenzy because in three weeks she was supposed to marry a fellow she now thinks is unsuitable—she isn't sure, mind you, but only suspects he's unsuitable. The invitations have already been sent, the arrangements completed."

"What did you tell her?"

"I thought she was more anxious about the commitment than anything else. But the point is, I couldn't just say, 'Do whatever you think is right.' She realized she was too involved to make a clear-headed decision by herself. People want—and need—guidance."

Elisha's father rubbed his eyebrow. He was taking his time getting to where he wanted to go. "Personal questions, family questions, these are the most difficult. Like whether to tell a child what to do, or say nothing and let him make his own mistakes."

He handed Elisha the receipt. "I wanted to ask you about this later, after sundown, but the way you rush out on Saturday nights, I wasn't sure I'd get the chance."

"What's this?" Elisha immediately recognized the receipt from the diner.

"Mother found it in the laundry. Apparently it fell out of your pants pocket. You ate there?"

"I don't understand."

"This past Tuesday night, it says. A diner in Midtown."

"Oh yes. I did… I paid for a friend. We were on our way to listen to music."

"This isn't a kosher diner, I presume."

"I had a coffee. In a plastic cup," Elisha lied. Badly.

"Coffee. On the way to listen to music. On a Tuesday night. I see. And this friend?"

"I guess he ate a meal."

"That's not what I asked."

"Oh. He's someone I know from music school. I play chess with him, too, sometimes. What's this interrogation about anyway?"

"Sometimes I feel I'm losing you."

"So now I'm dealing with the KGB?" Elisha leapt to his feet, his voice rising as well. "You examine receipts from diners? Ask about my friends?"

"I'm asking about you."

"This is outrageous. Look, I don't eat *treyf.* Okay? And I don't have to answer for every minute of my life."

"Elisha—"

"I don't believe this."

"Listen—"

"I won't live like this."

"I'm not accusing you of anything. I only wanted you to know I'm concerned. Concerned about the direction you're taking. You have responsibilities. People look to you. Especially now."

"Well they shouldn't. I have a right to live my own life."

"Oh yes, I forgot. Rights."

His father picked up a chess piece and fell silent. Elisha peered at the ceiling. After a few still minutes, his father broke the quiet. "Do you know about Moshe Mendelssohn?"

"What now?" Elisha said. "Yes, he lived back in the eighteenth century, and although observant he studied secular philosophy, helped bring about the Reform movement, thereby destroying Judaism, so forth and so on. Implying?"

Elisha's father held up his hands, parrying the onslaught. "Implying nothing. This isn't about philosophy. It's about chess. Mendelssohn was the greatest player in Germany in his time. But he quit playing."

"Too busy figuring out how to save—or was it, ruin—Judaism?"

"Relax, will you? Mendelssohn said he decided to stop playing because for a game, chess was too important, but to be spending his energies on it, well, chess was only a game."

"Your point?" Elisha said, still suspicious.

"No point, Elisha. It's only a story. I thought you liked stories."

Elisha nodded and looked up at the clock. Twenty minutes and he'd be off to Manhattan.

10

....

The root of sorrow is arrogance—to think one is entitled to all.

—the Besht

Katrina was staying at her mother's cavernous apartment on 77th Street off Park Avenue. The apartment belonged, in fact, to her mother's current boyfriend; they'd gone off to Europe for a few months or until, as her mother put it, "well, things don't always work out,"—whichever came first. "Yes, there's money...money is all there is," Katrina had once remarked elliptically to Elisha, the acrimony in her voice a warning not to mention the subject again.

"The door is open," Katrina shouted back to the bell, and Elisha stepped inside. His eyes widened to take in the luxuriously appointed rooms that adjoined the endless hallway. He tracked Katrina's voice to the living room, another humongous affair. A series of decorative prints plastered one wall, but on the adjacent one, cozying alongside an expensively framed reproduction of a bucolic Eakins painting of cowboys in the Badlands, Katrina had hung a Jimmy Hendrix poster in a there-goes-the-neighborhood gesture of defiance. From within a psychedelic halo, the guitarist peered down on Katrina's three-foot statue of Buddha in celestial repose on the living room rug, a stick of clove incense burning at its feet. Elisha traipsed cautiously into the room, carefully avoiding the precarious balustrade of books that weaved its way round antique vases sitting pretty on ornately carved stands.

"Elisha! You made it!" Katrina cried out, her glee suggesting she wasn't sure he would. She was lying on the couch, reading, her bare feet curled like kittens underneath her.

"Did they check your passport when you crossed from Brooklyn to Manhattan?"

Elisha said, "I'll have you know anyone who is anyone of significance is from Brooklyn. Or will be."

"Speak up," Katrina instructed and pointed to the turntable. "Or turn it down. I'm too lazy to get up."

Elisha lowered The Doors to human decibel range. He could now hear Katrina's dog Zorba scraping the floor in another room.

Katrina patted the couch pillow next to her. "As you see, my clothes have decamped on all the other seating possibilities, an improvement in the case of that horrid divan in the corner."

She sat up as Elisha sat down, exposing the ridge of her breasts under her sheer chiffon blouse. She followed the direction of Elisha's electrified eyes and noticed the open two top buttons of her shirt. She left them that way.

"I've been meaning to ask you," she said. "Do you believe in God?"

"Do I what?" Elisha could feel his groin tighten, answering its own call to attention.

She repeated the question.

He coerced his eyes away from her bosom. "If I believe in God? Why do you ask?"

Katrina said, "I've read Judaism is much more concerned with behavior than belief. And I've noticed that about you, too."

"Really? That's pretty good, 'cause I can't figure out what I believe."

Katrina said, "You always talk about Jewish practice, what you are and aren't permitted. And sometimes you allude to what you do all day in the yeshiva, the gratification that comes from studying Talmud, though I don't really get what that's all about. What was that line you told me from that rebbe?"

"I've tried many lines on you." He worked on keeping his eyes above her neckline; talking about religion didn't make the challenge any easier.

"The line about Paradise, smart aleck."

"You mean from the Rebbe of Mezeritzch? He said that after his death, he expected to be in Paradise, for even if admittance were denied him, he'd commence to teach Torah, and all the holy tzaddikim would assemble to hear him. And the place where he stood would be Paradise."

Katrina said, "That's the one. I like that."

Elisha wriggled in his seat. "What's with this interest in religion and theology?" Couldn't they talk about something else?

Katrina nibbled on her fingertips. "It's just I notice the only time you mention God or the afterlife is when they show up in Chassidic stories…like the one you just repeated. The rebbes are always arguing with the Master of the Universe, cutting deals with Him, carrying on shuttle diplomacy with souls in the afterlife. It's like a theological playground. Otherwise God's pretty much absent."

"And why exactly should this matter to me?" Elisha asked. Why did it matter to *her*?

"Well, you're the religious one here, but you don't talk religious. Unlike my father, for example, the newly devout Christian, who never stops telling me how famously he and the good Lord get along, in contrast, he's sure to add, to 'my New York intellectual daughter,' who's facing a sad eternal future if she doesn't repent."

Elisha noticed the sullen turn in Katrina's voice at the mention of her father but let it be. "You're right about Judaism," he said instead. "It doesn't focus on theology or what happens after you die. Judaism cares less about the philosophy that comes out of your mouth than the kind of food that goes in. We don't have…what's that word again?"

"Dogmas? Doctrines? But tell me, what do *you* believe?"

"What do you?" His eyes, despite his directive, again drifted downward toward Katrina's breasts.

"How typical," said Katrina. "Answering my question about you with a question about me."

"But you know why Jews answer questions with questions?"

"Why?"

"Why not?"

"You're impossible," Katrina said, stifling a smile. "You refuse to take me seriously."

She stood up to get a drink from the kitchen. Elisha followed close behind her.

"If only you knew how seriously I do take you, Katrina. But do you realize how complicated these issues are for me?"

Katrina spun around. "And do you realize how complicated you are? I want to understand these 'issues' as you call them, mostly because I want to understand you. And I don't."

"I know. As you said, I'm unusual."

"Stop it. I mean it. What you are is frustrating."

"I could write the book on frustration." Elisha bit hard on his lip.

Katrina ran her fingers across her mouth and stepped nearer to Elisha. "Yes, you're unusual," she said softly. "You're unusually interested in everything and that makes you unusually interesting. You're also smart and sweet and honest and handsome, too, and I love looking into your eyes…especially when you allow them to look back into mine. But then there's this barrier."

"You didn't mention my astounding clarinet playing."

"Yes, even your awful clarinet playing has potential."

"Well, thank you."

"Look, I know I'm this *shiksa* in your life."

"Please don't say that," Elisha said. He'd recently read Portnoy's *Complaint* and despised the book's caricature of horny young Jewish men, but hated even more the possibility he, too, was acting out a Jewboy-shiksa cliché.

"But it's true," Katrina said. "Your life is directed by this ancient tradition brimming with rules and expectations that rule me out. But I'm also learning how much good stuff there is in this tradition, and how it matters to you. It should. I respect that."

Elisha kept silent, agreeing but not wanting to.

Katrina brushed the back of her hand against her mouth. "That's what makes it...what makes you...so difficult for me."

Elisha walked slowly to the window.

"It's not easy for me either," he said.

Katrina stood behind him and took his hands in hers. "We can make it easier for each other."

Elisha gripped her fingers tightly and kept his head forward, as though by not facing her he didn't violate the prohibition against touching women. On the street twenty-two floors below, people looked like miniature wind-up robots darting between miniature wind-up cars, hurrying purposively to their destinations. But where was he headed? Where did he want to go?

"I'm so confused," he said with deep resignation. He withdrew his hands and began crisscrossing the floor. "Understandable or not, I can't continue on like this. In my head, I keep writing this letter to my father. A declaration of independence. No more charades. No more pretend. Tell them I'm sorry but the world has changed. I've changed."

"What is it you want, Elisha?"

"I don't know. That's the problem, isn't it? But I do know I can't live their lives." He paced faster, the pitch in his voice climbing, the Park Avenue apartment fading into his kitchen back home. "And the joke of it all? Tateh? I haven't strayed far at all. Have I ever missed a morning of putting on tefillin? Smoked a cigarette on shabbos? Eaten on a fast day?" He looked over to Katrina's body leaning against the wall. "Or…"

"Then what's the problem?" Katrina asked.

"It doesn't matter there. It's the same whether you deviate a block or a thousand miles."

Elisha took a few calming breaths and walked up to Katrina. "I'm sorry for getting carried away. This isn't fair. It's my problem."

"You don't get it, do you?" Katrina said.

Elisha looked to the side, unsure how to respond. He returned instead to their previous discussion. "You know when you asked me before about God? I recalled something the Rebbe of Kotsk once said."

"And what was that, my untiring Chassid?" said Katrina stepping close to Elisha.

"As a child he used to go out to the forest to pray. His father asked him, 'But isn't God everywhere?' The young Kotsker answered, 'He is. But I'm not everywhere.'"

"And you, Elisha, want to know where you are."

"And I don't."

Katrina put her arms around Elisha and her head on the crevice of his shoulder. After a moment, he leaned his head on her shoulder as well.

"It'll work out," she whispered in his ear.

"I don't want to squander my youth," he whispered back.

"You won't. You aren't."

Elisha hugged her more tightly. Could this be impermissible? Could she be impermissible? He put his cheek against Katrina's cheek hoping that might still the trembling in his chest. He was soothed; he was stimulated. He shut his eyes. He kissed her forehead.

Katrina lifted her mouth to meet his. Elisha brushed his lips against hers then again rested his cheek against her face.

"I'm sorry," he said. "I can't."

"You can't?"

"Not yet."

Katrina stepped back and pursed her lips. "Careful there, Valentino," she said. "That was almost intimate." She forced a smile.

"I'm sorry," Elisha said.

"I'll take you as you are," Katrina replied, then adding with an easier smile, "for now."

She sauntered over toward the hallway and disappeared into one of the rooms. "But I can take only so much gravitas," she shouted. "I have a job for you. It has the bonus of getting you out of here for a few minutes."

She returned to the living room with a dog at her heels. "Zorba needs to go out. Why don't you take him?"

"You've got to be kidding?"

He knew as much about getting a dog to pee as he knew about the rules of lacrosse. You might as well ask him about the fine points of sailing. He was petrified of animals, even of this little mutt who'd fit into his clarinet case with room to spare. Chassidim did not keep pets in their homes, not bird, sea life, or gerbil; the extent of his contact with other life forms was the four goldfish his cousin Genendel kept in a basin for a month and that was ten years ago. But dogs? Especially not dogs. Dogs growled alongside hunters, tsars, and fascists, put on this earth to terrify Jews.

Between gulps of laughter, Katrina showed Elisha how to hold a leash. "Leave it to him. He knows what to do."

Elisha waded into the street behind Zorba, their nostrils taking the first assault of the freezing air. The residue of the previous week's blizzard still cushioned the streets, and the round of flurries that had begun at dusk was now a full-fledged snowstorm. Up and down the block, the sound of shovels scraping pavement joined a chorus of tire chains churning snowdrifts. The glory of a snowstorm was short-lived in New York City. In a few hours the sparkling white purity would turn peppery with embers of drifting dirt and soiled footprints.

Elisha recalled that night in the library when he'd exchanged his stuttering first words with Katrina. He'd sunken back into the protection of the book stacks where he happened on a book listing the variety of Eskimo descriptions of snow. To avoid humiliating awkwardness, he'd memorized several of those words and still could recite two: *mannsguq*, for drifting snow and *katakartanaq*, encrusted snow that gives way underfoot. He wondered now if there was also a word for fist-sized balls of snow that whip you in the face while you try to figure out what the hell to do with a dog in the blustery midst of a gale. Elisha wrapped the leash tighter around his wrist and prayed the dog wouldn't sniff his incompetence and meander off on his own. As if on cue, Zorba pulled Elisha to a parked tire and sat on his haunches.

"Pee, will you?" Elisha beseeched silently, refusing on principle to speak full sentences to a nonlinguistic species. The dog just sat motionless in Zen-like disregard of the clueless Chassidic Jew to whom he was now tethered. "Tell me, Zorba," Elisha hissed at the dog, "is this supposed to be a comedy or a tragedy?"

"Both," Elisha could swear the dog hissed in reply.

Katrina was on the phone in the kitchen when the two shivering mammals returned home.

"That took a while," she said, her hand on the mouthpiece. "I thought you kidnapped the dog and took him to Boro Park."

Elisha said if he had, they'd pay her the ransom to take the dog back.

Katrina expressed a few indifferent ahums and mindless to-be-sures then hung up the phone hard, just shy of a slam. "That was my father," she said, joining Elisha on the couch. "He always calls at the wrong times. Come to think of it, his calling makes it the wrong time."

"You never speak about him," Elisha said. He could smell fresh perfume on her neck. The two buttons on her blouse were still open.

Katrina shook her head, her usual cheerfulness distilled from her cheeks. "There's not much to say."

"What's going on between you?"

"Let's not," she said, raising her hands. "We already did our family drama. One saga a day."

"That's not fair."

"Some other time."

"So you always say."

"But in any case not today. I've got a better idea."

Elisha tried to read her eyes but hadn't a clue what she had in mind.

Katrina said, "I think we both deserve to lighten up a bit, don't you agree?

"Sure," Elisha said, still wary.

"Like that rebbe said in the Buber book I read."

"You're going to quote Chassidic teachings again? I've created a monster!" He was, in fact, both pleased and discomforted by her incursion into his tradition.

"Is this a problem?" Katrina said. "You're welcome to read Tolstoy, you know."

"I'll stick with the Chassidim for now," said Elisha. "So what did this rebbe say?"

"I forget his name," said Katrina. "But he taught it's the task of every person to redeem himself from exile. And the essential exile is the one we have from our true selves. And the essence of personal diaspora is sadness."

"Listen to you!"

"I'll be right back."

Katrina returned a minute later from the back of the apartment, dimmed the living room light, and put on an album of Ray Charles ballads. "Better" she declared, and sat down next to Elisha. She held out two closed fists.

"Choose," she commanded.

Elisha tapped her right hand.

"Excellent choice. You win." She opened her hand to reveal a joint.

"What's in the other hand?" Elisha asked.

She opened her left fist. Another joint.

"You were destined to win," she said.

"You're going to smoke this, I take it," Elisha said, lifting his neck in what he hoped was a display of casual indifference.

"We are."

"I'm not so sure about the we part."

"Let me guess. You haven't before."

"Smoked marijuana?"

"No, run the marathon in your pajamas."

"But I've been around it. Outside the student building. In the park."

He watched Katrina light the thinly rolled cigarette and draw in deeply. She held out the joint to Elisha. "Here you go," she said between closed lips, the smoke still lodged in her lungs.

"Really Katrina. I don't think so. I held a girl's hand tonight...while trading insights of ancient rebbes. I even had a profound dialogue with a dog. Don't you think that's enough night's adventures for a Chassidic young man?"

Elisha fumbled the exchange and dropped the joint to the ground.

"*Oy vay*," Katrina squawked. "Like this. Thumb to thumb. Don't they teach you anything in yeshiva?"

Elisha managed the pass this time around, but struggled with inhaling. "I don't think this is for me," he said. He'd be disappointed but relieved, too, a familiar duo.

"Let me shotgun it for you."

"Do what? "

"I'll show you."

She fired up the other joint, placed the lit side in between her lips and beckoned Elisha to come close, pointing to his mouth. He didn't comprehend at first, but then put his lips on the cigarette as Katrina instructed and inhaled the smoke she blew into his lungs. He gagged the first time but not the second.

Katrina put the joint back in the ashtray. "Now without the stick," she said and put her hand under Elisha's chin. She leaned closer, drawing his lips to hers. Elisha looked for her eyes but they were shut. An ancient surge of thrill and trepidation coursed through his body from the top of his head to his ankles, and he shut his eyes as well. He kissed her full mouth. And again and again.

Later, Katrina stood against him, her arms underneath his winter coat wrapped around his chest. Good night, they whispered to one another. Ciao for now, let's hear it for the cow. Elisha tried to steady the whirlwind in his head, one thought sloshing against another, here, there, gone.

There is no Chassidic story about a first kiss but only because Chassidism forbids the kiss, not the story. He must remember—somehow, sometime—to forge a tale of a young man wrenched from the mouth he craved by the conclusions of a two-thousand-year-old heritage.

He looked at the clock in the hallway. He'd never before come home this late. He rehearsed his entry: he'd carry his shoes in his hand like a drunken husband, hope to sidestep the obstacles strewn in the dark as he tiptoed into the bedroom after a supposed late night in the office. He prayed everyone would be fast asleep.

Bracing for the winter night, he had one final question for Katrina. "What was the book you were reading when I came in?"

"It's called *A Spy in the House of Love*," said Katrina.

"Perfect. That captures precisely what I feel like tonight."

"Who are you spying for?"

"Me, I suppose. Who's the author?"

"Her name's Anais Nin. Spunky woman,. A girlfriend of Henry Miller. Are you familiar with Henry Miller?"

Elisha smiled. "Intimately."

11
......

A faith like a guillotine, as heavy, as light.
— Franz Kafka, *Parables*

Chanukah is a lesser festival in traditional Judaism, as compared, say, to the Biblical holidays of Passover or Succoth. The Talmud, uneasy with the political faction-alism of the Maccabees, devotes a scant two pages to the holiday; Purim, on the other hand, another holiday estab-lished by the rabbis, gets a full volume treatment. The European-raised Chassidim were therefore bemused by the excessive popularity of Chanukah among secular Jews in America, a vogue generally attributed to a hankering for a gift-giving holiday to run parallel with the Christmas of their Christian neighbors; others, alternatively, traced the festival's elevation to a post-Holocaust need to commem-orate Jews as victorious freedom fighters. But it is the mystical meanings of the Chanukah ritual that matter most for Chassidism—the lighting of the menorah, for example, as refracting Creation's original illumination. Chassidim also welcomed Chanukah because it afforded another occa-sion for the devoted to be with their rebbe as he led them in a communal performance of the mitzvah.

By the time Elisha and his family arrived at the shul, a phalanx of Chassidim milled about the entrance while a much larger throng was already inside jockeying for the best views. The heirloom silver menorah, which his grandfather had brought over from Europe, stood ready in the fore; at three feet, its eight branches reached above the window pane, fulfilling the rabbinical encouragement to share its luminescence with the darkened world outside.

As they made their way on to the shul's steps, Elisha's mother and sisters vanished into the women's section and a sea of Chassidic men split into two, forming a corridor for his father.

Elisha felt a tap on his shoulder.

"I didn't want to bring this up when Mother was around," his father said hurriedly in Elisha's ear. "And now's not the time to talk about this either. But you should know I heard you come in last night. Late, very late. I also noticed you slept late this morning. Very late."

"I couldn't help it. I got caught up—"

"I'm not pleased."

Elisha cringed at the hard edge of his father's clipped tone and the vexation in his narrowed eyes. He waited a few moments before following his father and brother into the synagogue.

"Last night was real," he'd said to himself when he'd awoken late that morning, an incantation against its impossibility. He repeated the words again now even more emphatically while peering out at the congregation of dark coats and pale shirts stirring like extras in an old black-and-white film, his own opaque suit blending into the colorless wave.

Suddenly, as if at some imp's directive, a flood of dizzying, hallucinatory hues rushed at him, the contrasting colored flashbacks of the previous night: the East Side apartment's indigo rug surrounded by the inharmonious lavender walls, the matching russet-browns of Katrina's skirt and Zorba's skin, her crimson blouse, the twinkle of her blue-green eyes. Elisha gripped the back of a bench for support.

On his right, locked in a suspicious stare, a young boy with sidelocks half his height tugged at his father's sleeve. "Isn't that the rebbe's grandson?" the boy asked, with the audible license of a child. "But he doesn't wear payis?" Elisha sent him an accommodating smile, but the child's stone-faced amazement suggested he was reading other, more devilish incriminations on Elisha's face.

Elisha turned the other way. Someone was scratching his left forearm.

"*Sholem aleichem*," the man said. "I haven't seen you in a year and a Wednesday."

"*Aleichem sholem.*"

"You don't remember me? Dov Ber? A cousin from Williamsburg."

"Of course," Elisha lied, then noticing the spacious gap between the man's front teeth said "of course," again, this time truthfully.

"So how old are you?" Dov Ber asked.

"Twenty. Soon twenty-one."

"Nu. *Shoyn tzeit.* It's definitely time."

Elisha looked up at the clock, feigning ignorance of his relative's intent. "Time for what?"

"Both my sons were already fathers at twenty-one."

"Mazel tov. But I'm in no rush to get married."

"Twenty-one is not called a rush. So, to the point. I have someone for you. An exceptional girl."

"Honestly, I'm not in the market at the moment."

His father must have approved this matchmaking venture—no one would suggest a *shidduch* for Elisha without having first cleared it with him. But a bleaker possibility struck him as well: his father himself had initiated the proposition. After all, what better way to deflect Elisha from his dangerous course? What better way to ensure he remain in the fold than by tying him with the bonds of marriage and a family?

Dov Ber said, "The girl is from Sao Paulo."

"Chassidim? In Brazil?"

"Oh, yes. There's a sizable Chassidic community there."

"My Portuguese is a bit rusty."

"You can learn. But I should also mention right away that…let me put it this way…hungry, you won't go. The family is very comfortable. You could remain studying Torah in a yeshiva for years."

"Money is not an issue for me."

"Don't be a child; money is an issue for everyone. You know what they say, 'Love is sweet—but it's tastier with bread.' But, you're right, of course. Wealth is not everything. Her father happens to be a well-respected Chassid and a learned man. And the girl, I understand,"—Dov Ber looked up at Elisha's clean shaven chin—"is not like our cloistered Chassidic girls here. She's 'with it' as they say, well traveled and cultured, suitable for you."

"Thank you, but as I said—"

"I see you're hesitant." Dov Ber puckered his lips in a conspiratorial smile. "If you were wondering, she's very pretty. Even my wife says so, and believe you me, she's quite the critic."

"Girls are always pretty to their matchmakers," Elisha said.

"Listen, I don't make light of this quality," replied Dov Ber. "The Chassidic books teach that all beauty traces to the Divine, especially the allure of a beautiful woman."

Elisha nodded in agreement. There was something divine about her face last night when it caught the glint of the moon through the window, something ethereal in her earthy laugh.

"It so happens the young lady will be in the States in two weeks."

"Thank you, but I don't think so."

"Meet her. What do you have to lose?"

Elisha performed an evasive tilt of his head. Wasn't that what he was weighing all the time—what was he gaining, what was he losing?

Dov Ber backed away in defeat. "Unless you're already seeing someone. In that case, God forbid I should interfere. But if it doesn't work out…"

The Chassidic flock pressed forward as Elisha's father strode to the menorah. He twirled the wick of cotton, placed it in the candelabra, poured the olive oil, and recited the benediction with an uncanny reproduction of the rebbe's enunciation, replicating each of his father-in-law's stresses and pauses. The Chassidim sang their dynasty's lugubrious version of the traditional hymn, *Ma'os Tzur* confirming their own Chassidic traditions would endure for at least one generation more. Brisker melodies followed, the rhythms quickened, and the animated Chassidim began to dance in orbiting circles, each person's hands atop the shoulders before him. Elisha stood aside, humming along to the tunes faithfully but with little enthusiasm, bringing his hands together so lightly you'd think his palms were infested with boils.

Uncle Shaya pulled at Elisha's rigid arm.

"Hey, a little life, please. This isn't a funeral."

Elisha, always heedful of his uncle's unpredictable moods, was pleased it seemed upbeat this evening.

"What can I tell you?" Elisha said. "I'm a serious young man."

"The truly serious know better than to take themselves seriously," said Uncle Shaya.

"Seriously?"

"Still the wise guy."

His uncle pinched Elisha's cheek. "Without joy, what's the point of all this?"

"Some think the point is the fear of God," said Elisha.

His uncle nudged him toward the dancing circle. "The Baal Shem Tov taught us fear of God without joy is not fear at all but melancholia."

Elisha considered the idea. "Well, maybe that's a better word for me. Melancholic."

"*Oy*, please," said Uncle Shaya. "You think you're a character in some nineteenth-century Russian novel?" This time he succeeded in moving his nephew into the whirling gyre of Chassidim. "Let's dance a little. There are times when you need to lose your mind and come to your senses."

Elisha put his hands on the thick shoulder blades of the person in front of him and adjusted his own shoulders to the grip of his uncle's brawny hands. Uncle Shaya was a terrible dancer—"two left feet," he gamely acknowledged. Elisha recalled another time his uncle acknowledged his clumsiness.

They were walking home together after shul; Elisha had turned fifteen according to the Hebrew calendar that day. "Can you walk shifting your feet like this?" he'd asked his uncle, demonstrating. "Right foot, then right foot again, left foot, left foot, right foot, right foot." A flash of terror had crossed his uncle's face then vanished as suddenly as it had appeared. In the *lager*, his uncle said, a Nazi guard ordered them to march in step like that, *Recht, Recht, Link, Link*. He wasn't able to do it and felt the blow of the stick explode on his neck. The guard made sure to command him to march the same way on the hike back, and again he couldn't manage those steps. Again lashes across his shoulders. He practiced, but to no avail. His feet wouldn't obey. Every day the guard would gleefully shout, "*Recht, Recht, Link, Link,*" and every day he'd get beaten. "Funny, isn't it?" Uncle Shaya said. Elisha shuddered. Yes, hilarious. Uncle Shaya had celebrated *his* fifteenth birthday…in a concentration camp.

"What's the matter now?" Uncle Shaya said, pounding him on his back. "We're supposed to be dancing, not daydreaming."

"Yes, let's," Elisha said. For the next minutes he'd lay aside his philosophical doubt, the traces of his other life, and abandon himself to the swirling rapture of these Chassidim, these people to whom one way or another he'd always be connected.

12
....

A wise man hears one word and understands two.
— Chassidic proverb

Elisha rose late the next morning, exhausted by the previous night's food and dancing, and ambled his way to yeshiva. This morning, as each morning, he was escorted on his route by WEVD, "the station that speaks your language." The radio in Hochberg's grocery store relayed the Yiddish wavelengths to Linick's Toy Outlet who passed it on to the tinny transistor radio on a back shelf in Schick's bakery, and on to the tailor shops, the Hebrew bookstores, and the string of apartments that lined Elisha's path. There was something here for everyone: breathless news reports of continuing Arab attacks on Israel; top tunes of the Yiddish theater sung by the likes of Molly Picon and Jan Peerce; story readings of Sholem Aleichem, I.L. Peretz, and Chaim Grade; a Talmud lecture for scholars compelled to earn their wages with a garment cutter's scissor or a diamond dealer's loupe; the comic, Galician one-upmanship routines of Dzigan and Schumacher; mock court cases starring cruel landlords and even crueler mothers-in-law; and Elisha's favorite, "The Yiddish Philosoph," a self-important blow-hard who interspersed his advice for the lovelorn with impassioned pitches for Carnation Instant Nonfat Dry

Milk. The familiar audio waves were a daily proof the European shtetl could flourish even in the wilds of Brooklyn.

Boro Park had not always been an acoustic home for Yiddish speakers. When the first Jews arrived to this patch of Brooklyn at the end of the nineteenth century, the mile long, mile and a half wide, former Dutch territory was still farmland, a rustic retreat from the distant city. This first wave of immigrants was intent on leaving their mother tongue with their mothers on the former side of the ocean; let their unwashed greenhorn cousins in their self-willed ghettos elsewhere in New York continue their Yiddishisms if they liked. These Boro Parkers were Americans and would speak like Americans. But they were Jews, too, and during the 1920s and 1930s they erected the grand institutional buildings that still stood in place: Israel Zion, the first hospital in America to serve kosher food, the splendid synagogues that cared for their communal souls, and the YMHA where they learned to care for their bodies for "one ought to be fit, to fit into America."

But then the German henchmen uncorked their venom across Europe and the surviving Chassidim, homeless and shell-shocked, straggled their way to New York City and when their resources improved, they began to trade the dense railroad apartments of the Lower East Side, Williamsburg, and Brownsville for the upscale one- and two-family homes of Boro Park. It'd been only a few years since Elisha and his mother took their seasonal walk three blocks north of their house to admire the Christmas ornaments, the rows of Italian homes garnished in red and green, each garden displaying an elaborate crèche, competing with its neighbors in decorative detail. But now the more assimilated Jews and their Italian neighbors had moved to the suburbs and their lawns and garages had been reconfigured into bedrooms to accommodate new inhabitants with their large Chassidic families.

Elisha stopped to observe a construction crew maneuver a dinosaur crane into the pit of a freshly dug foundation. "Another shul," a passerby cheerfully replied when Elisha asked what was going up. Boro Park already boasted several hundred synagogues, two per block, along with several dozen yeshivas; according to projections over the next decade, by 1980 that number would double.

This morning, as each morning, Elisha stopped at Zeitchik's for coffee and a buttered bagel. Other than widening the doorway to accommodate the flow of baby strollers, the luncheonette hadn't undergone a facelift in fifteen years. Nor had the rusty radio moved from its place above the stove in as many years; the volume knob, however, had disappeared in the interim and the Yiddish station blared all day like a trumpet call.

Mr. Zeitchik, the store's proprietor, sole waiter, and court jester, greeted Elisha without looking up from the cash register. It was only a few minutes past nine, but Mr. Zeitchik was long into his second cigar and long into his comic routines: "WEVD?" he said, laughing uproariously even before he delivered his punch line. "It's 10.50 on your

AM dial, but for you my dear customer, I can get it for 10."
Zeitchik's belt never adequately encircled his massive belly
and Elisha hoped he'd be there when the man's belly-roll
guffaws caused his pants to fall down to the floor.

A Chassidic woman waited impatiently for Mr. Zeitchik's attention. Could he call *Chaverim* for her? She'd
locked herself out of her apartment.

Chaverim was the new Chassidic organization that
assisted people in immediate need. Volunteers carried
shopping bags for the elderly, provided rides for drivers
stuck on the road, sent babysitters to parents who'd otherwise have to leave their children unattended. Elisha was
expected to contribute his time as well. His cousin Baruch
was in charge of scheduling young men to drive invalids to
their doctors' appointments; the moment Elisha passed his
road test, he'd be pressed into service. He'd protested that
he didn't have the time, but his cousin wouldn't accept the
excuse. "So who has the time?" Baruch had roared in return.
"You make the time. Like everyone else. Like everyone else,
you have responsibilities."

Mr. Zeitchik made the call. In a few minutes, a Chassid
arrived with a set of locksmith keys dangling from his belt.

Elisha barely noticed. He had other things on his mind.
He ate his breakfast slowly, digesting, too, memories of the
night past and daydreams of the nights ahead.

"Elisha, wake up!" Mr. Zeitchik howled.

"What?"

"Isn't that one of your esteemed ancestors he's talking about?"

"Who?"

"On the radio."

"No, which ancestor?"

"Listen, yourself," Mr. Zeitchik said, his head disappearing again behind the cash register.

An unfamiliar voice was speaking with the familiar pulses of Chassidic Yiddish. "So this is a Chanukah story about the balance of good and evil we humans can't always detect. It features Reb Moshe Leib of Sassov, the miraculous redeemer of captive bodies and captive souls.

The day of his bar mitzvah, Elisha had asked his father about the supernatural feats attributed to Reb Moshe Leib. Did they really occur? And all the other tales of righteous Chassidic tzaddikim—were they true as well? His father had replied, "Anyone who believes these tales are true is a fool, but anyone who believes they couldn't be true is an even bigger fool." He'd taken comfort in his father's permission not to believe, but these days wondered if he hadn't become the bigger fool.

"You listening?" Zeitchik piped up.

Elisha moved nearer to the radio, drawn despite himself to the wondrous tales of his rabbinical forefathers. "Yes, I'm listening."

"Good," Mr. Zeitchik said. "Because a story is never just a story."

Rivka Parnes had returned to Brody from Vienna where she had taken her daughter to be examined by the most prestigious cardiologist in all of Europe. There was nothing they could do, the doctor said. His judgment, "she hasn't much time," erupted in Rivka's ears like the death sentence it was.

Half a mile away, in the rear of a hardware store on busy Lemberger Street, a young man named Yechiel Tsurif was so absorbed in his artisan's craft he didn't notice his friend enter the room.

Had he heard the news?

"The Tzaddik of Sassov is coming to Brody for Chanukah," his friend said, bouncing on his heels. "He'll be with us to light the first candle tomorrow evening. All the rebbe would say was he was leaving his home to come here so he could redeem a soul."

Within an hour of his arrival to Brody, long lines of men and women had formed seeking an audience with the tzaddik. Waiting impatiently were Torah scholars and the scarcely literate, landowners with fur-lined coats and beggars wearing patches on patches, venerable Chassidim who'd been to the rebbe a dozen times before and hopeful first-timers, unswerving devotees and curious skeptics, all seeking a word of advice, a message of reassurance, a blessing, or simply the chance to tell their grandchildren they'd visited the Rebbe of Sassov. Among them, wearing a black kerchief pulled down to her tear-strained eyes, Rivka Parnes waited her turn.

She stood silently as the rebbe finished reading the petition she'd handed him. "As the tzaddik can see from my note, my daughter Bluma is deathly ill. The doctors say there is no hope."

"There is always hope," the rebbe said.

"Yes, of course. And if the rebbe would please pray for my daughter's health then surely this wish will be realized."

The Sassover Tzaddik shook his head. He asked for nothing. "God hears your entreaties, Rivka. I assure you, your Bluma will live and thrive and marry and, God willing, you will enjoy many years together with your many grandchildren."

Rivka Parnes smiled for the first time in months, the weight lifted from her heart. She thanked the rebbe and prepared to leave when the tzaddik called her back.

"Oh yes, there is one thing. Just the one thing. Your menorah."

"My menorah?" Rivka was startled. She owned several.

"The silver menorah, the one you inherited from your father," the rebbe said. Could she please bring it right away?

A few hours later, the shul was crowded with Chassidim thrilled to be with their rebbe when he initiated the first night of Chanukah. They also gathered around to admire the famed Parnes Menorah which stood on the table next to the rebbe.

"Yechiel Tsurif!" the Sassover Rebbe called out. "Come, come here. You are an artisan. I'd like to hear your professional assessment of this menorah."

Yechiel slowly picked up the candelabra, uneasy with all the attention now converged in his direction. "It's exquisite," he said. He ran his hand over the smooth lines and perfectly shaped knobs, appreciating craftsmanship that escaped the others.

The rebbe's gaze fixed on Yechiel. "I'm pleased you're fond of this menorah. I'd like for you to be at my side when I make the holiday blessing."

The Chassidim roared "Amen" when the rebbe completed the blessing and with one voice sang the holiday melodies. When the singing quieted, the rebbe turned to Yechiel Tsurif who'd been beside him throughout the ceremony.

"Nu, so what do you think of this Chanukah lamp?"

"As I said before," Yechiel said, "this is a true work of art. May the rebbe enjoy it until he is a hundred-and-twenty and greet the messiah with it in his hand."

"No, no," said the Sassover. "This isn't my menorah. It's yours. I will tell you why. And you will all understand why this is truly a festive Chanukah." He asked that Rivka Parnes come to the front for she too must hear what he had to say. A hush descended as Reb Moshe Leib began his tale.

Years ago, there lived in Brody a devout Chassid of the holy and pure, Reb Zusha, may his name be a blessing for us all. This Chassid's name was Yechiel Tsurif—your grandfather, Yechiel. As you surely have heard, he was an outstanding silversmith admired throughout the region and from whom you inherited your artistic skills along with his name. Well, Yechiel Tsurif may have been a brilliant craftsman, but he was also a hopeless businessman and barely scratched out a living.

Now, as I mentioned, this Reb Yechiel was a devotee of Reb Zusha and whenever possible would spend the holidays with his rebbe. As is the custom of many Chassidic rebbes, Reb Zusha distributed silver coins to his Chassidim when they set out to return to their families and Yechiel Tsurif prized these silver mementos above all other possessions.

When Reb Zusha died, Yechiel Tsurif grew increasingly anxious about his treasured collection of coins. What if it were lost or stolen or inadvertently used to make an ordinary purchase? Yechiel alighted on an inspired solution. He would melt the coins and use the silver to sculpt a menorah. As you can imagine, this became a labor of great love fusing his artistic talent with Chassidic devotion. The striking result stands before us on this table.

Affluent Jews beset Yechiel Tsurif with generous offers for his menorah and the most adamant of all, Nuchim Parnes, the richest Jew in Brody, offered two, three times more than anyone. But Yechiel rejected all tenders. The lamp was priceless, he said, and not for sale.

Years passed, and Yechiel Tsurif's daughter reached the age of betrothal. An excellent match was arranged with a young man renowned for his piety and scholarship. There was, however, the one hitch: money for a dowry. Yechiel would have to support the young man in full-time Torah studies for several years, a cost Yechiel Tsurif could certainly not afford. The poor artisan sought loans from friends and acquaintances, but the funds were insufficient to secure the marriage. Desperate, bearing the awesome responsibility for his daughter's future, Yechiel Tsurif knocked on the door of Nuchim Parnes.

He explained his situation. He needed a loan to pay for a wedding and to subsidize his potential son-in-law in his Torah studies.

"A loan? A loan he wants." Reb Nuchim suppressed a chuckle. "And what do you intend to provide for security? The chickpeas in your kitchen cabinet? Your estate...your hovel? Let's forget this loan business. Whom are we kidding?"

Yechiel Tsurif wanted to flee then and there but understood walking out empty-handed meant no marriage for his daughter. "Reb Nuchim, please… without your help…"

"You want my help?" Nuchim Parnes said. "Okay, so let's talk business. You want something I have. Money. You have something I want."

Yechiel Tsurif's temples thumped, his chest tensed. He dreaded what would follow.

"Yes, your silver menorah. You're well aware I've been eyeing it for years."

Seeing Yechiel Tsurif blanch, Nuchim Parnes said, "Be realistic for once. It's your good fortune I have such a craving for your menorah. In exchange for it, I am prepared to pay the entire cost of your child's wedding."

The two men stood looking at each other.

"So, Yechiel Tsurif. Do we have a deal?"

Nuchim Parnes pressed his offer. "I appreciate what this menorah means to you. And I also want to partake in the great mitzvah of helping a young Jewish woman celebrate a wedding and build a new home. So I'll add to the bargain. Not only will I pay for the entire wedding, I'll finance the first two years of your future son-in-law's studies. All for a menorah." He stretched out his hand to consummate the arrangement.

An hour later, a heartbroken Yechiel Tsurif returned holding a box in his hands. He loved his menorah, but he loved his daughter more.

Nuchim Parnes kept his end of the agreement and more. The wedding was a glittering celebration—a wealthy banker could do no better—and the dowry, too, arrived as promised.

The Sassover halted and sipped from a glass of water, but the Chassidim did not stir. "Yes, there is more to the story," the rebbe said, anticipating their curiosity.

A few years after the wedding, Nuchim Parnes died, and his soul arrived at the Heavenly tribunal. The lawyers for the defense presented a solid history of good deeds, his meticulous care in fulfilling the commandments along with his philanthropy for the needy. But the prosecution presented a negative catalog no less compelling—there were questionable business dealings and arrogant outbursts toward his employees. Back and forth, the trial swung, tilting one way then the other. When the arguments were done, the scale tipped decidedly: against Nuchim Parnes. He would be sent to the region of the infernal.

But just as the sentence was to be pronounced, a commotion erupted in the rear of the heavenly courtroom. A blind angel stumbled into the room shouting for a halt to the proceedings.

"I am the angel Nuchim Parnes created when he provided for Yechiel Tsurif's daughter's wedding!"

The angel staggered to the front of the tribunal. "Place the weighty mitzvah of aiding a needy bride on the scale, and let's see where matters stand." The scale was now preponderate in the other direction. The soul of Nuchim Parnes was directed to enter paradise.

Alas, this would not be the end of his trials. According to Kabbalah, each time we perform a mitzvah, we create an angel who will be our benefactor, and the most important mitzvah we do creates the angel who will escort us into the Next World. But the actions we commit in this world are rarely wholly good or evil. Intention always counts. So when we perform a good deed with flawed motivation our corresponding angel is corrupted as well. The blemish corresponds to the blemish in our action.

Nuchim Parnes performed the wonderful mitzvah of providing for a wedding, but his mitzvah was compromised. By demanding the menorah in exchange for his charity, he banished the light from Yechiel Tsurif's home. And so the angel he created was also bereft of light. Nuchim Parnes's sponsoring angel was blind.

Do you know what's been going on all these years? Ever since the verdict, Nuchim Parnes and his blind angel have been seeking the entrance to Paradise. They roam from place to place, push against walls, two lost companions, hostages of the dark, searching, searching.

The Sassover picked up the menorah and handed it to Yechiel. "Take this. It is your patrimony. Redeem the soul of Nuchim Parnes. Now that the mitzvah is made whole, sight will be restored to the blind angel, and he will be able to find the Gate of Heaven."

Yechiel's hands trembled as he accepted the menorah, but the Sassover Tzaddik laughed as he clapped his hands. "Ah, to free a soul from captivity!" Rising to his feet he called his Chassidim to join him in a dance.

And those in the room that night swear that never have Chassidim danced with such joy as they did that first night of Chanukah in Brody.

13
....

He who doesn't see God everywhere sees God nowhere.

—the Rebbe of Kotsk

Elisha hadn't noticed the skeletal woman drinking a coffee a few stools away, her wrist slim enough to fit into a Mafioso's pinky ring. Were there anorexic angels, too? Emaciated angels created by people who stinted when speaking kindly to others, their comforting words expelled from behind half-closed mouths. What about crippled angels? One-armed by-products of the charitable deeds performed by those who donate with one hand behind their backs, their philanthropy a hedge against possible sanctions in the afterlife.

Elisha wished he could spend the rest of the morning right there at Zeitchik's counter strolling the corridors of the celestial spheres rather than at the crammed table in the yeshiva. How nice it'd be to sip his coffee and visit with the blind angel who'd be waiting for him on a tree stump off the heavenly road.

"Let me tell you my side of the story," the angel would say as Elisha approached. "Do you have any idea how relieved I am to be finished with that old man? Shlepping him around, day after day, decade after decade, that fat old Mr. Pomposity, that sanctimonious, supercilious, snobbish…better don't get me started."

Elisha asked for a refill and rehearsed the conversation he'd have with Katrina that evening. He'd retell the tale of Blind Angel and Katrina would be tickled by the idea of tentative angels battened to the impulsive decisions of humans down here on earth, sympathetic to the notion even our petty actions have cosmic significance. He'd complain again about her concessions to fairy tales, and, to buttress his credibility, quote the levelheaded Kotsker Rebbe: "Can the tzaddik resurrect the dead? No, that's God's business. Our job is to resurrect the living." But Katrina would just shake her head and quote, "There are more things in heaven and earth, Horatio, than are dreamt of in your philosophy." Why was it, Elisha mused, the people who mattered most to him had such tolerance for mystery and magic? He had no good answer to that question, he admitted, and gathering his coat, he bid a good day to the top of Mr. Zeitchik's head still hidden behind the register.

The hours Elisha spent in Boro Park diminished with each passing day, while the hours with Katrina increased with each passing evening. They'd meet before Katrina's waitressing shift and after, before classes and after, sometimes conspiring to skip school altogether and roam the city's obscure neighborhoods in search of imported trinkets before settling into a café for a few hours more to dissect God, government, Gogol, and *The Godfather*.

Katrina dazzled him with her exuberance; her impulsive abandon blazed such contrast to his own pensive sobriety.

One school evening, to his embarrassed admiration, she jitterbugged in the student lounge to a Leonard Cohen dirge then insisted on teaching him the steps. One Sunday morning, she recited a continuous run of nursery rhymes the entire train ride from Manhattan and all the way up the steps of the Statue of Liberty, inveigling him to join her in a fresh batch of children's tunes on the way down. One late afternoon in the park, she drew him into an animated hour-long conversation with a group of Puerto Rican children about the nefarious motives of Batman and later in her living room, on her flute played variations on a theme by Grieg, "our Norwegian composer," and sweetly applauded Elisha's own feeble attempts to do the same with his clarinet. And most remarkably, thanks to her prodding, Elisha discovered one night at Max's Kansas City he was a natural dancer if only he stopped watching to see if he was watched. "You don't need anyone's permission to celebrate your passions," she'd tell him again and again.

But Elisha couldn't fully let go. He muttered frail appeals to a natural lack of spontaneity, his natural self-consciousness. He pleaded he needed to preserve his dignity, protect his public persona. And precisely on those days when he held back, reticent and unsure, Katrina would sneak up on him from behind, fling her arms around his stomach, and tease the outer lobes of his ear with her tongue. "It's me," she'd whisper, "your inner muse here to help you unleash Elisha."

And, to be sure, there'd been an unleashing. He now wore a checkered golf cap in Manhattan, but nothing at all on his head in movie theaters, jazz clubs, or at the Rossalimo Chess club where he whiled away many of his free hours. Indeed, most telling was that day he sat bare-headed with Katrina in a café when a familiar-looking Chassid walked in to use the restroom. Elisha had flinched, but only momentarily; gone was the reflexive cardiac panic, the urge to scurry under the table for cover, and Elisha knew he'd crossed another boundary.

He ate dairy in nonkosher restaurants. Fish any day now. Prayer had become increasingly difficult, the words cardboard on his lips. Each morning he'd close the door to his room and wrap his phylacteries on his arm and head as the Torah commands, but remove them after two minutes and read a magazine for ten—time enough to have completed his prayers for anyone monitoring the clock. On the Sabbath, he'd stumble into shul, banter with his comrades at the rear table for an hour or so, wish a good shabbos to his grandmother, peek in on his bedridden grandfather, then meander the streets until it was time to go home. "You now win the shteibl LIFO award," Fuleck said, yielding his top-ranking honor. "Last in, first out."

He hadn't had a haircut in months.

Elisha had considered withdrawing from yeshiva entirely, but concluded the idea was imprudent. First, and most crucially, his father would be devastated—why incur even more of his already deepening displeasure? Second, although the war in Vietnam was dwindling, the appetite for new recruits remained voracious. Third, he still enjoyed studying Talmud, although he no longer was sure why.

But he did show up to yeshiva later and later each morning and leave earlier and earlier each afternoon. He wasn't surprised when he received word the rosh yeshiva, the dean of the school, wanted to see him in his office.

Rabbi Aronowitz was one of the few renowned Talmudic scholars of Lithuania to survive the war, a reputation that immediately catapulted him to the pantheon of rabbinical luminaries in the United States. The rosh yeshiva was also rumored to have been something of a mathematical prodigy and even to have written a commentary on Euclid when he was twelve, though no one had actually seen the work. Elisha and his friends wasted many high school hours debating whether Rabbi Aronowitz would have been as celebrated as Einstein had he persevered with his mathematical studies, and, conversely, whether Einstein would have been a laureate of Torah had he devoted his brain cells to Talmud rather than physics. No doubt the next batch of high school students was retreading the same conjecture.

"I'm told your attendance has become a real problem," Rabbi Aronowitz said to Elisha as he entered his office. "Alas, I've heard even more worrisome reports."

Rabbi Aronowitz squirmed in his chair, irked at having to involve himself in disciplinary matters. His kindly face seemed incapable of appearing angry, but was cast in perpetual exhaustion. Elisha harbored the notion that the furrowed lines scattered above the rabbi's brows were Hebrew letters that spelled out some holy message. He could read nothing there now but concern.

"I've been exceptionally busy," Elisha said. "As I informed the rosh yeshiva, I'm taking classes in college."

"I know all about it," said Rabbi Aronowitz. "I wasn't happy when you started and, as we see, for good reason. I'm surprised your father gave you permission."

"One needs a profession to make a living."

"Others, yes. But not you. You have a glorious lineage to maintain. Elisha, you have the potential to be a great teacher of Torah, a leader among Israel."

"I'm not sure about that."

"It's terrible to squander your talent."

"I keep up."

"Keep up? Torah is a full-time occupation, not a stroll in the marketplace. So what *is* the problem? I know there are young men who have difficulties at home, don't get along with their parents, and take it out on their Judaism. But I don't think that's the issue here."

"It isn't. I treasure my parents."

Rabbi Aronowitz grabbed his beard and looked to the side. "You're a young man," he said haltingly. "With desires. That too, sometimes…"

Why not be honest? The rabbi was not a petty man, and he'd dealt with personal challenges before. One of his daughters, a professor of political science at UCLA was no longer observant, a persistent source of shame for the rabbi.

Elisha tapped his foot on the floor. Rabbi Aronowitz was right about desire: her arms were certainly an allure, her lips a convincing argument. But the truth was, physical craving wasn't what drove him from these study halls. His uneasiness ran deeper, reaching down to the basic tenets of his tradition. Without those convictions, why spend eight hours each day pouring over a page of Talmud?

"Questions are natural," Rabbi Aronowitz continued. "The solution is more Torah study, not less. Trust in the Almighty and in the teachings of our sages, and this confusion will work itself out."

This was the standard response to skepticism, the catechism Elisha had heard so many times before: religious disquiet can only be calmed by more religion. But unlike the others, Rabbi Aronowitz believed it. Elisha stood silently and waited impatiently to be dismissed.

The rosh yeshiva lifted himself from his chair signaling the end of the interrogation. He, too, was eager to get this inquisition over with; his task was to teach students to navigate through difficult passages of legal texts not monitor their bodily comings and goings. He had one parting remark for Elisha. "Someone, I'm not sure who, but someone wise, said, 'Seek not to understand that you may believe, but believe that you may understand.'"

Elisha thanked the rosh yeshiva as he walked out the door. He didn't have the heart to tell him the quote belonged to Saint Augustine.

"Coronary Jews," was how Elisha and his fellow students described Jews who observed none of the tradition but claimed to be "a Jew in my heart." He was less cynical now, old enough to notice that people always mock what they're about to become. But a coronary Jew? He knew too much Torah for that. He knew that Judaism had to be lived not only with sentiment, but also with one's mind and limbs. And he understood, too, that he couldn't continue as he was now: three toes inside his traditional world, the rest of his body leaning outward, half observant, half heretical, each morning revisiting his limits, each evening choosing to conform or transgress. This religious randomness was exhausting. You accepted or you rejected. There was no choice but to choose.

In the past, the choices came easy—guilt would draw his borders. But the pinch of remorse had become dull and unreliable. Only at home did it retain its sting; a spasm of contrition ripped through him each time he let himself notice the hurt in his parents' eyes. Perhaps most painful was seeing the satisfaction on his brother's face when he carried a Talmud into their father's office for a study session; that was supposed to be him, Elisha, the older, wiser son in that room. Now Elisha and his father exchanged little more than monosyllabic nods, each aware of the conversation they both so sorely missed. Elisha discovered how homesick one can be even when one is at home.

14

....

*Evil is not only he who hates his fellow man, but he
who hates himself.*

—Rebbe Nachman of Breslov

They'd already sat down for the Passover Seder when the door-bell rang. Who'd use the bell in violation of the laws of the holiday? Certainly not the mailman at this time of night, and it was too late for an encyclopedia salesman. Too late even for the Jehovah's Witnesses who peddled their missionary wares to the bewildered Jews of Boro Park. No one was surprised when Elisha got up to answer the door. Who else dared bring his outside life home on this Pesach night?

"Katrina!"

As he feared, his outside life was standing right there in a loose jacket over a plain white T-shirt, a sensible white skirt well below her knees but wearing, too, the pink, green-laced sneakers she went nowhere without.

"I had the night free," Katrina said, cheerfully. "You told me what a major event this meal was so I thought I'd pay an unexpected visit."

"What a surprise," Elisha said, in a strangled voice. The buzz of conversation behind him screeched to a foreboding silence.

"What's the matter?" Katrina asked, reacting to his stark reserve. "Aren't you going to invite me in?"

"Actually, Katrina, this isn't a good time for a visit."

The door separating the foyer from the dining room was half open. Katrina craned her head and peered inside. The pupils in her eyes expanded as she absorbed the live diorama, her eyebrows lifting so high they seemed ready to float off into space. Elisha knew what she saw: embroidered pillows on the dining room chairs prepared for reclining during the meal and matching embroidered white table-cloths over a table long enough to accommodate twenty-five place-settings. What did she make of the married men in their pressed *kittels*—white robes that made them seem like…priests?…doctors?…imperial wizards of the Ku Klux Klan? Could she see the women clustered at a second table, dressed in their holiday attire, some wearing headscarves, the others wigged? Elisha was certain all of them were craning *their* necks for a better view of her.

He turned and confirmed what he dreaded most. Katrina's direct line of vision was fixed at the head of the table where his father sat silently, hardly moving, waiting, waiting, looking straight back at Katrina.

Elisha moved a step to the side, desperate to block the visual crossfire. "As you can see, Katrina, I wasn't kidding when I said I come from a very Orthodox family." He'd tried to impress her on how different he was from the others in his family, yet here he was so patently at home in his home. "This really is awkward," he said.

"Awkward? Why? I thought this was a holiday? A festival calls for festivity. Here, I brought you dessert from Astoria."

"Thanks, but—"

"It's your current favorite. *Koulouria*, those butter cookies with a light sugar glaze? It's not bread; I know you can't eat that on Passover."

Elisha waved his hands in front of him. "Thanks, but these cookies aren't permitted on Passover either. Nothing leavened. Please keep them in your bag." That's all he needed, Katrina passing Greek cookies around the Seder table.

Behind him the murmuring mounted. His aunt Gittel, intrigued: "Who is this girl?" His cousin Hencha, twining her pearls: "A *shiksa,* no question, did you notice the eyes and turned-up nose?" His cousin Freyda: "And straight hair. Not one of ours, that's for sure." From the men's table, his cousin Yossel, disconcerted: "And Elisha used to be so devout"; and Mayer: "I always said, this is what happens when you let them go to college"; Aunt Gittel again: "She's a friend, nothing wrong with that, but I agree, this is not the right time for a visit." Too bad his uncle Shaya held his Seder in his own house, Elisha thought. He could sure use his support tonight.

Elisha turned to signal his father that he'd join them in a minute. And then to Katrina, "I appreciate your stopping by. But, really, this isn't the best time." Please, please, let this be over quickly.

Katrina brought her lips together, dissolving the chipper smile on her face. She was bewildered by his reaction.

"I'll see you in a couple of days when the holiday is over," Elisha said, as brightly as he could. "And I promise to explain in obsessive detail all the eight thousand laws of Passover."

Katrina was not amused. "I don't understand the problem. What's the big deal? I've never met your family and I've never been to a Seder."

"It's not that simple." Goodness, what eyes she had.

Elisha hurried another look over his shoulder. His young cousin Fayga and sister Deena were standing a few feet away, their eyes as wide as the Seder plate.

Katrina said, "What do you mean, it isn't that simple? They'll observe me, and I'll observe them. The visitor from one weird galaxy arrives at another weird galaxy. We'll all play anthropologists. Your field of expertise."

"Our Seders aren't ordinary holiday meals," Elisha said. "They're more like a service with prayers and rituals. They aren't like your Thanksgiving meals."

"What would you know about my Thanksgiving dinners?"

"Not much, I admit." Elisha's family had attempted a Thanksgiving dinner once when he was a child. The meal consisted of chicken soup and roast beef as a backup in case the turkey failed—an astute precaution as it turned out—along with potatoes and coleslaw as side dishes, for who knew cranberries in Cracow?

"By the way, how did you find my house?" Elisha asked, eager to smooth the edge of his rudeness.

"A bit of sleuthing. Sharp suit by the way." But Katrina was looking at his black velvet yarmulke, much larger than the one he wore in Manhattan.

She stretched her head for another peek into the living room. "Your family really is legion. Wow! So many kids. Which one is your brother?"

Must we do this? Must he turn around and point? "He's the teenager with the black yarmulke or more likely, the one still wearing his black hat. With glasses."

"Thanks a lot, Sherlock. That rules in just about every male at the table."

"Next to my father at the head of the table."

"Oh, I see him," she said, converting her fist into a telescope. "He kinda looks like you…like you the first time we met in the library when you were in hot pursuit of a hat. I mistook you for Charlie Chaplin."

Elisha heard footsteps and with a slight swivel caught his aunt Hencha ambling to the nearby couch as if to fetch something from her coat pocket, a poorly masqueraded ploy to get a better view of her nephew's who-knows-what. Elisha shifted impatiently from foot to foot. They'd been standing in the doorway for less than two minutes in clock time but several life-cycles in panic time.

"Elisha, *oder yuh, oder nein,*" his mother called in Yiddish. Yes or no.

"Please, Katrina," Elisha begged with his eyes, his posture, his entire being. Allow him his two separate lives.

She said, "Okay, you can stop freaking out. I'll leave."

"I don't mean to be impolite."

"I'm sure you don't. We can meet later when you're finished. I'll wait in a local coffee shop."

"I don't think that'll work. We don't finish the Seder until well after two in the morning. And there are no coffee shops in Boro Park."

Katrina puffed a cheek full of air and hunched her shoulders.

"All right. Even I know when to stop pushing. Enjoy your Seder. I really did think this was a good idea," she said, her voice soft and conciliatory. "I just wanted to see you."

"And I'm so sorry I can't invite you in."

And then his father did just that.

"Would you like to join us?" he said. "Please. It's late, and we need to move on."

She looked to Elisha for directions.

Elisha jerked his head. "I don't think this is a good time," he said aloud.

"I don't think so either," Katrina echoed. "Perhaps some other time." She remained petrified in place, as if a wave of volcanic lava had suddenly washed over her.

Elisha's father stood and motioned Katrina toward the table. "Please."

"Thank you," Katrina said. "Just for a few minutes."

"It'll be okay," she whispered to Elisha without much conviction.

Elisha brought Katrina to the women's table, avoiding eye contact with anyone. "This is Katrina, a friend from school." His mother made room next to her and asked her daughter to bring an English translation of the Haggadah from the drawer.

"You needn't bother," Katrina said. "I'm just staying for a short while. And like that Chassidic story about the young orphan, I'll just open the Hebrew pages and let God choose the words I'm supposed to say."

Elisha's father gave Elisha a startled look, but a stifled smile followed in its wake.

Twenty minutes later Elisha escorted Katrina to the front door.

"You okay, kiddo?" he asked.

"Fine," she said. "They're really sweet. Will you be all right?"

"I'm not sure."

"A bit of drama, huh?"

"The drama just begins."

"'Leish, I meant well." She leaned in a few inches and whispered as quietly as she could, "I wish I could hug you good night."

Instead she beamed a kiss with her lips. "Time to scat, cat."

"Take care, bear."

Elisha returned sheepishly to his seat. "I apologize," he said, his eyes on his plate. "I don't know why she showed up here tonight."

"Did you see her hippie sneakers," his cousin Fayga squealed.

"And a purple head band," chimed in his sister Deena with equal zeal. "She was nice."

Elisha turned toward his father whose eyes were already on him. "Let's continue with reading the Haggadah," his father said.

But his brother wouldn't allow Elisha's humiliation to pass so easily. "You could have the decency not to bring your goyish life into our house," he said to Elisha across the table. "At a Seder no less."

Two years younger than Elisha, Jacob to his older brother's Esau, Avrumy had never veered from the correct path. The past year he'd altered his wardrobe to parallel his steady rightward religious progression, the brims of his hats expanding to sombrero proportions and in an exhibition of religious cool, the *tzitzis,* the ritual wool tassels he first tucked neatly in his pants pocket now reaching his thighs. Gone were colors: the once sky blue shirts of his early adolescence had faded paler and paler into the purity of white, while even his weekday suits darkened in the opposite direction and were now all black, and only black.

"Avrumy, nice outfit," Elisha had commented at the start of the holiday. "You do like things black and white, don't you?"

His brother replied, "This is how people dress who still care about their Jewishness. As opposed to people who'd rather look *groooovy*."

Elisha wanted now to say to him aloud, "You think father is proud of you? You don't understand him. He respects complexity. Non-Jewish girls visiting his son on Pesach is not exactly the kind of alternative he has in mind, but neither is simplemindedness." But what would be the point? Besides, Avrumy had home court advantage.

The reading went slowly. Moishy, Beirish, Sarahle, Shimmy, Fayga, Deena, each child insisting on his or her turn to offer commentary on the text. It was an hour before they reached the section of the Haggadah recording the remarks of the four sons.

Mayer coughed for attention. "I have something to say about the errant son." He shot a look in Elisha's direction. "People ask, why do we continue to print new Haggadahs every year? After all, isn't everyone's drawer already overflowing with them? I once heard a good answer. We assume the wayward son of last Pesach has surely repented and is no longer wayward. So we need a new Haggadah to depict a new contrary son." Underneath his breath, he groused, "But the errant son must want to repent."

Score one for Mayer.

Elisha's father glared icily at his cousin before turning to the rest of the table. His silence had been disconcerting, but now he, too, wanted to offer a remark on the reading.

"Our great-grandfather, the Rebbe of Ropczyce, asked why the Haggadah listed the comments of the four sons in this order: wise son, sinful son, the simple-minded son, and the son too dimwitted to even articulate his question. Said the rebbe, 'The wise son pleaded he didn't mind spending the long hours of the Seder next to his delinquent brother—the fellow's wrongheaded, but at least he uses his mind. But please don't force him to spend the evening next to a simpleton."

Score one for Elisha.

"But the Ropczycer had something else to say about the rebellious son," his father continued, addressing Elisha directly. "I like this insight best of all. What is the transgression of the unruly son? It's that he detaches himself from the community, says the Hagaddah. He considers himself an outsider. 'Well,' says the Ropczycer, 'we have something to say to this young man. We tell him, you know what? Becoming an outsider isn't that easy. This isn't a unilateral decision, up to you alone. Our tradition includes you in our Seder, like it or not. We make room on the inside even for the would-be outsider. You, too, have a seat at the table, right here next to your brothers.'"

Elisha and his father gazed into each other's eyes—no one else in the room mattered now. His father was letting him know he'd always be welcomed home; there'd always be a seat for him at the table. Elisha blinked hard and looked away. How he wished he could assure his father he wouldn't lose his son to the lures of his unfathomable generation, that he could count on his always sitting at his side. But Elisha said nothing, unable to promise those words of comfort.

15

....

If religion has given birth to all that is essential in society, it is because the idea of society is the soul of religion.

—Emile Durkheim

Elisha was sipping a leisurely coffee, late again for the prayers, when his mother entered the kitchen dressed for shul. Although women are not required to attend services, she, the rebbe's daughter, felt obliged to make an appearance on the Sabbath and holidays.

"I want to thank you for being so gracious the other night at the Seder," Elisha said to her.

"Big choice you gave us."

"Nevertheless."

"Nevertheless, do you have any idea how distraught Tateh is? How on-edge he is about where you're heading?"

"I have an idea."

"You're the world to him."

"You're only making it more difficult."

His mother's sigh shook her entire body as if a gust of wind had uprooted the core of her being. She reached up and grabbed a lock of Elisha's hair.

"Don't you think it's time for a trim? Even though I'm sure your new friend approves of this forest on your head."

"I like it this way, too."

"Why do you need this mop? To proclaim your new life to the entire world?"

"This is hair we're talking about, not the essence of my existence."

"I'm not so sure."

"Please, this conversation, parents complaining about their kids' hair? It goes on in every household in America."

A stupid remark, Elisha realized immediately. This is consolation? That his mother has the same problem with her son that all other American mothers had?

In shul Elisha paid attention to the words in the prayer book for the first time in months and only at the end of services did he notice his uncle Shaya beckoning to him.

"It was a chore flagging your attention," his uncle said. "Your nose was glued to the siddur."

Elisha grinned and promised it wouldn't happen again.

Uncle Shaya was heading over to Beth El to hear Cantor Koussevitzky chant the *Hallel* prayer. Would Elisha join him for the walk? It'd been a long time since they'd had a private conversation.

The yellow-domed Temple Beth El was built in 1902 and remained Boro Park's most palatial synagogue. The synagogue's affiliation was modern Orthodox, so modern it featured a choir and no Chassid would ever pray there, but its other attraction enticed Jews of all denominations: Moshe Koussevitzky, the world's greatest living cantor. Boro Parkers gloried in their one unrivaled claim to dominance—their shuls had long headlined the most prominent cantors in the country.

Uncle Shaya and his fellow aficionados could tell you—and would, if you so much as hinted any interest— which shuls and which years featured Rosenblatt, Hirshmann, Pinchik, and Kwartin, and with an iota more prodding, Uncle Shaya would proffer a critical discourse on the innovations of Chagy, the baritonic strengths of Karpov-Kagan, the falsetto obligatos of Waldman, and why, of the four cantor Koussevitzky brothers, Moshe's bravura vocalization placed him at the acme of the pantheon.

The entire subject bored Elisha. He'd lost interest ever since Solly Roitman introduced him to Buddy Holly, Del Shannon, and Elvis Presley; his current musical tastes had erased any patience for liturgical chanting, though, admittedly, he'd recently discerned a similarity in the keening of the cantor and the wailing of the blues singer.

Elisha tightened his coat belt as they began their nine-block journey. Although the calendar showed spring debuting in less than ten days, the temperature that afternoon begrudgingly grazed forty Fahrenheit at its warmest. His uncle blew on his hands and said, "New York City winters are like guests from hell who refuse to leave long after their welcome." But he was coatless as usual, remarking vaguely that as a boy he'd learned to deal with the cold.

What was Elisha working on these days, his uncle asked. Elisha could sense from his uncle's intonation the question was introductory—clearly some other agenda waited in the wings. But he was happy to expound on his latest intellectual preoccupation: Emile Durkheim's theory of religion. Elisha expounded on the French sociologist's notion that the prime function of religion was social. Religion, Durkheim argued, was a central source for solidarity and also satisfies our universal need to distinguish between the sacred and profane. "Chassidism meets both these qualifications, doesn't it?" Elisha said. He allowed his attraction to Durkheim might have something to do with the fact Durkheim, too, was the son, grandson, and great-grandson of devout rabbis and had spent his younger years studying Talmud.

Uncle Shaya slowed his stride and turned to Elisha. "Your father and I had a brief discussion about you yesterday."

Elisha braked to a full stop. "So, he put you up to this little walk!"

"Absolutely not."

"I should've guessed."

"He didn't. I promise."

"Then what do you mean by you had a discussion about me?"

"He's worried about you. I'm sure that's no revelation."

"It's not."

"I heard about your visitor at the Seder. It must have been awkward."

"You might call it that," Elisha said carefully, unsure where the conversation was heading.

The two resumed their walk. Did Elisha remember their conversation years earlier on the porch? All the tough questions Elisha had asked him about God and evil, his annoyance with any beliefs he deemed inconsistent.

"I've become a bit wiser since then," Elisha said.

"As you later witnessed in a bar lounge, my contradictions weren't only theoretical. And I want you to know I always appreciated your discretion." He'd had his struggles, Uncle Shaya said. His battles with the demons.

Elisha was aware of his uncle's fast and furious resume. After liberation from concentration camp, he'd spent two months in a DP camp, followed by two months with a Zionist youth group in Bucharest, three months in Rome pretending to be a normal teenager, and a year in Palestine working on a religious Kibbutz before crossing the ocean to live with an aunt who'd arrived in New York before the war. Eighteen years old, suffering an inner life no longer accessible to others, Uncle Shaya enrolled in night school at Seward Park High in the Lower East Side while studying in a yeshiva during the day, graduated in two years, completed college with a major in mathematics and four years later received his PhD in applied physics from Columbia University. Fourteen years after his last day of starvation in Auschwitz, he was lecturing on jet propulsion to the elite scientists of the newly formed National Aeronautics and Space Association. He'd slayed his share of demons all right.

"I wanted to ask about your girlfriend," his uncle said.

"She's not a girlfriend. She's a friend and a girl."

"Your father was impressed with her."

"He was?"

"I suspect that's partly why he's so concerned about your relationship with her."

"He shouldn't be."

Uncle Shaya put his hand on his nephew's shoulder. "That woman you saw me with at the Waldorf?"

"She looked Hispanic."

"Actually, she was from Ceylon."

"What about her?"

"I don't remember her name."

He'd met her at the conference earlier that afternoon and had never seen her again after that night. "That's the point. I don't remember her name."

"I'm not following," said Elisha.

"It's one thing to discover the world beyond ours; it's another thing to live there."

"You're being cryptic."

"Elisha, listen to me. You wouldn't call me a fanatic, would you?"

"Cryptic, yes. But, no, definitely not a fanatic."

"Your father and I have our differences about the dangers of participating in the modern world. I'm a lot more liberal than he on that score. But we agree that freedom in America is in its own way a major threat to the Jewish people. Not that we don't appreciate it or want it otherwise. But it's a danger."

"Here we go—the danger of assimilation."

"It is a serious danger. Intermarriage will spell doom for American Jewry. There are fewer Jews now in the world than before the World War thirty years ago."

This apocalyptic prediction was nothing new. "We've had this problem before," Elisha said. "And survived."

"Here's what's new about America," his uncle said. "It's not just that Jews are willing to marry Gentiles. It's that Gentiles are willing to marry Jews. That's all fine. Everyone marries everyone in this country. And it's not a problem for everyone. If lots of American Catholics marry Lutherans and raise their kids Lutheran, there's still hundreds of millions of other Catholics. But we Jews are so few. We can't afford to lose our children."

"And the solution?" said Elisha. "We remain in our ghettos, our eyes fixed to the ground, seeing nothing, hearing nothing beyond the walls?"

"Come on now," Uncle Shaya said, irritated, almost angry. "You know very well I don't believe that. I'm only pointing out a concern."

"Cautionary advice?" Elisha said, equally annoyed with the conversation's direction.

"Yes," his uncle said. "Cautionary advice."

16
....

By believing passionately in something that still does not exist, we create it. The nonexistent is whatever we have not sufficiently desired.

— Franz Kafka

"Oxford?"

Elisha replaced the brochure on the hallway table. "Well, I don't say, Madam. You and the queen, two of a kind."

"I'm exploring possibilities," Katrina said from the other room, her voice low and doleful. She was standing in profile, the heel of her hand pressing hard on the windowsill.

"I want to apologize," Elisha said.

"For insulting the queen or me?"

"I acted atrociously on Passover."

"You didn't. Forget it already, won't you?"

"There's no excuse," Elisha said, walking toward her. She turned her head toward the window.

"If anyone needs to apologize, it's me," she said. "I should have known better."

Elisha had never seen Katrina this subdued. Her eyes were swollen. She'd been crying.

"You have a family," she said.

"Oh, I sure do."

"You don't know what you have."

"Well, I certainly don't know what you have. You never divulge anything about your own family."

"What's to divulge? I just spoke to my father. If you call him family."

"What's going on, Kat?" He took her hands in his.

She said, "I keep thinking how it would be if you visited us in Racine. Thanksgiving, right? God help us. Even before the divorce."

"Everyone time you mention Racine, I wonder if you're inventing the place."

"It's the center of the universe. The Brooklyn of the Midwest."

"I can picture your house. A stately Victorian manor with gable ornamentations and a majestic porch. A grand yard, of course. And glass windows in the tower."

Katrina couldn't contain a small laugh despite her mood. "Yes, we'd ferry you across the moat to our immaculate castle. It's a house, Elisha. An ordinary, run of the mill, decent-sized house. But, speckless, oh yes. Not a smidgen of dust ever floated free, no smudge ever lived through the day. Even the Sunday paper has its funeral out in the trash before the stroke of noon."

Elisha pointed to the books and clothes strewn about the room. "That explains your current décor."

"When I was a kid," Katrina said, "I used to beg for clutter, some disorder that indicated real lives were taking place in my house. The boredom crept like vines across the rooms, strangling the lot of us. My only means of escape was reading. I spent my childhood in bed cuddling with a stack of books."

"My competition."

"It's a close contest," she agreed. She described what his reception at her home would be like. Unless there was a blizzard, her father would be out golfing and her mother would cordially invite him to join her for a martini—not the first of the day, he could be sure, no matter what time he arrived.

"Do you know why Jews don't drink?" Elisha asked, determined to buoy her spirits.

"No, why?"

"Because it dulls the pain."

Katrina allowed herself another cursory laugh. She said her parents would be expertly civil to him and wouldn't even take the trouble to be anti-Semitic. No one would give two shits about his beliefs. They didn't care about hers either.

"Points for tolerance at least," said Elisha.

"Trust me, it's not tolerance. It's indifference."

Katrina tightened her fingers around Elisha's. "I witnessed a family in Boro Park. An unrestrained, joyous family, where a ten-year-old girl asks a question about some ancient text and the entire table stops their conversation to consider what she had to say. Your family talks, Elisha. Right across the generations. Do you know how rare that is?"

"No, I don't."

Katrina ran her hand against his chin. "And you. I watched you."

"And saw?"

"I saw someone who wears his respect for his father on his sleeve. And I can see why. He seems very wise."

"He is. Katrina, this is making me very uncomfortable."

"I'm sorry. I guess it's the contrast that's upsetting me. My father called to say he was in New York. He wants to get together tomorrow evening."

"That's good. You haven't seen him in quite a while."

"He invited us for dinner. Details to follow."

"Us?"

"Us. I told him I had a previous engagement. With you. He said to bring you along."

"You think this is a good idea?"

"I can use an ally."

Elisha had no idea what impression he'd make on her father nor what impression he was supposed to make. Shouldn't she go alone?

Katrina put her hand on Elisha's cheek and left it there. "You'll be fine. But can we forget about families for now?" Her voice was low and silken. "Not school, not work, not the future. Can we concentrate on us for a change?"

"Smoke again?"

"No, better. Much better." She brought her lips to his. A light dimmed in the building next door accentuating the flecks of emerald in her eyes.

Elisha said, "Did I ever tell you all beauty traces to the Divine."

"Is that a typical Chassidic pick-up line?"

"Yes, I use it on all the girls."

She put her mouth on his throat and whispered, "I can't figure out what your limits are with regard to intimacy."

"I can't either. But I do know you are beautiful."

She unbuttoned the top of his shirt and ran her tongue on the side of his neck.

She said, "I like that I was the first girl you ever kissed. I love being your first."

"I chose well."

She combed her fingers through the budding hairs on his chest.

They kissed again with their mouths open, her hands drifting to his lower back, his on hers. She brought them to her breasts.

"Elisha," she said. "I don't know if you'll get to paradise in the next world, but you are entitled to a bit of it in this one."

She took his hand and led him to the bedroom. "It's time," she said. "Time for our own little Eden."

17
....

Pretending to be amused when a fool tells a joke is also a kind of charity.

—Rebbe Yechiel of Alexander

What does one wear to the Palm restaurant? Katrina had only told him not to expect a diner and used the word *upscale,* which didn't convey much. Nothing about a dress code. So a suit, Elisha figured; better to be overdressed than underdressed, better her father think him a young man about town than a callow Brooklyn bumpkin. On the other hand, what made this wayfarer from the badlands of Wisconsin the greater sophisticate than a denizen of Brooklyn, the fourth biggest city in the country? All right, then, a suit. But no tie. He'd arranged to meet Katrina beforehand so she could approve his attire, and besides, she wanted them to walk in as a team.

"Erik Nelson," her father said, rising from the table to greet Elisha with a handshake firmer and longer than Elisha thought reasonable. He was taller than Elisha had surmised from Katrina's family photographs and the sleeves of his sports coat inched up to the middle of his forearm when he extended his hand.

"Pleased to meet you. I'm Elisha."

Mr. Nelson leaned across the table and buzzed his daughter on the cheek. "They let you in with those ridiculous sneakers?" He repeated Elisha's name, enunciating each syllable, as if he were hearing it for the first time.

"So what kind of name is that?"

"It's biblical. Elisha was a prophet. Elijah's assistant."

"The Old Testament. Yes, Katrina tells me you're a religious Jew."

Elisha flung a look at Katrina. Your dad's wasting no time. Straight to the Crusades. But he'd handle him, not to worry. For God's sake, the man's wearing a flaming red tie bedecked with purple and green golf clubs.

"Not many people I know would call me a practicing Jew," Elisha said.

"Practice makes perfect."

Katrina said, "Must we begin the meal with a theological inquisition? Here's a more momentous matter: what to eat?"

"She's just like her mother," Mr. Nelson said to Elisha with an unkind little laugh. "Gets right down to business—to her business."

Katrina noticed Elisha scanning the tag line atop the menu, *Classic American Steakhouse*, and preemptively divulged Elisha didn't eat meat.

"You one of those vegetarians types?" her father said. "I should've guessed." He suggested the lobster and rolled his eyes when Elisha explained he kept kosher and couldn't eat seafood either, but the tuna would be fine.

"This *is* a steak restaurant, you know," Mr. Nelson said, his eyes commencing another circumnavigation in their sockets.

In a valiant attempt to keep the conversation benign, Katrina informed the table the original Italian owners didn't intend to specialize in steak but in cuisine from their native Parma, Italy, and called the restaurant "Parma," which, due to their accents, transformed into Palm. And for the next half hour Elisha vanished into the ether. His oddity established and confirmed, Elisha's presence was of no more interest to Katrina's father than the unbidden sommelier lurking in the corner.

Mr. Nelson devoted his discussion to matters Racine and matters Mr. Nelson. Elisha politely listened to a detailed report on the road construction on Mr. Nelson's street begun six months ago. He learned about a brewing scandal involving the new mayor and his mistress, the details far less enticing than one might hope. And, more boring still, how Katrina's cousin had lost his job at the Modine plant, apparently drugs again. Mr. Nelson had to pull a netful of strings not to mention a wad from his wallet to get the young man into a rehab center affiliated with their Lutheran church, "a venue it wouldn't kill Katrina to visit on occasion."

And so it went. Mr. Nelson recounted how he'd been rehired at the SC Johnson corporation from which he'd been dismissed back when he'd had that drinking problem and was now working on their Glade account: "There's nothing like traveling on an expense account," he assured them.

Katrina smiled for the first time that evening when her father mentioned passing through Sturgeon Bay where Katrina developed her "superb sailing skills," and their camping expeditions in Fish Creek. He informed her that Marshall Gillo, her Horlick High history teacher, had died that week. Did she know he was the younger brother of Hank Gillo who led the NFL in scoring with 52 points back in the 1920s? Football. Boy-talk. Mr. Nelson remembered there was another male sharing the water pitcher.

"Elisha, bet you weren't aware Racine once had a pro football team? The Racine Legion. They eventually became the Detroit Lions."

"No kidding? That is truly amazing!" Elisha said, but his hyperbolic exclamation gave him away.

"So what are you majoring in?" Katrina's father asked, his attention still fixed on Elisha. "Something wooly and useless like my daughter? What was it again, Katrina?"

"Comparative literature."

"That's right. Stories. Other people's stories. You know, she was an excellent math student. Could have been a scientist, or something useful in the medical profession. I don't get it."

Elisha wanted to ask him why he spoke of someone sitting right next to him in the third person, but couldn't decide how to couch the question.

"You all have it too easy," her father said downing his glass of club soda in one gulp. "When I was seventeen and had enough of subzero cow milking on my grandfather's farm, I got a job at Walkers fixing jacks and mufflers from eight in the morning to six at night." He glowered at his daughter. "No silver spoon for me. Born with a plastic spoon in my mouth is more like it."

"Don't you think this sermon is getting a bit tedious?" Katrina said. Her eyes shifted away toward a painting on the wall.

"I'm sorry, what did you say you were studying?" her father said to Elisha, ignoring Katrina.

"Anthropology."

"That's like sociology, right?"

"They're related."

"Well then, perhaps you can explain to me why New York City has so many fags. Homosexuals. I was down in Greenwich Village last night. Men holding hands. Detestable."

"Please stop," Katrina said. Her nostrils flared in disdain.

"It's not my word. It's God's word. 'Thou shalt not lie with mankind, as with womankind; it is abomination.' Ask your biblical friend here. That's from the Old Testament."

Elisha looked over at Katrina. Should he respond? She shook her fist under the table. Go for it.

"Well, in fact," Elisha said, "the Hebrew word for abomination, *to'eva,* is used many times in the Bible and for various prohibitions like graven images." He flitted a glance at the cross around Mr. Nelson's neck, but pointed to the mussel shells on the table. "And the Bible calls those detestable. I don't suppose you consider it immoral to eat unslaughtered meat and seafood?"

Katrina put her hand above her nose and sneaked a smile at Elisha. "Teach him to mess with the rabbi," she mouthed.

Her father retreated into his seat and declared with much less vigor that queers and lesbians were just part of the decadence of sexual freedom gripping the youth of America—Jews, Christians, no difference, it was dragging the entire country to the ground.

Katrina, emboldened and delighted in her father's comeuppance, said Elisha was also a wonderful storyteller. "Stories of different nations. Chassidic tales."

Elisha shot Katrina a puzzled look. He was in no mood to launch into the usual five-minute intro to Chassidism, and happily Mr. Nelson hadn't asked him to.

"Why not tell us one of those tales?" Katrina said. "A little something to catch its flavor." Her eyes were charged with determined amusement.

"You *are* serious?" Elisha said, but he, too, was intrigued by the sheer weirdness of the situation, this yeshiva boy who'd spent the morning studying Talmud in the study hall now sitting in a steak restaurant telling a Chassidic story to this man from Wisconsin who cared nothing about these tales—and why should he? But Elisha had the perfect short tale to tell. A story about storytelling. Perhaps the most famous parable in all of Chassidism.

When the great Rabbi Israel Baal Shem Tov saw misfortune threatening the Jews, he'd visit a certain part of the forest, light a fire, say a special prayer, and the misfortune would be averted. His disciple Reb Ber would go to the same place in the forest to intercede with heaven when another catastrophe loomed and cry out, "Master of the Universe, I do not know how to light the fire, but I am still able to recite the special prayer," and again the miracle would be accomplished. Still later, Rabbi Moshe-Lieb of Sassov, in order to save his people once more, would go into the forest and plead, "Lord, I do not know how to light the fire, I do not know the special prayer, but I know the place, and this must suffice," and the miracle was performed.

When it fell to Rabbi Israel of Rhyzhin to overcome misfortune, he'd sit in his armchair with his head in his hands, and entreat God: "I'm unable to light the fire, and I don't know the special prayer, and I cannot even find the place in the forest. But what I can do is to tell the story and this must suffice." And it was sufficient.

"And the point being?" asked Mr. Nelson, utterly confused.

"It's a story about storytelling, father dear," said Katrina. "How telling a tale is the equivalent to prayer. You're big on prayer, aren't you?"

She turned to Elisha. "Come to think of it, maybe reading the stories of writers like Tolstoy is my form of prayer."

Elisha walked Katrina the forty blocks to her current apartment in the East Village. Her mood was sour. "That was just a taste of my dad," Katrina said. "I'm sure you found him most appetizing." Elisha dutifully tried to make amends for her father and suggested that deep down he meant well.

"Bullshit!" Katrina shouted. "Listen, I'm the lit major, the authority on deep-downing obnoxious characters. People always parrot that means-well crap. 'Yeah, Stalin killed a couple of million people, but deep down he meant well.' Well, guess what? Deep down my father doesn't mean well. He's as miserly with his emotions as he is with his money. And he's a bigoted s.o.b."

Elisha held her tightly, paying no attention to the stares of the passersby on the busy street corner. She leaned her head on Elisha's shoulder.

"You know, 'Leish, you're really a rabbi, at heart. I don't mean in the professional sense. I mean in your soul. It was clear to me as I listened to you tell that story to my father."

"What makes you say that?" Elisha said.

Katrina lifted her head and shrugged. "I don't know. But when you tell Chassidic stories or talk about your heritage, there's something in your intonation. The way the words seem to have traveled through the centuries, through you, if you know what I mean."

She put her arm in his. "At some point, you'll have to face it, you know. It's in the blood. You're your father's son."

"Thank you," Elisha parried, "but I think the rabbinical line stopped with my father."

Katrina was still in his arms two hours later in her room when he said good-bye.

"Take care, Voltaire," she said. "And thanks for being such a great sidekick this evening. It wasn't easy. It never is."

It'd once been easy with his own father, Elisha thought as he made his way home. Would it ever be again? He took some solace knowing he'd always cherish his father no matter what quarrels between them might erupt, for a rupture was surely waiting, unpleasant, hard, but inevitable.

18

....

Anyone of sufficient elevation can perform miracles.
But to be a truly decent human being...now that is
an accomplishment.

—the Choizeh of Lublin

Elisha came home from a night in the city to the eerily quiet Boro Park streets. Too late to find Chassidic men trudging home from their night study sessions, too early to see them gathering for the dawn morning prayers. This was the hour the neighborhood slept.

The door of his parents' house was double locked. Odd. Despite the recent rash of incidents, they bolted a second latch only when leaving for extended vacations. A growl of premonition rumbled in the pit of his stomach. Elisha tried the side alleyway tiptoeing between the slats of wood still lying there a month after the neighbor's house reconstruction. The key worked.

All the lights in the house were off except for the permanent glow from atop the oven. But a second glint flickered in the kitchen. Elisha stepped gingerly toward the dangling cigarette.

His father was sitting erect in his chair glaring at the clock on the side wall. 3:45. His father's face was wooden, impenetrable, and unyielding. He said nothing.

"We had a little get together," Elisha said faintly. And to himself: Do not be intimidated. And to his father: "A birthday party for friends…it was too late to call…why are you looking at me like that?"

Not a word from his father. Elisha, nonplussed, continued, "And what's with the double lock? I come home late one night…big deal…the train was creeping…I'm nearly twenty-one-years old, for goodness sake."

"One night?" his father said, his voice chillingly steady. "And two nights ago? And four nights ago? And the weeks before?"

"I stay out a bit late these days. I have midterms to study for. I have a recital coming up. I'm busy."

"A quarter to four in the morning."

Elisha took a deep breath. "Look, Tateh," he said, "I'm living a life you don't approve of. But I'm still within bounds. Why all this drama? I don't understand your waiting up like this."

"You don't understand," his father spat out the words as if he'd bitten into something bitter. "You don't understand what it's like to hear from people that your son walks around without a yarmulke—"

"There are times when I—"

"With a girl on his arm."

"You know very well—"

"Eating in nonkosher restaurants."

"You're making a mountain of nothing. I eat out. I told you I did. But I don't eat nonkosher. And I have a friend who happens to be a girl. Katrina."

His father snuffed out his cigarette, and though the room darkened, Elisha could see his father's lips clench and the slow shake of his head.

"I don't know what's become of you, Elisha. I don't know how this happened."

His eyes stayed fixed on his son as he removed a packet from his pocket and placed it on the table. His hand remained on top, enclosing it, the palm twitching. What was this about? This was no simple restaurant receipt. Elisha looked up at his father's moist eyes. He was biting his lip. He withdrew his hand from the object.

A condom.

"What the heck?" Elisha gulped. "What are you suggesting?"

"I'm suggesting nothing. Avrumy found this in your desk. He was looking for scotch tape."

"Looking for scotch tape? In my drawer? What the hell is he doing snooping around in my desk?"

"This isn't about Avrumy."

"Listen, someone gave it to me as a joke."

"A joke? I don't need such jokes in my house. I don't need my son to come home in the middle of the night—"

"As you see, it hasn't been used." Elisha wasn't sure who he was trying to protect with these frantic lies, his father or himself.

"This can't go on," his father said.

Elisha fastened his stare on the block of ash attached to his father's cigarette. What should he say?

His father said, "Have I not allowed you enough freedom? You wanted to go to college in Manhattan. Okay, go. You were finished with engineering, an anthropologist you want to be. Fine. Be an anthropologist. You spend less and less time in yeshiva. You cut off your payis. Then no more hat. Then dungarees and this…this hair you haven't cut in months. Look at you. But okay, I let you be. What could I do, anyway? But everything has its limits. As long as you live in this house, there are limits."

"Well guess what?" Elisha shouted. "Did you ever consider that your limits may not be mine? I refuse to stand here on the dock like a condemned villain. And do you—"

"This is still my house," his father said. "And as long as you—"

"—think other people my age have to justify to their parents why they come home late? Most don't even live with their parents."

"If that is what you prefer…" His father wiped a tear from his eye, but Elisha let his own flow down his cheek.

"I'm going to try to get some sleep," his father said. He stood up and retrieved an envelope from the inside pocket of his jacket draped on the chair. "I've told you a hundred Chassidic stories, but this one…now…is more important than any. Elisha? I pray you, too, have your limits."

Elisha sat down, removed the pages from the envelope and held them up to the light above the oven. The pages, typed in Yiddish, were yellowed with age, the ink already faded. The story was entitled "The Outsider" and the byline Lev Tahur, the pseudonym his father used when he wrote for a Yiddish magazine during those first years after his arrival in America. Elisha reached for one of his father's cigarettes and leaned back heavily in his chair.

Bitter was the day when Stanislaw Wyszynski became commissar of Krosno and its environs. The Jews were now ordered to furnish an additional tax beyond their already heavy financial burden, and those who could not afford the payments were turned out into the streets. Club-wielding ruffians attacked Jews without pity, aged Chassidim a favorite target of relentless taunts.

At first, the Chassidim of Krosno sought to escape their misfortune through the customary means: a day of fasting and prayer, further appeals to the commissar and then to his superiors who, of course, proved no more sympathetic to their plight. No one was surprised when Reb Abish, the most respected Chassid in Krosno, said the time had come to try bribery. Perhaps, once again, avarice will trump malice.

With the money raised from the meager means of the desperate community in his pocket, Reb Abish and two Chassidim made their way to the tavern where

Commissar Wyszynski reveled in his nightly bout of drinking.

"Please accept this donation in recognition of our civic devotion," Reb Abish said, placing the stack on the table next to the commissar's cards.

Wyszynski looked straight at Reb Abish and twirled his horseshoe moustache. A snarl creased his ruddy face.

"This will pay for tonight's vodka," he said laughing. "But you accursed Christ killers must be stupid if you think I can be bribed by the likes of you. I have better ways to get your pitiful zlotys. Now get the hell out of here before I chase you out with my whip."

Even more despondent than before, the Chassidim of Krosno decided to seek the blessing of their rebbe, the Tzaddik of Dynav.

The Dynaver rebbe listened with a broken heart to the travails of his Chassidim, but offered little solace. "I fear my prayers will be of no avail."

The Chassidim stood forlorn when suddenly the tzaddik raised his head, his eyes shining like a ray of light across a cloudy night.

"And why not?" he said, tracking his own supernal thoughts. "You need the blessing of Naftuli Geiger."

The Chassidim had never heard the name before. Was he one of the *Lamed-vovniks,* the thirty-six people in every generation whose covert righteousness sustains the world? The rebbe said only he might be found in the village of Yavenik and wished them success.

The next morning, with unwavering trust in their rebbe's words, Rebbe Abish and his two compatriots arrived in the tiny hamlet, one of the many villages that dotted the Chassidic landscape of Polish Galicia, and headed immediately to the local shteibl. This Naftuli Geiger must be a devout rabbi from afar who'd recently moved to the village, and someone was sure to lead them to him. But they were greeted with only blank stares. No one had any idea whom he might be. Their inquiries in shuls, schools, and the marketplace were equally fruitless. With heavy hearts, the disappointed Chassidim trudged to the *krechma* to spend the night.

The roadside inn was deserted except for a group of Gentile villagers drinking in the drab dining room. The fatigued Chassidim sat at a table of their own and ordered tea. Aware their strange presence demanded an explanation, they said they were looking for a Jew named Naftuli Geiger, but not one of the peasants recognized the name. No one, that is, except for a man with one arm sitting alone at the far side of the room.

"They mean Tadik." He gave the Chassidim directions to Tadik's shack on the outskirts of town.

The others in the room were incredulous. "Tadik? That good-for-nothing drunk rascal is a Jew?"

The Chassidim were even more astounded. Was their hoped-for savior a local lay-about? Why would the rebbe send them to receive the blessing of an alcoholic lout? Most likely, they decided, Tadik was a clandestine devout Jew, who only appeared inebriated, but, in fact, spent his evenings at home studying Torah and fulfilling its commandments.

But when they reached his home, they were met not by the sweet sound of a Jew chanting sacred scriptures, but by silence. Only a small light in the back signaled someone was home.

Tadik was asleep, huddled in a corner surrounded by empty whiskey bottles and stale vomit. Trying to wake him was like trying to teach Kabbalah to a goat, but the Chassidim pulled and prodded and finally cajoled him to open an eye. "Who in…God's hell… who are you people?" he wheezed. The Chassidim explained their presence.

"You ask for a blessing?" Tadik growled. "You come to mock me? Scoundrels. A swig of dog's blood…is what…you get. Now away and let me be." He turned to the wall. They had problems? Everyone has problems. What's it to him?

But the Chassidim made it clear they would not leave without his blessing. And seeing no other way to be done with these people, Tadik said, "Okay, bless you. Good-bye."

But the Chassidim hadn't come all this way to be cast off with a flitting two words from a pitiful inebriate. "You need to concentrate," they said.

"Damn," Tadik said, managing to sit up. And in a voice suddenly steady and sober, he said, "Fine. Attention,

Heavenly Father: on my behalf may the Jews of Krosno be spared further humiliation and pain. Will you now leave me to my sleep?"

The crowd at the Krosno station descended on Reb Abish and his colleagues the moment they returned, everyone shouting the good news. Commissar Wyszynski had been implicated in an extortion scandal and dragged off in handcuffs. His appointed successor had promised to install an honest administration that would immediately abolish Wyszynski's draconian anti-Jew laws.

Pleased but bewildered by the course of events, Reb Abish traveled the next day to the rebbe to learn the secret of what had transpired.

The Dynaver rebbe was delighted to hear about the turn of events in Krosno, but sighed when told of Naftuli's condition. "I was hoping he might have changed," he said. "No doubt you're wondering why I sent you to him. I will tell you." A dozen Chassidim crowded around the rebbe's table to hear the story of Naftuli Geiger.

"Naftuli's father was a Chassid of my father, the holy Bnei Yissoscher, may he rest in peace," the rebbe began. "Naftuli would often join his father when he came to us for the holidays. The young man was certainly no gifted Talmud student, but he was kind and devoted. He worked at a textile outlet outside the city of Rzeszow, and one day the young daughter of the local *poretz*, the region's overseer, came to purchase fabric. She took a liking to Naftuli and was soon making repeat visits to the warehouse after store hours. It was not long before the affection turned mutual. The warehouse visits led to secluded walks and clandestine trysts, and you might guess where this eventually led. The young woman told her father she wanted Naftuli as her husband.

"My son-in-law a Jew! Impossible," the poretz declared. But his daughter was obstinate: the boy was her true love, she insisted. The poretz finally relented, and one brisk morning showed up at the warehouse. Would Naftuli please go for a ride in his fiacre?

"Let me get straight to the point," the poretz said. He couldn't fathom why his daughter would be interested in a Jew, let alone one with neither money nor education. "But she is headstrong and determined to marry you, so what's a father to do?"

Naftuli wanted to say how the feelings were reciprocal but the poretz interrupted him in mid-sentence.

"Your sentiments are of no interest to me. You can be sure, however, no Jew will be my son-in-law. You will, therefore, convert to Christianity. Do you have a Polish name?"

"My nursemaid called me Tadik," Naftuli said uncomfortably.

"Tadik, short for Thaddeus. Fine. Let's get this over with quickly. You will be married in a few days. I will

207

see to all the necessary arrangements." Without another word spoken the coach returned the shaken young man to the warehouse.

Tadik faced an excruciating decision. On the one hand, would he ever have this opportunity again? To live a life of leisure, to give orders, not take them, to ride in ornate coaches, not walk the roads with dogs and goats? But could he really abandon the faith of his people? Still, hadn't Jewish rituals become rote, tedious, meaningless exercises for him? Conversion would be arduous, but, Naftuli concluded, with time he'd settle into his new life.

Three days later, two heavyset men showed up at his workplace and ushered Naftuli to a carriage waiting outside. A half-hour later they arrived at a church a few miles beyond the town, and Naftuli was brought up to a small room in the attic. One of his captors leaned in close to him and spoke into his ear. "Tomorrow morning the priest arrives and administers the necessary rites, and you will be converted to the Holy Roman Church. In the afternoon you will be married. They've even prepared a wedding suit for you." The two men left Naftuli sitting on his bed, locking the door behind them.

At seven o'clock the next morning, the priest knocked on the attic door, turned his key in the keyhole, and entered the room.

Reb Duvid'l Dynaver sipped from his glass of water and looked up at the circle of Chassidim pressing even closer now and continued.

The priest had entered the room but found it empty. For that night, alone in the dark, Naftuli confronted once more what he was about to do. This time his heart had its say as well as his head. What was he doing in this Christian house of worship? How could he mouth words he didn't believe in? Was material comfort so important to him he'd betray his people and his heritage? No, this was beyond the limit. Skillfully fashioning a rope from the room's drapes and bed sheets, Naftuli secured the cord to the window and in the faint night made his escape.

The repercussions were swift and severe. Word went out throughout the area no one was to hire Naftuli Geiger, and Naftuli was forced to move beyond the long reach of the poretz. He made his way to Yavanik where he kept a low profile and used his Polish name.

In the early days after his escape from the church, he'd attended a few services, but felt disconnected, a loner. He'd became an outsider from both the Jewish and Gentile worlds. Alone in bars, staring at the stale bread on his plate, Naftuli took to drink and drink took to him.

The rebbe exhaled slowly, dismayed. "How I wish this story had a happier ending for Naftuli. For now… well, Reb Abish, you saw for yourself."

"I did," Reb Abish said, no less perplexed. "But why did you send me to him for a benediction? Why would his blessing matter?"

The Dynaver rebbe said, "We are taught not to take lightly the blessings of the ordinary person, even the sinner, though most of us mouth our thanks for their good wishes, paying it no mind. But we should. You see, Chassidism also teaches that an unrewarded deed bestows on the doer of that deed a power to affect events. We can never be certain who bears this power and sometimes the bearer himself is not aware of his spiritual strength. The blessing of a drunk lost in an intoxicated haze might carry more weight than the blessing of the holiest tzaddik in the world.

"When Naftuli turned his back on apostasy and a life of ease, the Heavens conferred upon him a special gift: should he offer a benediction, it would be fulfilled. But it never dawned on him to bless anyone for anything. That is, not until a group of Chassidim from Krosno showed up in his rotten shack."

The Dynaver rebbe stood up, his face radiant. "I thought perhaps Naftuli's power was on reserve for just this occasion, to assist a Jewish community in distress. And so it was."

The Rebbe pointed to the clock on the wall. It was time for afternoon prayers.

19

....

There is a great difference between still believing something and believing it again.

—Lichtenberg

The story thrummed in Elisha's pocket when he arrived at Rossalimo's the next day. Reverberating, demanding, he couldn't get it out of his mind. He'd reread it on his way to the city and again his hands shook as he turned the accusing pages. Why did it unnerve him so? And what was making his father so unnerved? Surely not that his son would become a dissolute Tadik staggering in a vodka vapor from one saloon to another, ignorant and uncaring about his tradition. Wasn't his father's concern something much worse: that his beloved first-born might wed someone not of the tribe?

Elisha did fantasize living with Katrina, trading pecks as they went off to work in the morning, rushing home to their shared nights. But marriage? Could he stand on an altar under a cross and look down to pews filled with the seared souls of his saintly grandparents? Or even line up behind the Rodriguezes and in front of the Johnsons for his turn with the Justice of the Peace? The very idea was surely beyond the pale.

And yet. Elisha put his hand on the envelope containing Tadik's story. And yet, his father's anxiety was not absurd.

Only a year ago, could Elisha have foretold the life he lived now? Eating in restaurants from which he'd have previously refused a cup of coffee; praying only once a day if you called that praying; and spending evenings in the arms of a young woman who taught him to jitterbug and whose mother drank martinis for breakfast. He'd embarked on a path that led somewhere distant—how far would he travel before turning off?

Elisha stepped inside the club. Perhaps here in this home away from home he'd find some distraction, a few hours of escape from this inner turmoil that roiled without respite.

The Rossalimo Chess Studio on Sullivan Street was a shteibl of its own. Laid out in rows of rickety tables and broken chairs, its members/congregants sat and stood and strolled, each according to his own urges. Elisha instantly felt at home among its cast of characters with their improbable, hidden histories, submerged talents competing with inflated reputations, talkers and shushers, board-game gladiators nursing ancient feuds whose origins even they had long forgotten, scholars of the game and poseurs, blatant cons and covert philanthropists, the occasional celebrity visitor and the otherwise homeless, the newly converted, the tyros, the jokers, the misanthropes, and the dreamers. In this sacred sanctuary, luck had no dominion and connections offered no privilege; politics, religion, and social class ceased to be of consequence from the moment you thrust your first pawn forward. Elisha found comfort here.

He was pleased to see Mr. Jellerup at his usual seat this late in the afternoon. Karl Jellerup was Elisha's favorite competition, always ready to "provide youth an opportunity to contest the sagacity of age." Elisha missed the durable wisdom of the older men at his table in the shteibl and found homesick succor in Karl Jellerup's own wary experience; his rants against the young generation's conceits and its assault on reverence cheered Elisha with its familiarity. Piecemeal, begrudgingly, Elisha revealed his background to Mr. Jellerup and to him alone, even on occasion venturing to retell a Chassidic tale. "You tell wonderful stories," Mr. Jellerup said to him, "but why all these caveats and skeptical asides? Young man, you should learn to have greater respect for mystery."

This afternoon Mr. Jellerup was in the midst of a game with the religious Jew who'd been stopping by the club the past few weeks. Unfailingly polite, the unobtrusive gentleman played a few matches, exceedingly well, thanked his opponent for his time, and left. Mr. Jellerup deemed him inscrutable. But he was not to Elisha who, by the cut of the man's beard, the angle of pinch in his hat, and the inflection of his humming while cogitating his next move, could place him precisely along the axis of Chassidic Jews.

Elisha struggled not to reveal their common background, not let on that his anonymity was only a disguise. The urge to connect was strong, but Elisha held fast to his camouflage. Why jeopardize this oasis, the one place he could introduce himself without dragging along a trunkload of presumptions? Trevor might have spilled a wisecrack that'd unmask Elisha's Chassidic background, but he was at home in Vermont dealing with a bout of mononucleosis. And Mr. Jellerup, the seasoned veteran, never discussed private lives in public.

Elisha took a seat nearby and was soon absorbed in the battle between the two intrepid combatants, rooting for them both. Only after several minutes did he notice on the outskirts of his attention someone calling to him. It was the fellow he'd played the week before, looking once more as if he'd slipped off the cover of *Rolling Stone* magazine. From headband to sandals, he was accoutered in full Northern California ceremonial dress, the prematurely gray ponytail that reached down to the wheels on his Harley-Davidson T-shirt, three strands of ruby beads wrapped around his neck, a hemp bracelet dangling a silver trinket, Native American no doubt, and his glasses, mandatory Lennon-rimmed issue. In a concession to the wet weather, he'd allowed himself red socks adorned with little white umbrellas.

"Peace, brother," he said, his voice better matched than his clothes to his forty plus years of age. "Raymond. You do remember me?"

"I do," said Elisha with little enthusiasm.

"How about a chance for some revenge?"

There are two schools of thought about chess: one advises you to play the board; the other recommends you play your opponent. Proponents of play-the-board warn against psychologizing your adversary because intentions are easily misunderstood; better to concentrate on your next best move. Champions of play-the-person remind us chess is a game between compromised human beings, and as elsewhere in life, our personalities determine our moves.

In Raymond's case all would agree: play the man. Throughout their previous meeting, Raymond prattled on about his plans to help liberate the Western world from its mental enslavement to mind-body dualism, his sermon swarming with words like chakra, channeling, aura, and therapeutic touch. Two moves into the rematch, and Raymond was babbling again, this time something about a new age that enfolds all thinking into a single consciousness, a concept he said was pioneered by the ancient Sufi mystics. With practiced pronouncements, he expounded on the importance of spontaneity. But for all his revolutionary talk, Raymond played meticulously according to the book, never veering from the recommended moves. He hadn't an original idea in his head or in his game. Elisha declared mate after fifteen moves.

"You know, I respect that man over there," Raymond said, pointing to the man in the black hat. "The Amish refuse to relinquish their souls to technology and get devoured like everyone else in the jowls of capitalism."

"The Amish, huh?" Elisha said, riding Raymond's blunder.

"Sometimes known as Pennsylvania Dutch. The old-fashioned, plain dark clothing protects them from losing their identities."

"I see," Elisha said. He waited a few beats, and then added, "He's not Amish, by the way."

"What makes you think not?"

"He's an Orthodox Jew."

"You sure about that?"

"Trust me. He's Chassidic. And he's fine with technology and capitalism."

Raymond leaned obtrusively in the man's direction. "What's the deal with those people anyway? Walking around like they lived in Europe two centuries ago."

"So unlike the Amish."

"They're different. The Chassids are just into being different for the sake of being different. Listen, I'm Jewish. So, it's not—"

"Not what?" Elisha stopped him, his annoyance unsheathed.

"Spirituality matters to me. *Genuine* spirituality."

"And you, of course, are *genuinely* spiritual."

"You should study Kabbalah," said the would-be guru.

"You study Kabbalah, Raymond?"

"Yeah, wild stuff."

"I didn't know you read Hebrew."

"I don't."

"Aramaic?"

"What?"

"Oh, you read a book about Kabbalah."

"I have. More than one. Articles, too. You should look into it, my friend."

Elisha thanked him for the tip and said he needed fresh air. "What a shmuck," he fumed under his breath as he walked out into the night.

He drifted through the downtown streets. Little Italy, the East Village. Somewhere in Chinatown, he considered calling Katrina, see about meeting her later, but kept walking instead. Why had that jerk's comments about the Chassid so upset him? And why was he himself so determined to shroud his identity? It was the same old challenge, wasn't it, figuring out which part of his life was deceiving the other.

Elisha wandered for hours. His head was clogged with competing thoughts, his heart, his gut, every part of his body clamored for its say. Near Wall Street he dialed Katrina's number but hung up before her phone rang. This was the time to work things out, come to some decision. Perhaps Uncle Shaya was right about visiting the outside world but not living in it. Perhaps his father's apprehension was warranted, and he was hurtling down a highway without brakes or destination. He poked around the graves in the Trinity Church cemetery and stopped in front of Alexander Hamilton's grave.

"So what do you think, my esteemed Alexander?" Elisha said, wanting to express his thoughts to someone else, dead or alive. "Aren't they right? You can't just walk away from the family you treasure and chuck two thousand years of a tradition because of an itch in your groin or a notion in your head. True, more than an itch and more than a notion are propelling me to the exit sign, but aren't the motives of a twenty-one-year-old suspect?"

He'd give his Chassidic life another try. A final try. He'd be realistic. It couldn't be as before. His yeshiva friends maligned the entire secular world; bankrupt of the holiness of Torah, its ways were vacuous, they averred, sunk in moral decrepitude. Elisha knew better. He'd already walked too many miles in its provinces, ingested too much—you can't lump 99.99 percent of human experience into one hopeless heap. He'd return to Boro Park for now, do the best he could, but the outside world would be a part of him as well.

And Katrina? Piety by day and her tongue at night? The dissonance would be impossible, a contradiction he could not sustain. But if not the warmth of her body, he'd keep the treasure of her friendship. She'd be bewildered once again by this latest turn, but abide by the new rules. He was less sure he could.

For the next months Elisha sought to recapture the religious diligence of his earlier years. He hauled himself to shul for morning prayers, a sunup prelude for full days in the yeshiva where he lapped in the warm sea of Talmud. He rekindled old friendships with the best and brightest of the students, quickly joining them in the first tier. His teachers voiced their admiration and Rabbi Aronowitz expressed his own satisfaction with approving nods.

Elisha was no less conscientious about his college studies. No more dallying in the student lounge dissecting Mao and Dylan or gossiping about their professors' amorous ambitions. He didn't even linger in his beloved library. Elisha went to class and went home.

But he also kept intact the bridges to his more recent life and made sure to cross them on occasion. He'd visit with Trevor, who'd returned to New York in full health and full political passion, and joined him twice for a night of jazz club hopping. Alone in his room, Elisha practiced his clarinet, floating musical smoke signals from his Boro Park window to the sawdust haunts in the Village, New Orleans, and Paris, reminding them all he was still paying attention. He visited museums rarely, hadn't been to a concert in months, but read novels and history when he could, and the past week even reread a collection of Kafka stories.

And Katrina. Only with Katrina did he break the new-old rules. Not often and not without pangs of self-admonition and self-censure. But the flesh *is* weak. He called himself a hypocrite.

"You're not a hypocrite," Katrina said. "What you are is an intellectual hypochondriac."

"Now there's a concept."

"It's true, Elisha. You're forever checking in on your beliefs, appalled by every little blemish. Any minor dent in an argument becomes a crater proving your entire way of life is wrongheaded."

"Consistency is important."

"Important, but not everything."

"I'm trying to get it right."

"Well, get over it. It's tiresome."

"What's tiresome?"

"This perpetual angst of yours about getting it right. Questions aren't fatal. You won't die from them."

And did he think his physical distance was easy for her? But she was willing to comply with his arbitrary, nonsensical, self-imposed strictures, keeping apart on his observant days and guzzling her body on his deviant nights. She let him decide the extent of their intimacy—for now. She'd go along—for now.

20

In this burning country words must serve as shade.
                                        —Yehuda Amichai

During a shabbos lunch on a sweltering June day when your shirt collar stuck to your neck like Velcro and your shoes were saunas for the feet, Elisha's father wiped his brow with a napkin and placed his knife and fork on his plate.

"I have an announcement."

He put his palm on his face, the index finger under one eye, his thumb under the other, held it there for a moment before letting his hand begin a slow descent of his beard to the bottom of his chest.

"I'm going to Israel in two weeks."

He hadn't been there in years. He hadn't yet prayed at the Western Wall. The Gerer Rebbe's grandson was getting married and this would be a good time to go. He stroked his beard again, another exaggerated hiatus.

"And I'd like to take Elisha with me."

"So you decided to take him after all," Elisha's mother said, continuing to serve the salad. She commented on the still worrisome military situation in the Middle East, but seemed pleased. She herself had never been to Israel, but given her father's condition, being so far away from him now was out of the question.

Elisha's father related in a gust how difficult it was to get plane tickets, this being the peak of the travel season, but Srully the travel agent called twenty minutes before shabbos to say he'd pulled strings, got them a group rate, don't ask, a whole *megillah*, plenty of details to arrange, passports, inoculation shots, money transfers, in any case, bottom line, it's all worked out.

Elisha, stunned by this invitation, managed nothing more articulate than "Wow, I can't believe it."

"You deserve it," said his father. "These last months you've been a new person, or, should I say, your old self."

Elisha thanked him with a grin that spread across the Atlantic Ocean. He'd been dreaming about visiting Israel for years, but never more urgently than these past months.

The affinity he shared with other Jews for the young Jewish state had become a lasting infatuation five years earlier, during the biblical days of war in June 1967. In the hours prior to that conflict, Elisha beheld the incredulous, mortified look on his parents' face when they raised their eyes from their newspapers. The Arab armies were sharpening their knives and the tremor-weary Jews could feel the slash of steel scraping their post-Holocaust skin. His parents wondered aloud: Again? Scarcely more than twenty years after the gassing and again the world will wriggle and shrug and cluck its tongues at the sight of Jewish ashes? No, not again. This time would be different. This time the cosmic tremble ended in cosmic redemption. This time, the first time in two thousand years, the smoke cleared and the Jews were not supine. They were standing, victors.

Everywhere the Jews were delirious. Their mouths were full with headlines; they spoke to one another like newsreels, free of burdensome nuance and nervous hedging. They swapped war stories—who would have imagined?— Jewish war stories with happy endings! New heroes decorated the walls of their homes and schools; a general's eye patch became their badge of honor. True, Israel had also reaped an unfamiliar politics with someone else suffering the role of the vanquished, but those were thorns for later pruning. And all around Elisha, up and down the streets of Boro Park, the religious argument recovered ancient prophecies and with unnerving confidence heralded Israel's triumphal destiny.

But for young American Jews like Elisha, the glory was alloyed. They, too, had feared and then celebrated, but whom were they fooling? Their swagger was derivative, their tough-guy prowess fashioned with armor from shoulders across the sea. And they well understood: the bravery and spilled blood belonged not to them but to their cousins who actually held the hilltops and slew the enemy.

Elisha knew a few young men in his neighborhood who'd recently emigrated to Israel. Could he join them? What would await him there? Would this be an escape or a return? He had this daydream of Katrina in a Jerusalem park, stopping to discuss Gogol with old Russian immigrants, they speaking in Odessa-laced Hebrew and she with a Wisconsin Hebraic drawl. Fantasy costs nothing.

But this trip would put these reveries in peril. For the truth was his return to Chassidic life was not the success his father thought it was. Over the past weeks, he'd become restless once more; the old doubts, never deeply buried, had resurfaced, ever more jagged and demanding. Elisha had kept the Israel card in his hip pocket, the ace solution to his religious dilemmas. There, he supposed, he could shed his exilic clothes and sprint guiltless with the other young men and women forging their new Jewish identities.

But what if he were an outsider there as well? The Israel detour was, he understood, the final hurdle before his exit from his traditional life, and now he'd be pressing his body against it. And if it failed to hold him in? What if what mattered was what he was, not where he was? His ocean-wide grin shrunk to a thin grim line of his pressed lips. This trip would provide answers he could no longer avoid.

Elisha had never before been on an airplane and, as wide-eyed as the ten-year-old across the aisle, marveled at the billowing carpet of clouds below. In the next seat, his father riffled through a *Newsweek* he'd found in the chair pocket. "Look at this picture," he said. An anniversary article of the six-day war showed a photograph of an Israeli soldier standing atop a tank. He was wearing a white knitted *kippa* on his closely cropped hair, phylacteries wrapped on one arm and a machine gun slung over the other.

"Wonderful, no?" his father said. "Even in battle he wears his tefillin."

"You could put it the other way," Elisha said. "Even when he worships, he carries his Uzi."

"You elevate the gun, not the praying."

"They're equally…"

"Equally?"

His father emitted a low groan and shut his eyes. Elisha returned to gazing out the window.

A minute later, without warning or segue, his father lifted his body from his seat and reached for the overhead compartment. "Forget sleep. It's a shame to waste the time." He sat down with two Talmuds in hand. "I so enjoy our learning together."

So did Elisha. He relished not only studying Torah with his father, but the very idea of studying Torah with one's father, as his father had with his father, stretching back generation to generation into the distant past. Would he study Torah with his own son?

Father and son opened their books and plunged into the text, resuming a fifteen-hundred-year-old discussion and transforming the coach section of El Al into their private study hall.

From their lodging in Geula in the heart of Ultra Orthodox Jerusalem, Elisha and his father hastened each morning at dawn to pray at the *Kotel Ma'aravi*, the Western Wall. The twenty minute walk took them through the tortuous Arab *shuk,* past the hard glares of the shopkeepers raising the shutters of their stalls. The Wall dated back to 70 CE when Titus let stand a retaining wall of the Second Temple as a token of the destruction of Jerusalem; two thousand years later, in 1967, a Jewish conquering army had reclaimed the site. Legions of the local pious and the would-be pious along with scores of American Jews and Christian tourists donned cardboard yarmulkes and assembled day and night for their respective "religious experiences." The adjoining plaza functioned as a bizarre religious bazaar, boisterous and booming—no wonder some referred to the Kotel as the "diskotel."

Elisha spotted an unoccupied corner of the wall and leaned his head against its timeworn stone. Men and women had cried their hearts out here for centuries and the Wailing Wall—its alternative, tear-stained name—listened to each entreaty but promised nothing in return.

What was his plea? He wanted the impossible, didn't he? Individual adventures, but also the embrace of community. Freedom to doubt, but also the certainties of traditional faith. His family's approval, but also the touch of Katrina's fingers on his cheek. But even God cannot perform contradictions. Even God can't create round squares or make it possible for a young man to travel two diverging roads at once. Elisha placed his hand on the wall and his mouth against the wall, saddened that his lips could express no prayer.

Afternoons and evenings were devoted to courtly visits with Chassidic leaders, the protocol no different in Jerusalem than Brooklyn. Dressed obligingly in his dark suit and black hat, Elisha received the luminaries' blessings and stood to the side as his father and the rebbes exchanged Chassidic Torah and Chassidic gossip. The rabbis were invariably polite to him but, sizing up his modern appearance, suspicious as well. Three times in one day he was treated to the same admonition: "You have holy ancestors, Elisha, but pedigree is like a zero. The more zeros, the bigger the number...but only if you put a one in front of those zeros. Without that one—without yourself—you remain a zero."

And in every conversation, the rebbes would bemoan the ignorance of Israel's youth. "About Julius Caesar, they learn. Napoleon, they know. But Hillel and Shamai? Maimonides? The Baal Shem Tov? Nothing. Shakespeare they read. But the Pentateuch? Talmud?" Yet, there was hope, they insisted. Look around and see how the seeds of the old European Chassidic dynasties were taking root all over the primordial soil of Eretz Israel.

But this resurgent Chassidism was also inventing its past. One feisty older dignitary from a Polish town near Elisha's father's birthplace complained of the flood of imposters opening up storefront shteibls across the country proclaiming themselves Chassidic rebbes.

"It's the same in America," Elisha's father said. "When Satan realized he couldn't be everywhere, he made sure there'd be clergymen everywhere."

The old Chassid rotated his head to face Elisha. "An ambitious fellow once disclosed to the Tzaddik of Stolin he'd had a dream in which he was a rebbe with five thousand followers. The tzaddik replied, 'Young man, I'll be impressed when five thousand people tell me they'd had a dream in which you were their rebbe.'"

The repartee went on like this for an hour. These meetings were always too long and always too formal, but Elisha could at least expect an exchange of wit and Talmudic insights. Little of that pleasure accompanied the visits of the droves of cousins who came to pay their respects to his father. He'd meet even more relatives at the upcoming wedding, they assured him.

In America, too, Chassidic weddings had become massive affairs. Two thousand people had attended Elisha's own parents' wedding even back in the early postwar years when the number of Chassidim in America was miniscule. The upcoming wedding of a grandchild of the Rebbe of Satmar was expected to draw twenty thousand; rumor had it, Madison Square Garden had been rented for the occasion. The following week's wedding in Jerusalem would be a mammoth affair as well. "They've chartered planes from America, Antwerp, London, and Paris," his father said, and with a half wink at Elisha added, "even Brazil."

"Who's getting married again?" Elisha asked. "The Prince of Prussia and the Princess of Scotland?"

"Not so different," his father said. "For us Chassidim, the wedding of grandchildren of major rebbes is a royal ceremony."

Elisha asked to take his royal leave and went out for a walk. He waited at a red light as a young couple on a Vespa pulled up alongside him. The girl wore tight jean shorts and white boots, her legs folded around the driver, a long-haired young man wearing a pink shirt opened to his navel. The girl looked over toward Elisha, and smiled. Elisha noticed the dimple, the one dimple. She held up her fingers in a "V."

"Peace," Elisha called, and could hear her surprised laughter as the bike roared down the street. He followed her boots until she was out of sight.

He'd had enough. He needed a break from the faithful Chassidim recreating the past; he craved a spell of faithlessness with those creating the future. He told his father he planned to visit with Shmulik and Gita in their home in Holon, on the outskirts of Tel Aviv. After all, they were cousins too. His father folded his arms on his chest, "Shmulik and Gita?" He began a sigh but instead wished his son a good trip.

Shmulik delivered directions in a Polish-Israeli glazed English, but sensing Elisha's uncertainty, repeated the instructions in Yiddish before hanging up the phone. He was eager, he said, to see what had become of his "inquisitive little Chassidic cousin."

Leafy trees lined their street, casting serrated shadows on the long row of stucco rooftops. The manicured front lawns were replicas of suburban landscapes everywhere, but to Elisha this itself was a Jewish miracle. Shmulik and Gita's house was next to last on the block, identical to its neighbors but for its sky-blue façade and the careful alignment of flowers, none of which Elisha could name. He looked up at the doorpost. Was there a mezuzah affixed as required by Jewish law? He was comforted seeing it there. But his shoulders stiffened when he rang the bell and a dog barked.

"*Shtok,* Sasha," a voice called out and mercifully the howling ceased.

Elisha was in the sixth grade when he first met Shmulik. For weeks he'd anticipated the visit from this Israeli relative, a kibbutznik who'd be broad-shouldered yet lean and wearing one of those floppy kova temble hats he'd seen in photography books of the early Zionist pioneers. But the man who burst into their house that day, booming, "Sholem aleichem, you all," was short and compact, wearing thick glasses over a pencil-thin moustache, and a crumpled taupe jacket over brown polyester pants. Shmulik had bear-hugged his father forcing him to gasp for breath.

"Ah, you veak Americana," Shmulik teased with a hearty whoop. He even had put his arms around Elisha's mother who didn't seem to mind his forwardness. Was such *joie de vivre* allowed in their family? Elisha had wondered if it had something to do with his not wearing a yarmulke.

"Don't mind Sasha, she's really a kitten," Shmulik said, as he greeted Elisha in a warm embrace, and ushered him into the living room. Shmulik's arms were still muscular, his grip still tight. The German shepherd sniffed at Elisha's ankle and moved on.

Through the open door of a bedroom, Elisha noticed a large photograph of their teenage daughter Sivan standing on a swing wearing a pink halter-top and cutoff jeans, a cascade of brown tresses reaching down to her lower back. How marvelous, he thought—a cousin of his could dress like that. He remarked on the psychedelic "Make Love Not War" poster that hung on the wall; Trevor had the identical poster hanging in his bathroom. "Unfortunately," Shmulik said heavily, "in Israel we don't get to choose between these options."

Gita greeted Elisha in the kitchen, waving one hand while balancing a tray of tea and cake in the other. They took seats around a table in the kitchenette whose décor belonged to a previous decade, the themed wallpaper of long-stemmed flowers overlooking a green linoleum floor, an echo of the kitchen pattern in his parents' home. Shmulik and Gita's East European accents paralleled his parents' too, and they shared the same fatigued body gestures. These people were living his parents' counter-lives, Elisha realized, the lives they might have lived had they, too, abandoned the Chassidic shtetl for secular Israel where they would raise children in jeans and halter tops instead of black suits and ankle-length dresses. For that matter, he was the offspring of Shmulik and Gita's alternate life had they remained in the Old World of their youth.

"So?" Gita asked. "What does our American think of our country so far?"

"It's certainly not America," Elisha said. "People here talk to their dogs in Hebrew."

And what had he seen so far?

"Rabbis and graves." Elisha replied, the impatience in his answer a surprise to his hosts.

Shmulik said, "You ask me, Chassidism will never take hold in this country. Maybe pockets here and there and graves everywhere, but in this land we have no need for the beards and payis of the exile."

All week Elisha had heard his other Chassidic relatives contend the opposite with equal passion. Without Judaism, they said, what's the point of Israel? To have another country, another Bolivia or Belgium? But before Elisha could respond, Gita came to his rescue.

She wanted to hear about the upcoming wedding. The followers of Ger comprised the largest Chassidic sect in Europe before the war and were again the largest Chassidic sect in Israel. She'd grown up as one of them. But in the

1930s Gita had joined a Zionist youth movement and emigrated to Israel where at *Shomer Hatzair*, a kibbutz so vehemently antireligious it boasted lobster feasts on Yom Kippur, she met Shmulik, another Chassidic runaway.

Although Gita was Elisha's mother's age, she seemed older; years of squinting in the sun had bequeathed ridged wrinkles around her eyes and decades of pursed lips circling cigarettes had formed multiple creases around her mouth. But she spoke with a youthful impetuosity that sounded almost girlish. "I knew the current Gerer Rebbe's father. A man of few words but unwavering judgments. My friend Dora Dymant never forgave him for that."

"That name is vaguely familiar," Elisha said.

Gita squinted at Elisha, doubtful. "She was Franz Kafka's last lover. He died in her arms. Franz Kafka, the writer?"

Of course he'd heard of Kafka, Elisha assured Gita. Elisha hid a smile as the memory of Katrina handing him Kafka's book of stories flashed through his head. So that was why the name was familiar, he realized. He'd seen it in a Kafka biography. But what had Dora Dymant to do with the Rebbe of Ger?

"He prevented them from marrying," Gita said.

Elisha, already sitting upright in his chair bolted still higher. "The Gerer Rebbe and Kafka?"

"I should write her story someday," Gita mused.

"You should," Shmulik said, balancing a sugar cube between his teeth while he sipped his tea, the same way Elisha's father did. "This woman forgets nothing. She remembers the number on every combination lock she ever owned."

Gita took a prolonged pull on her cigarette. "I'll give you the gist," she said, pronouncing gist as an alliteration of give.

The Dymants lived next door to Gita in the village of Pabianice, just southwest of Lodz. Both families were fervent Gerer Chassidim. Even though Dora was considerably older, she shared with Gita her rebellious dreams and plans. As soon as she could, she left the shtetl, moving first to Krakow and then Berlin where she met Kafka. He was thirty-nine, she twenty-four. Dora wrote to Gita about the remarkable storyteller with whom she'd fallen in love, and how they planned to move to Palestine when his health improved. Despite her defection from Chassidism, Dora remained a dutiful daughter and wrote to her father asking his permission to marry Kafka. Her father brought the letter to the Gerer Rebbe who answered in a word: "No."

"And the reason?" Shmulik asked before Elisha could.

"He didn't say. Dora and Kafka were so disappointed. Kafka died less than a year later."

"Did she have any of Kafka's work?" Elisha asked, recalling how he'd asked the same question about his Aunt Leika.

"That's the great irony." Gita had asked Max Brod the same question when she'd visited him in his house in Tel Aviv. "Max Brod was—"

"Kafka's best friend," Elisha interrupted. "The one who promised to fulfill Kafka's request to burn all his manuscripts. Only a few had been published during Kafka's life. Thankfully, Brod reneged on his promise."

Gita was impressed. "How do you know all this? Not bad for a Chassidic young man."

Brod had asked Dora to give him Kafka's writings for publication. She had in her possession many stories, dozens of notebooks, as well as diaries, letters, who knows what else. Understandably, she refused, wanting to publish them herself. Then, in 1933, the Gestapo barged into her apartment, carted away all Kafka's papers and burned them... just as he'd requested.

Elisha couldn't wait to relate this story to Katrina. She'd appreciate his elation at once more finding his distant worlds intersecting.

"And speaking of heretics and their problems with authority," Shmulik said, "are you familiar with your namesake in the Talmud?"

Of course he was. Elisha ben Avuya was one of the four rabbis, along with Akiva, Ben Zoma, and Ben Azai, who "wandered into the garden" to study Kabbalah; other commentators say the garden alludes to Hellenist philosophy. Ben Azai became insane, Ben Zoma died, Rabbi Akiva remained the great leader of Israel, and Elisha turned into a disbeliever. The Talmud refers to Elisha as The Other yet includes his legal rulings in its discussions, making room inside the law for this outsider. Having his name was always a secret source of mischievous pride to Elisha.

"As long as we're on the subject," Elisha said to his cousin, "how did you become a renegade?" He was sure Shmulik had been asked this question a hundred times before, but he doubted his answer mattered to anyone as much as it did to Elisha. Shmulik and Gita were part of his family history, too. And he was standing at the entrance to a frontier they'd pioneered.

"Guess," Shmulik said.

"I have no idea. Spinoza?"

Shmulik laughed, "Me, Spinoza? I'm no intellectual. Even the Zionism came later."

"What then? Sex?"

Shmulik was surprised at Elisha's direct, uneuphemistic wording. He smiled at Gita but shook his head at Elisha. "No, not even sex. It was Beethoven."

"Beethoven? As in Ludwig Van Beethoven? I didn't know he, too, was a lapsed Chassid."

Shmulik said he was sixteen or so, a Chassidic boy— "not like you, but sheltered like you can't imagine"—when one winter evening, he'd wandered into a Cracow music hall to warm up. The orchestra was playing Beethoven, Symphony Number Seven; that he'd never forget. He stood in the rear hidden behind a pole, spellbound by what he heard; his heart, his pulse, even his toes were exploding. He couldn't take his eyes off the conductor. Like a magician he was. He asked his yeshiva teachers to explain how this secular creation could be so spiritual. Could the soul who composed this music be so elevated even without any connection to Torah? His teachers scratched their heads. They muttered this way, they muttered that way, they nodded their heads, they shook their heads, they said, yes, it's all very nice and wonderful, but essential it's not, for in the end, this music is but another distraction from what really matters, the devotion to the holy teachings. In other words, they had no answer. "Well, that started me on the path out. I realized my religious tradition couldn't account for everything, not even everything sacred."

"But you had ignorant teachers," Elisha said, suddenly eager to defend the Chassidic tradition.

But Shmulik wasn't going to argue the point. "Listen, let's not pick away at this. The truth is we don't really know why we make the choices we do. Why did I leave my Chassidic life while all my six siblings remained? Who really knows? We each choose our path and then choose a story to explain our choice. So Beethoven. That's my story."

Elisha lay in bed for hours pondering what story would explain his own choices. He managed to sleep only after consoling himself he was still too young and his tale had not yet been written.

He woke up to an empty house. A note on the kitchen table from Gita invited him to help himself to breakfast and stay in touch. It was eight in the morning; one in the morning in New York. Elisha picked up the phone, entered the AT&T code, and dialed Katrina's number. He wanted to tell her she was on his mind. That he wished he was holding her in his arms. That he was reaching decisions and couldn't remain much longer as he was when he left. That it was all becoming clearer.

He let the phone ring ten times before hanging up. He carried the disappointment with him back to Jerusalem and the evening's Chassidic wedding.

Teams of Chassidic marshals on walkie-talkies were strategically stationed at the wedding hall, ushering the guests to their appropriate sections: boys to the makeshift bleachers, unmarried young men to the upper tiers, older men to the lower; a group of women performed the same duty at the ladies' entrance. Two strapping young men greeted Elisha and his father and brought them to their reserved seats in the front row directly across from the wedding canopy. Elisha surveyed the swarm of bodies around him and up in the rafters. Only here and there did he notice another shaven face.

The singing was already in full throttle when they arrived: "Aiy, aiy, aiy," thousands chanted for ten minutes before moving on to the next refrain; on an improvised stage on the side of the arena, a band of Chassidic musicians gallantly tried to follow along. As the time neared for the ceremony to begin, the singing grew lustier, the clapping and stomping more emphatic.

And then the music stopped. The singing and thumping ceased in an instance. The ceremony had begun.

The groom shambled down the aisle held up on either side by his father and soon-to-be father-in-law. The boy's soft, ruddy complexion made him appear even younger than his nineteen years. A minute later his thickly veiled bride made her way to the platform escorted by her mother and future mother-in-law. The young couple stood next to each other under the canopy, their eyes facing the floor. They'd met only once before, six weeks earlier, for a few minutes, heavily chaperoned; for both, that was the first encounter with someone of the other gender who was not immediate family. In a few hours they'd be having sex with one another.

The ceremony culminated with the customary breaking of a glass to signify that even at this moment of the greatest joy one must remember human suffering. "Mazel Tov!" twenty thousand voices boomed and the dancing began in earnest. So it would continue throughout the night, circle revolving around circle, gyre within gyre.

But Elisha would not be among them. He delighted in their ecstasy, but he'd find his own elsewhere. It hit him now with a burst of clarity. This was no contradiction after all: he could cherish their lives but want a different one for himself. He watched them dance for a few moments and recalled the words of the Rebbe of Breslov: "A person must dance every day, either with his body or with his thoughts." He walked slowly to the exit, his chest tight, his breaths short. And then he remembered something else the Rebbe of Breslov had said: "All the world is a narrow bridge. But the important thing is not to be afraid." He turned around to look again at his fellow Chassidim, before heading out into the Jerusalem streets. He would not be afraid.

Somewhere along a deserted avenue he found a telephone. It would be late morning now in New York, time for Katrina to be rousing after her late night. He had so much to tell her, so much to ask her. But again the phone rang and she did not answer.

21

....

We are sinful not merely because we have eaten of the tree of knowledge, but also because we have not eaten of the tree of life.

—Franz Kafka

The day after he returned to the United States, Elisha placed two phone calls.

First to Katrina. Her phone was busy.

He next called Trevor. Elisha reviewed his trip and promised to provide photographic documentation if, for a change, he'd correctly rolled the film in his camera. And he had something important to report. "I'm no longer Orthodox."

Even as the words eked out from behind his teeth, they seemed to come from elsewhere, a ventriloquist's illusion. Was this how it sounded when others first acknowledged they were alcoholics, or homosexuals, or adulterers, or members of the communist party? "I'm no longer observant," he repeated under his breath, but the words still hung ungainly from his mouth like borrowed clothes. He considered explaining to Trevor why, given his background, he could only be a lapsed Orthodox Jew but never a devout Conservative or Reform Jew, but the fine distinctions of Jewish denominational skirmishes would be of no more interest to Trevor than local soccer team rivalries in rural Ecuador.

"You still there, pal?" Trevor asked, ending the prolonged silence. "Because while you were painting the ceiling or whatever kept you busy in never-never-land, the skies opened and an idea descended into my overwrought brain."

His roommate was moving out for several weeks, perhaps permanently, and would Elisha like to move in for a while... or, who knows, even longer? As a bonus, provided Elisha swept on occasion and washed a dish or two, Trevor would allow Elisha to fondle his cello on lonely, horny nights. "Move in, daddio. We'll have a blast."

Elisha promised to take the offer seriously. The rent would be doable, at least at the start. He could tutor chess and math, and there were those bar mitzvah bonds that had recently matured and were lying fallow in the bank vault. The problem would be in the declaration itself. Did he have the gumption to move out? Chassidic young men never, ever forsook their parents' home before marriage. Detours invite deviance. The transition from parental home to one's own domain always included a spouse and the imminent expectation of children. Elisha tried saying the words, "I'm moving out," but the sentence even failed to reach the front of his teeth. He was determined, though, to push those words out into the cold air and follow right behind.

He tried Katrina again and spoke with her for two hours before yielding the phone to his sister. He walked to a public phone booth for another hour of talk. Katrina had been productive. She'd read two Chekov plays in Russian and joined a chamber group playing Baroque composers.

She'd knitted a scarf, well, almost, until she messed up the yarn. She was nearing a decision about what to do after graduating this semester; the Peace Corps was no longer an option. Elisha said he'd tried to call her from Israel. She'd been out a couple nights with old friends, she replied.

And she had a question for him. Could he get free next week for four days? For a trip to the country.

Four days? Elisha calculated. Neither school nor yeshiva was in session. Four days alone with Katrina. He'd work it out somehow.

"Gotta scram, lamb," she said. "Work."

"Hugs for the bugs," he said.

The quickest way to get to Moosehead Lake from Manhattan was via the Mass Pike, a nine-hour drive, but no more than eight if Katrina was driving. And she'd be doing all of it, every country meter, as Elisha had only received a learner's permit a month earlier and in his practice runs had forged no further than from one barricade of the Kingsway Bowling Alley parking lot to the other. The vacation was subsidized by Katrina's mother who'd vacationed in the area a few weeks before and upon learning her former husband had treated Katrina and Elisha for dinner was determined to outperform her ex's largesse. She'd even lent Katrina the Chrysler for the trip. Elisha had only to make sure to bring a substantial sweater for the cool nights and a bathing suit for clear-water rafting, though not a necessity for swimming if the cabin was as isolated as her mother indicated. And did he have access to binoculars for bird-watching?

Rafting? Skinny-dipping? Bird watching? Elisha insisted he wasn't at all fazed. He was no city slicker, he bragged, even before they reached the Cross Bronx Expressway; why, as proof, one summer in camp he'd single-handedly captured a cricket and put it in a jar under his counselor's bunk bed where despite a frantic search it remained undetected for two nights, and not only that, but once on an overnight trip, he'd snapped a picture of a deer grazing in the woods, although, truth be told, he'd kept his distance and you needed a magnifying glass to make out the deer among the branches. True, this Maine lodge would be the farthest he'd ever been from a supermarket or synagogue, barber shop or bakery, but he'd be fine, just fine, even without a telephone or radio, no problem at all, so what are a few tiger bites on your arm? He did worry, he admitted, what one does in the case of an appendicitis attack out there in the wilderness.

When they crossed into Connecticut, Elisha read from the guide book Katrina's mother had left in the glove compartment: *Nestled among scenic mountain ranges at the doorstep of Maine's great north woods, Moosehead Lake is the largest lake east of the Mississippi contained within one state. Henry David Thoreau explored the region with Indian guides in the mid-1800s.*

As Elisha read on with patent and accumulating anxiety, Katrina laughed so hard she had to stop the car on a New

Hampshire highway. Undaunted, he continued: *A fox sits with pricked ears on a mountain top. A bear scampers in the woods. An eagle soars overhead. In the distance, a moose snorts. Fish furtively gulp at midges on the water's surface.* "What's a midge?" Elisha interrupted himself. He continued: *Bees buzz. Flowers bloom.* In a sidebar, the writer rises to lyrical rhapsody: *Light dims across the ridges to the west, while to the east, the last crest of the range turns into a flurry of sun-struck spikes of firs and eucalyptus.* Elisha said these were the sort of descriptive passages he always skipped when they blocked his way through a novel.

Clusters of spruce and tawny grass spread out below in sprawling meadows—would Katrina please translate? He knew more words for elation than for names of trees, more synonyms for agony than names of plants. Chassidism, he declaimed, was a winter sport. He was of the stock of indoors men; the outdoors belonged to coyotes and Cossacks.

Katrina kept her vision straight ahead as, clear through Vermont, Elisha addressed her profile, the side with the dimple. The romanticization of nature was idol worship, he inveighed, the deification of the created over the Creator. No wonder you could draw a direct line from German romanticism to Heidegger and the Nazis. If she thought he was overstating the case, well, let's just say nature is even more overrated than people. And nothing in the world is more tedious than people talking about nature, the sun-scarred would-be Druids ejaculating over an awe-inspiring sunset dipping below the mountain, how it makes them feel at one with the universe. Well, explain to him, please, why these folk don't erupt with the same stupefaction when they're in the middle of an earthquake or attacked by feral predators? Why aren't they warbling hymns to the glory of nature when they're infected with a nasty bacteria that forces them to dash to the bathroom every five minutes? As for the pristine and serene, he preferred the obscene.

When their automobile crossed the Maine border, Katrina warned Elisha if he didn't shut up she'd put his Brooklyn street smarts to the test by leaving him on the road to fend with raccoons and New England moose hunters. He said he hadn't yet gotten to the good part about nature and sucked on her neck.

The two cottages they passed on the final dirt road were no longer visible when they reached their destination. Their cabin stood in a wooded lot at the mouth of the lake, and Katrina and Elisha remained outside for a few minutes, their arms atop each others' shoulders, breathing in the rustic air. Katrina asked Elisha if he noticed how the white oak shingles carpeting the saddleback roof reflected wedges of sunlight filtered through the leaves. He said she had to be kidding, but he could smell pine.

They'd landed in an enchanted forest. The quiet quickly imposed its calm on Elisha's frantic rhetoric. He rocked himself on a chair on the porch, the peace so pronounced he could hear himself think, but why think when you could be still and indulge the flirtatious breeze caressing your face. That first night, they lay on their backs in a field and drew constellations in the sky with nearby sticks, made love, counted stars into the thousands, and made love again before falling asleep in each other's arms and legs.

Elisha awoke first and from the tawny field collected a cache of flowers which he compared to the entries in the *Flora and Fauna of Maine* coffee-table book in the reading room. He brought his harvest to Katrina, still half-asleep, and proudly informed her the tough-looking things with the soft silver-green needles were called white pine and were the largest conifer in the northeastern United States (neglecting to mention he hadn't an inkling what a conifer was). She named the other flowers in his hand, freesia, anemone, and baby's breath, and to encourage his botanical education, offered a ten-minute sensual massage for every flower or tree he correctly labeled. Elisha studied the flora book with the scrutiny he'd apply to a page of scripture.

Depending on the moment's mood, he listened to one of the three tapes he'd brought along: Bach's *Goldberg Variations* for his mind, Shlomo Carlebach's Chassidic songs for his soul, and Charlie Parker ballads for his body. From the kitchen window he watched Katrina dart up and down the surrounding hills like a jaguar released from her cage, squealing with joy, and greeted her with hugs and cookies when she returned, her hair laced with twigs and her overalls coated in dirt gathered from rolling on the earth for the sheer delight of it.

On their afternoon hikes, Katrina pointed out chickadees, hummingbirds, plovers, and terns, rattling off their species' nomenclature as though calling out to her own children. She was even better at butterflies, she said, without a trace of arrogance; she'd become interested when she learned that Vladimir Nabokov, her favorite living Russian writer, was a prominent lepidopterist and had organized the butterfly collection of the Museum of Comparative Zoology at Harvard; Elisha said that might explain how she was able to help him escape from his own cocoon. She showed him how to mark a trail, and he taught her how to skip stones in the lake. From branches and moss they crafted wreaths for each other's heads and pranced across an adjacent dell performing absurd elf imitations. Elisha couldn't remember the day becoming night becoming day so seamlessly, nor could he remember ever being this happy.

On the third morning he tracked the trill of a flute to a patch of grass under a tree where Katrina sat cross-legged, the wreath of twigs on her head, playing the Irish tune she'd sung to him on the way up, called appropriately "The Lark in the Morning." He watched, he listened, and he decided. He'd move out of Boro Park. He'd do it without delay. The decision felt less like an epiphany than the ineluctable conclusion to a long, tortuous argument.

There she was, the catalyst that had showed him the way out. He'd be leaving because of her, but not for her—this was his journey. The road was sure to be curved, the forks many, the destination as yet undetermined. But how lucky he was to have her travel with him if only for part of the way. He stood breathing in the pungent morning air before turning back to the cottage.

Later, coming up next to her in the lake, he asked, "Of these three, which do you prefer the most and which the least? Things, people, or ideas?"

Katrina dunked into the water, her naked body still visible in the late afternoon shimmer. She resurfaced fifteen feet away. "I do like tinkering with stuff," she said. "And unlike a few other people I know, I do appreciate nature. But especially the nature of people."

"So people most?"

"Yes. And things least. How about you?"

"I'm with you on the things category. Engineering wasn't ever happening."

"And most?"

"Ideas, I'd have to say. Even when I study anthropology, it's the conceptual parts I like best. That's the difference between us."

"People versus ideas?"

"You're interested in ideas because people have them. I'm interested in the idea of people."

"I've suspected as much," Katrina said. "It's not me you're drawn to as much as the idea of me." Her laugh was small and forced.

"That's simply not true," Elisha protested, but Katrina had already dived back into the water and was gliding toward him.

"Let's race back to the shore. Ready, set," she said, and began swimming without getting to "go." Her strokes were swift and clean, learned and practiced on her high school swim team. Elisha jumped in behind her and propelled by a competitive determination reached the finish line an arm's length ahead of Katrina; he suspected she'd purposely slowed up toward the end.

They dried themselves and lay on the blanket, her head on his chest. Above them, a reluctant sun edged its way to the rim of a faultless blue sky. How sad, they agreed, they'd already be on the road home when the sun reappeared the next morning. Katrina suggested they play a couple of rounds of truth or dare, but Elisha said he disliked the game. "Why advantage the mean-spirited and nosy?"

Katrina said, "All right, no dare. Just truths. I'll start." She sat up and drew her finger against her teeth. "Those calls you tried to make from Israel?"

"I was so eager to talk to you."

"I was out."

"Apparently."

"With an old boyfriend."

Elisha sat up immediately but inched backward, uncertain he wanted to hear more.

"His name is Erik," Katrina said. They'd been going steady during the last two years of high school and through much of her first year of college. She'd wanted to break up with him and that was partly why she'd moved with her mother to New York City and transferred to CCNY. Erik didn't see it the same way. He'd kept the lamp burning.

"So he came to see you."

"He was visiting relatives. And as luck would have it, you happened to be abroad."

"His luck. Yours too?"

"Listen to the tone of your voice, Elisha!"

"It's just a question."

"We spent a couple of nights together."

Elisha swallowed air.

Panic isn't the fear of danger, but the fear you can't control your fear, and it was the depth of his anguish that bewildered Elisha most. But what did he expect from her?

"What do you expect?" Katrina said, reading his thoughts with startling accuracy. "I was lonely. I missed you. You'd gone off to your observant life. It'd been a long time since someone held me without worrying he was violating the fundamental laws of the Divine."

"That's no longer true of me."

"And…it's not like…you and I…are officially boyfriend and girlfriend."

Elisha stared into his hand. "I'm not sure I know what that means. And Erik?"

"Back in Kenosha, Wisconsin. There's nothing between us."

"A fling for old time's sake."

"You're jealous."

"I have no right to be."

"I'm sorry, Elisha. But it wasn't a big deal. As you see, not even big enough to keep from you." She took another breath. That was done. She reached out and tweaked his nose. "Your turn. Truth."

"You think I can match that?"

"We'll see."

What terrible secret could he disclose? That he stole a look at the *kohanim* during the priestly blessing? That he'd masturbated to the fleeting image of high school girls in tight sweaters? To most humans on the planet, his guilt-racking transgressions didn't even qualify as trifles, as the merest of misdemeanors. "Okay, here's my revelation," he said. "I'm peeved as all hell by your Erik escapade. I have no business feeling this way. But I do. It hurts. More than I would've imagined."

Elisha spun a twig between his fingers, and looked over Katrina's shoulder, avoiding her eyes. "I knew I hated this game," he said, and walked off on his own.

22

....

*Only when you walk a new path can you be certain
no one has yet spoiled it.*

—the Rebbe of Kotsk

Elisha told his parents over dinner he was moving out and
in with a friend. He'd hinted at his decision for days but
the shocked look on their faces made clear that his warnings
had gone unnoticed. Elisha immediately sought to soften
the blow: Trevor was a vegetarian, so the apartment would
be effectively kosher, but he'd bring his own dishes anyway;
no more full-time yeshiva, true, but there was a legitimate
part-time yeshiva in Manhattan in which he'd continue his
studies; he'd come home for shabbos and holidays. The
move was temporary, he said. Elisha wondered how much
of this his parents believed.

"I see," was all his father said before walking out of the
room.

Elisha overheard his mother on the phone with Aunt
Malka the next day, gallantly spinning the news as best she
could. Elisha would be staying with a friend during the
week, she had her reservations, but it wasn't such a bad
idea what with the stories one hears these days about the
dangerous subways, especially at night, especially in *that*
neighborhood. But the look on her face let him know she
wasn't fooled. Not for a moment.

Trevor lived in a divided one bedroom on La Salle Street, a few blocks north of Columbia University. The best light came through the kitchen window that overlooked a court-yard the locals had arrogated for their private dumping grounds; the forest of air-fresheners Trevor had hung in each room was no match for the stench of rotten bananas and rancid melons. When it got bad, and it got bad often, the place smelled like a junkyard on a windless day.

Outside, every day, an orchestra of sirens, garbage trucks, and mothers swearing at their children and each other provided an unyielding audio backdrop to whatever other cacophony was taking place. In the late afternoon, the boom boxes held center stage blaring Tito Puente knockoffs, an opening act to the night's conga drumming, courtesy of a toothless Puerto Rican who'd requisitioned the building's front steps as his personal arena.

Trevor had decorated his apartment with makeshift throw-aways. The living room's centerpiece, a rickety, torn sofa, blended perfectly with the other discarded street debris even the hard-up neighbors deemed unworthy for keeping.

"Welcome to the lap of luxury," Trevor said, helping his friend with his suitcase.

Elisha's education in home living began instantly. He'd never cooked anything more complicated than scrambled eggs. He'd never managed a load of laundry. He'd never washed a floor or cleared a stuffed toilet. He'd never written a check. There was a flock of questions he'd never expected to ask: Where in the grocery store did they shelve sponges?

Which is better, canned peas or frozen? What exactly is a fuse box? Does anyone understand how to read a utility bill? Freedom hurls a nasty learning curve.

At first Elisha phoned his parents daily to reassure them, to reassure himself, the connection between them was alive and well, but like a charge seeping steadily from a battery, the calls dwindled to every other day, then twice a week, and now Elisha marked his calendar to remind himself to call on Fridays and wish his family a good shabbos. His father never called him; his mother rarely. And when she did, she'd bolster the fading pretense that Elisha had resettled only bodily and only temporarily by providing detailed litanies of the latest family happenings: his sister Deena won the school Bible tournament and his brother Avrumy did well on his entrance interview at the Talmudic academy in Lakewood, New Jersey, the country's premier post–high school yeshiva; and his cousin Bashi's wedding was next week ("which, I'm sure, you'll find some excuse not to attend"). Elisha listened politely to the family updates, but didn't bother to feign any interest with follow-up questions.

Before hanging up, Elisha guaranteed his mother he wasn't yet emaciated and was going to sleep on time, and no, he couldn't make it home this shabbos either but he'd try for the next. "How is Tateh?" he'd ask, and his mother responded mechanically with, "He's fine," sometimes appending, "and how do you think he feels?"

When he did come home, Elisha and his father maintained an arctic civility, each devising excuses not to be in the same room as the other. Conversation was limited to the necessary, impersonal and brief, accompanied by icy stares across a deep and deepening divide.

But one shabbos day, his father's seething disappointment burst. Elisha had straggled to the table twenty minutes after the others had settled in. He'd been reading in his room, he said, with no trace of apology, and begrudgingly nodded to the guest at the table, a young man Avrumy had befriended in summer camp. Ephraim—for he no longer wished to be called Evan, but only by his Hebrew name—had been raised in a secular household in Baltimore, but in his last year of high school had come under the influence of a charismatic Orthodox rabbi. To the chagrin of his parents, both physicians, Ephraim abandoned pre-med college plans to devote himself totally to Torah studies. The young man was well-spoken and inquisitive, eager to learn as much as he could about Jewish law and Chassidism.

Is it true, he asked, giraffes are kosher? Yes, they are. They chew their cud and have split hoofs. Eel? No, fish must have scales and fins. And the rationale for these criteria? With a mischievous lunge, Elisha launched into the anthropological explanation for the biblical kosher laws as a matter of species conforming fully to their natural class—amphibians are therefore not kosher for they live in two climates, nor are lobster and crabs, for they are sea animals that also crawl.

He eyed his younger brother, avoided looking at his father, and with a roguish grin said to Ephraim, "I hate to break this to you, but many biblical prohibitions have their basis in the ancient codes of other Middle Eastern societies. Not all the laws of the Torah are a Jewish invention."

The table responded with appalled silence and turned to Elisha's father for guidance on how to react to Elisha's unveiled sacrilege. His father's said, "How comforting to have a scientific explanation for everything," and invited the assembled to join in a Chassidic shabbos melody. Elisha heard the controlled fury in his father's voice, but Ephraim, undaunted, had another question, if he may, on this topic of music: Was it true the Chassidic Yiddish tune, "*Golis, Golis,* exile, exile," was really a Hungarian folk tune? Is that permissible?

"More than permissible," Elisha's father replied. "There are certainly sacred sparks in Beethoven. The Rebbe of Breslov taught that every blade of grass had its own unique melody, and so, too, does every idea, even the ideas of heresy. It's the tzaddik's task to hear that melody and uplift its purer spirit."

Elisha was familiar with his father's style of rebuke, a quote from the sages delivered to all but carrying a special message for his intended target. Elisha appreciated the delicacy of these anonymous reprimands, leaving it to the listener to discern the coded lesson. But his father's reference to heresy was no more subtle than Elisha's own incitement. Elisha dared a quick glance at his father and caught him doing the same in his direction. Their eyes spoke the same words: the time for restraint had passed.

Elisha's father recounted for Ephraim how the Hungarian peasant song became a Chassidic standard. The Rebbe of the Kahlev was walking in the meadow one day when he heard the plaintive singing of a shepherd: "Forest, Forest, how endless you are, how you keep me from my beloved." When the rebbe arrived at shul, he sang that melody with new words: "Exile, Exile, how endless you are. Were it not for you, our people would be one with the Divine Splendor."

From behind a broad smirk, Elisha interrupted: "So, as you see, Ephraim, Chassidim also sing peasant songs. And for some reason we're supposed to find this tidbit extraordinary."

Another stunned silence swept across the table. Elisha's father raked his fingers through his beard, laboring to regain his composure. "In fact, there's a deeper insight here," he said to the young guest, ignoring his son's latest antagonism. "An insight that escapes those who view things only on the surface." The Kahlever Rebbe wasn't simply applying Yiddish words to a folk song. As the rebbe explained, the shepherd's grieving for his maiden and the Jewish people's thirst for oneness with God are radically different sentiments, but they share the same root of human longing. And this was a melody of yearning.

Elisha said nothing more for the remainder of the meal and retreated to his room without joining the others in the recitation of grace after meals. A half hour later, his father stood at his doorway.

"Don't do us any favor by coming home for shabbos."

"I offered a different point of view. This isn't allowed?"

"We don't need your condescension."

The sides of his father's mouth drooped and his short breaths rebounded across the room. Elisha recalled his father quoting to him a remark of a Chassidic rebbe: "Long ago, I conquered my anger and placed it in my pocket. When I have need of it, I take it out." His father was reaching into his pocket.

"I wasn't being condescending," said Elisha.

"You don't want to be here? You don't want to partake in our lives…"

"I never said that."

"Then don't be here."

"I won't."

23
....

When I was young I admired clever people. Now that I am old, I admire kind people.
                    —Abraham Joshua Heschel

One mid-November night, New York received its first harsh lick of the coming winter. Elisha zipped up his too-thin jacket, wishing he had on the winter coat that hung in a closet in Boro Park. It'd been more than three months since he crossed the threshold of his parents' home.

But it wasn't only the coat he missed. He yearned for a few minutes of his shteibl-mates crackling local gossip and galactic politics. Were Fuleck and Bumshe still smuggling in put-downs of each other as they traded commentary on Holy Scripture? He ached for the restorative halt of an authentic shabbos, an oasis in the week that succeeds, he now could see, only when others around you share in the pause. Now and then on a Saturday night, he'd listen to a Talmud lecture on the Yiddish radio, the hour a nostalgic tease in sorry contrast to the give-and-take of a steady study partner, especially when that partner was his father; his ears still resounded to the delicious cacophony of a hundred voices debating fine points of text in the yeshiva study hall. And what would or could replace the embracing camaraderie of his Chassidic community?

How could he run free when he felt like this: untethered yet still entwined? But a new life takes time to be born.

Time, however, was the cause of the other chill that had wafted into Elisha's mood. Two weeks earlier at dinner in her apartment Katrina told him the good news.

"I've been accepted to Oxford."

"Congratulations!" Elisha had exclaimed, reflexively proud.

"I found out this morning. I couldn't wait to till you."

Elisha raised his wine glass. "This is exciting," he said, but his refusal to meet Katrina's eyes betrayed his delight.

The conversation went hard that evening and hard for days to follow.

Didn't he agree, Katrina asked, disappointed with his disappointment, that this was the time to grab opportunities before they flitted away?

Yes, of course he agreed, he'd answered. But she was the one flitting away. They'd be apart for so many days, so many weeks, so many months; he wouldn't be graduating college for at least another year and half.

Katrina reminded him that they'd come a long way since Kitty Hawk and airplanes now flew over the Atlantic. And she wasn't going until the end of summer. "Can't we concentrate on the present?" she said. "On our time together now?"

"It's not that easy," Elisha said.

It wasn't. For the next week, Elisha began each morning by marking the calendar on his wall as if he were a condemned prisoner counting off the days until the hanging. Katrina would not be staying—there'd be no stay of execution. He looked up the anthropology department at Oxford…but who knew where Katrina would be twenty months from now…where he'd be…where they would be?

Katrina was right—the trick was not to worry about the distant future. This past week he'd managed pretty well. And when his dread seeped through and he held tight, she'd whisper in his ear, "We're okay, we really are." And he'd press his cheek to hers, resting in the warmth of her words.

Trevor was waiting up for him.

"You've got messages," he said. Raymond had called to reschedule his daughter's chess lesson. "I had to tell him I was in the middle of a transformative cello practice to get him off the phone. Man, that guy can talk. And your mother called. Twice."

"Twice?"

"She sounded even more glum than usual. You're to please call her back as soon as possible."

Elisha looked at his watch.

Trevor replied, "She said to call no matter what time you came home."

Uncle Shaya had been in a car accident. From the stops and starts in his mother's monotonic delivery Elisha could tell she was pacing the room, clutching the telephone with both her hands, the line coiled around her arm; we each dispense bad news with a distinctive delivery, and Elisha read his mother's fluently. The prognosis was grim, she said. Uncle Shaya was in the intensive care unit at Mount Sinai hospital and they weren't allowing visitors yet. She didn't try to dissuade Elisha from stopping by the next day, anyway. "I know you two always had a special relationship."

Elisha stared at the wall but felt as if he were peering down a steep, unlit stairwell, a dark feeling of eerie conclusion. Once again his uncle skids off the traveled road, once more he veers from the straight and narrow. An accident, they said; Elisha had other suspicions. His gums went sour against his tongue. The club of adulthood Elisha had been so eager to join had peculiar bylaws and now this one: Accept as a fact of life that people, including those who should know better, manage to sabotage their lives. Protesting "it isn't fair" is a childish, naïve yelp. But that was precisely what Elisha wanted to scream down into the stairwell, that it wasn't fair, that his uncle had no business destroying himself, no business finishing the ugly work perpetrated on him by others during "those years."

He called Katrina. Would she go with him to the hospital? She ought to meet Uncle Shaya; he ought to meet her.

Visiting hours were long over when they arrived at the hospital, but Elisha had learned the trick of the resolute stride that inhibits guards from impeding your way. The visitor's room was deserted but for a Filipino orderly splayed on the couch asleep and Aunt Malka staring at the television set high on the wall.

"It's not good," she said solemnly when they entered her peripheral vision but not taking her eyes off the fluttering screen. "He'll be glad you're here."

She turned around and her eyebrows lifted above her reddened eyes when she noticed the young woman at Elisha's side.

"This is my friend Katrina. I wanted Uncle Shaya to meet her."

"Thanks for coming," said Aunt Malka, forgetting to shake Katrina's hand. "He's not exactly spiffed up in his usual best. But he'll be happy to make your acquaintance."

Aunt Malka turned to her nephew and clucked her tongue. "Perhaps you can explain to me what he was doing taking pictures while driving. And on such a treacherous road."

"Pictures?"

"His Polaroid, the latest gadget. Any new toy and he has to own it."

"Where did this happen?"

"Not far from the waterfalls near the bungalow colony. It was already getting dark."

A trip to the falls had been an annual summer highlight. When he was eleven, Elisha found a pearl-inlaid penknife on one of the ravine's jagged cliffs and kept it in his pocket as a souvenir for the next two years; it still had a place of honor in a drawer back home. To reach the falls you had to maneuver down a dirt road, a difficult trail to navigate even without simultaneously manipulating a camera on your steering wheel.

"Don't stay long," Aunt Malka called after Elisha as pushed open the door to the ICU. "He's very weak."

Uncle Shaya was lying still, a network of tubes flowing in and out of his mangled body. "It reminds me of those aerial shots of Los Angeles's intersecting freeways," Elisha whispered to Katrina. They commented on the whiff of formaldehyde in the room but couldn't trace its source. Along the wall, monitoring machines whined an antiseptic hum. Elisha pulled the drape around the three of them—"Like being in a voting booth," he said, with the forced cheerfulness of hospital visitors. Uncle Shaya wiggled a few fingers in greeting.

Elisha introduced Katrina to his uncle. "See?" Elisha said, skimming his hand over his uncle's bandaged feet. "I told you he was the best-dressed one in the family."

"Don't believe anything he says," Uncle Shaya said. He spoke with difficulty, resting for breaths. "Elisha is a chronic storyteller."

"Don't I know?" Katrina said.

"But he does have discerning taste. I'm pleased to meet you, Katrina."

"Discerning, eh?" Elisha said. "Always trying to impress the ladies with the big vocabulary."

Katrina warmed to the easy banter between uncle and nephew and said she'd heard much about Uncle Shaya. She hoped they'd meet again soon in less austere surroundings.

"I almost forgot," said Elisha, trying to regain the lighter mood. "For your discerning taste. Cantor Pinchik." He withdrew a tape from his pocket and put it on top of the unopened hospital dinner on the adjacent table. "But what's with the photography? Dedication to art is one thing, but this is a bit much, don't you think?"

Uncle Shaya motioned for Elisha to come closer and took his nephew's hand in his.

"I took my last shot," Uncle Shaya said, his voice barely audible.

"You wanted this, didn't you?" Elisha said.

"I've always had trouble with rules."

Uncle Shaya grew quiet for a while then pointed to his young visitors. "Root for each other."

"We do," said Katrina.

"Then help him reconcile with his father. I always blame myself for causing them to separate. They need each other."

"I think so, too," Katrina agreed. "And I'll try."

"I'm glad," Uncle Shaya whispered. He tightened his grip on Elisha's hand and closed his eyes. "And you, young man, remember what's important."

Elisha promised he would and left his hand in his uncle's until a peaceful sleep announced it was time to leave.

24

....

We don't see things as they are; we see them as we are.

—Talmud

Elisha was sitting on his bed, his back against the wall, adjusting his radio, ignoring the book on his lap.

Today was his twenty-second birthday. And this week would be nine months since he'd last seen his parents. Three quarters of a year. Long enough to have a child. Long enough to lose one.

He spoke to his mother sporadically on the telephone, but to his father not a word in all this time. The first months of silence had been wrenching. Everywhere he imagined sightings: was that his sister across the street? Mr. Laufer from the shteibl in the grocery aisle? His yeshiva study partner Levi in the front of the bus? Once, during a statistics class, the image of his father's face was so vivid, so pained, Elisha packed his bag and left the room.

He armored himself with distance, forced himself not to listen to Chassidic music, made sure not to read books or movies that referred to events in the Holocaust. He no longer studied Durkheim and topics relating to religion and society; his new focus was the emotionally safer economics of culture. It was working, he told himself. Being alone without family isn't all bad, is it? You develop character.

267

And you gain all this free time. Severing ties to his old world was fine with him. This is what he told himself, what he told Katrina and Trevor. Neither believed him.

For a while, back in the beginning, Katrina urged him to make amends with his parents. "Why suffer like this?" she pleaded. "Just talk to your father. Why be so obstinate?" But Elisha said it was a matter of dignity—he didn't need his past, only his future. "And I'll thank you, Katrina, to please stop suggesting otherwise."

Elisha looked up from his bed and saw Katrina's face leaning into the doorway. She was dangling a rose between her teeth.

"Where's the rest of you?" he asked.

Katrina twirled into the room. "Ta ta. Happy birthday, prince." She held out a package wrapped in blue paper and purple ribbons. She'd tied one of the purple ribbons to her hair. "Here's to twenty-two." She was taking him out for dinner to celebrate. "What's with the radio?"

News from Israel, Elisha said. That morning twelve Israeli soldiers disguised as maintenance staff had stormed a hijacked Sabena Boeing at Lod airport in Tel Aviv and released the 100 people who'd been held hostage. With his arms and fingers, he depicted blazing machine guns.

"A twenty-two-year-old male," Katrina said with a smirk. She handed Elisha the package and the flower. "Here's something less aggressive. A book."

"I've had one of those before. They're wonderful," Elisha said.

Katrina sat down on the chair across the bed. "It's a new translation of *Metamorphosis*. To mark your ongoing metamorphosis."

"I remember the first time you lent me a book by Kafka," Elisha said with a theatrical groan. "It's been a *Trial* ever since."

Katrina brushed her front teeth with the side of her finger…a telltale sign some seriousness was on the way.

"What?" Elisha said.

Katrina took her time before responding. "I want to tell you something before we go out."

Elisha waited.

"I met with your father."

Elisha jolted forward in his bed, his feet reaching the floor.

"You met with my father!"

"I did."

"With my father?" Elisha repeated, enunciating each syllable as though confirming he'd heard correctly. "Without telling me?"

"The day before yesterday."

"This is outrageous."

"If you calm down…"

"Who called whom?" he demanded.

"I called him."

"How could you, Katrina?"

269

"Calm down and I'll explain."

Elisha grabbed a pencil from the nearby desk and twirled it between his fingers. He nervously bounced his leg up and down, his torso rocking slowly front and back. "I can't believe you'd do this. Whose side are you on anyway?"

"I didn't think there were opposing sides here."

Katrina leaned in closer, her voice dropping to match the shrinking distance between them. "You're unhappy, 'Leish. You don't do miserable well. It's ridiculous, you two not speaking with one another."

"That's something for me to decide, don't you think?" Elisha said. His eyes ran through a series of twitches displaying anger, disappointment, fear, and even a sliver of delight. He collected himself. "Okay. Go on. Tell me."

"I want to help, 'Leish."

"Help? That's pretty presumptuous, don't you think?"

"I knew what you'd say if I suggested it. Just listen to you now."

"So you called him."

"I was petrified. I had no idea how he'd react."

"How did he react?" Elisha's heart churned, still angry but curious.

"He recognized my name immediately and asked if everything was all right. He sounded frightened. I mean, why else would I be calling? I assured him you were fine and asked if we could meet. I told him you had no idea about the call."

"And, of course, you know how to get to the house," Elisha said. "Even if it's not a holiday."

Katrina ignored his sarcasm. "A young Chassidic man let me in and asked me to wait a moment. Your father was bringing a tray with beers to some workers on the porch. I heard him say something, I think in Polish, and they all burst out laughing. He was still grinning when he came back into the house, but his expression changed real fast when he saw me.

"I followed him into his office. He kept the door ajar. The young Chassid—he seemed pretty awkward—"

"Zevulun. We call him Zevy. He's my father's assistant of sorts, but it's more like charity. Not someone capable of holding a real job."

"He sat in an alcove outside the room. You're not permitted to be alone in a room with a female not of your immediate family, isn't that right?"

"Correct," Elisha said, and pointedly turned his head toward the closed door behind Katrina.

Katrina said, "You'll be relieved to hear I was dressed appropriately. Skirt down to my knees. Blouse fully buttoned. Shirt sleeves down to my elbows. But I saw your father's eyebrows rise when he glimpsed my sneakers."

"So what did he have to say about me," Elisha asked.

"Actually we didn't talk about you at all. Not at first. He asked about the book sticking out of my backpack."

"*The Gambler?*"

"He thinks Russian literature is wonderful. And he recommended I listen to their music if I wanted to dig even deeper into the Russian soul. 'Make sure though,' he added, 'you balance all this morbidity with something more cheerful.' Your father laughs easily."

"Not like me, huh?" Elisha said.

"You're, shall we say, a bit more intense. Do you know that picture of your family on the shelf in his study? How old were you, eight? You're adorable, but already you have that gravity on your face. This weightiness. And your suit pants are at least two inches above your ankles."

"You *are* observant. Yeah, about eight. I refused to wear a new suit, wedding or no wedding. But Katrina, on with it. You didn't spend the hour talking about Dostoevsky."

Katrina settled back into her chair, her fingers again against her lips. His father had done most of the talking, she said. He assured her that his disappointment was with his son, not with her. That he had no doubt I'd done good things for you. But you had made choices and choices have consequences.

"Consequences? Like what? " Elisha said.

"Your father thinks—this is your father talking, not me—it's ludicrous how people nowadays think they can reject their traditions and still expect to be embraced as if nothing had changed, and even demand everyone respect their decision. 'Discarding one's heritage isn't like choosing between ice-cream flavors,' he said."

"My father thinks I discarded my heritage?"

"I told him how you hadn't. I mentioned the elation that overcomes you when you look into your Talmud and remain lost there for an hour. How despite claiming never to listen to Chassidic music anymore, you do—and when you do, the world around you disappears. I told him about your constant spouting of Chassidic anecdotes and words of wisdom."

"That's not what counts for him."

"No, it isn't. 'It's all very nice,' he said. 'Music, stories, snatches of Torah study, but that's not what's fundamental. There are basic rules. There are limits.' I watched as your father ran his hand down his beard so slowly I thought it would be nightfall before he reached the bottom. He looked up at me and said, 'And, I'm afraid, beyond friendship, you, Katrina, are beyond the limit.'"

Elisha stopped fidgeting and gripped his pencil tight in his hands. His eyes were wide and unblinking. "And what did you say?"

"I wasn't sure what to say. I wasn't going to get into a theological discussion about the essentials of Judaism. But I said that we were only good friends. Two twenty-two-year-olds not thinking about life-long commitments."

"Only good friends?" Elisha said.

"What did you want me to say?"

"Is that how you see us?"

"You know very well I see us as more than that."

Elisha searched her eyes for confirmation of her words. He thought he saw it and nodded his head, relieved.

Katrina said, "And I told him about my leaving for Oxford."

"He must have been pleased to hear that."

"I don't know. He said it would be hard for you. We talked about your sensitivity and the veneer of disinterest you try to hide it with."

"Spare me."

"I said I was certain your tie to tradition was more than sentimentality. That it reflected who you are, your deepest roots. And I told him you missed him terribly."

"You said that?" Elisha said, alarmed.

"I did." Katrina lifted her chin defiantly.

Elisha stood up, paced across the room a few times, then landed leaning against the far wall. "Why would you say that?"

"Because you *do* miss him terribly."

Elisha went silent for an entire endless minute. "How did you leave it?" he asked.

"Unresolved, I guess. I said surely there was some way for the two of you to work something out, for him to let you back into his life."

"What makes you think I want that?" Elisha shouted.

Katrina gave him a long, unflinching look then turned away. She picked up where she'd let off. "Because you do. Your father thanked me for coming and walked me to the door. Before I left he asked me if I'd ever heard of the Baal Shem Tov, the founder of Chassidism. I told him I had.

He took two long breaths. He said a man once asked the Baal Shem Tov what to do about his son who had strayed from the path of Torah. The Baal Shem Tov answered: 'Love him more.' Your father tilted his head to the side and brushed his eyes with the back of his hand, then turned back to me. 'The problem is this,' he said to me, a whisper so broken it made me shiver. 'The problem is I don't know how to love Elisha more than I do. And do you know why? It's because I don't think it's possible for a father to love a son more than I love him.'"

Elisha was swaying slowly on the balls of his feet, his eyes fixed on the ground.

Katrina said, "I wish I could have held your father, comforted him. Me comfort him? When I'm the problem."

"You're not the problem," Elisha said quietly. "You know that."

"Or comfort you," Katherine said, and walked over to Elisha.

"I don't need comforting," Elisha said. "I'm fine."

Katrina held him anyway. "I needed to tell you beforehand. Not have it lodged in my esophagus all night. It's done. Now let's go celebrate your birthday."

25

....

I did not travel to Reb Dov Ber of Mezeritzch to study Torah, but to observe how he fastens his shoes. For it is in a man's actions that his Torah is manifested.
—Reb Leib Saras

Raymond was complaining again about his daughter. "I don't get her," he said, across the untouched chessboard.

Elisha offered a sympathetic mumble. His mind was elsewhere.

"You're her chess tutor. Maybe you understand how that girl thinks."

"Well, you know how teenage girls are..." Elisha answered in a wooden monotone. He'd spent the morning shopping for luggage with Katrina and had been sullen the rest of the day.

"Is everything all right?" Raymond asked. "You're staring off into space."

"I'm fine," Elisha said, and he had been, until this morning when he was reminded of Katrina's looming departure, three months to the day. A recurrent stomach pain had gripped him all day. And he'd again felt a humid sweep of loneliness wash over him, a loneliness of the worst kind...self-imposed, imagined, and unnecessary. He coughed into his fist and turned toward Raymond. "You were saying?"

"Why does my daughter seem so distant, so unappreciative?" And he was so attentive to her, he said. Wasn't he meticulous about not missing their scheduled time together?

Her name was Aurora. Living proof, Raymond once bragged to Elisha, that already fifteen years earlier he'd been thinking cosmically. But Aurora told Elisha her mom said it was her idea, in remembrance of a night under the Northern California stars. Raymond and his wife had separated two years ago.

"I always remember to tell her I love her," Raymond said. "Regularly."

"Regularly?"

"Yes, parents should regularly say I love you to a child."

"Like on a schedule? Maybe that's the problem."

Elisha had been tutoring Aurora several months and her progress was astounding. She was precocious, clever…and angry. "I love my father and all," she fumed in a teenage froth, "but if only just once, just friggin' once, he held me without being so damned proud of himself for being—how does he put it—'so connected.' I don't want him to 'connect' to me because it's the goddamned right thing to do."

Elisha understood her frustration. He'd observed Raymond interact with his daughter, the stiff hugs and studied declarations of affection.

Elisha sat back in his chair and looked straight at Raymond. A thought crossed his mind and a smile crossed his face.

"I was once in a store with my father, and we noticed that sign that you sometimes see, YOU BREAK IT, YOU OWN IT. My father said to me, 'You know, that's where stories are different. With a story, you fix it, you own it.'"

"Your point?"

"Do you like stories, Raymond?"

"Sure."

"Good. I have one for you. One I'm about to own. It's about a Chassidic rebbe, an ancestor of mine. It might help. Did I ever tell you I'm a descendent of Chassidic rebbes?

"No, but I suspected something like that."

"Sure you did."

"You have this ancient aura."

"It seeps out sometimes, I guess. So here's this ancient tale."

Reb Mordkhe of Chernobyl stood at his window and looked out at the raging storm. A gust of wind crashed into an already pummeled tree; the young birch teetered above a pile of branches strewn on the ground below. Reb Mordkhe thought of his community and the battering they'd been undergoing these past months. The crops had failed, and heavy snows made trade impossible. This had been the worst year in a string of worst years.

The Chernobyl tzaddik trudged to his study and sunk heavily into his chair. His own home was destitute as well. When was the last time his family had enjoyed a full meal? It was their deprivation and the poverty of his community that saddened him, not his own. For the tzaddik drew his nourishment from the sweet nectar of Torah—the pangs of hunger evaporating in the rapture of performing a mitzvah. But something else was causing the shadow of distress to cross his holy visage.

The holiday of Succos would begin that evening, and for the first time Reb Mordkhe would not be able to consecrate the holiday with his own *esrog*, the mandatory citron. Due to the acute shortage, the cost of this fruit was far beyond the budget of the penniless tzaddik. The Jews of Chernobyl had purchased an esrog for their communal use: each congregant would recite the benediction before passing it on to his neighbor. The tzaddik always looked forward to performing the blessing over the esrog with full Kabbalistic intentions, and without his own esrog, this year's benedictions would be rushed and unfulfilling.

But brooding was sinful, was it not? Did he not teach his followers that when a Jew wholeheartedly desires to perform a good deed, the Heavens come to his aid? Sitting quietly in his chair, Reb Mordkhe of Chernobyl prayed that somehow this year, too, he'd sanctify the mitzvah with all his Chassidic fervor.

In the next room, his wife, the Chernobyler Rebbetzin, formed a prayer of her own. She stood in the kitchen and surveyed the bare breadbasket and empty cupboards. The coffer was now void of a single kopeck. Last week her daughter had asked for money for a new dress. She was a young woman of marriageable age and her single holiday outfit was torn beyond repair. The rebbe explained he'd given away his last rubles to someone poorer still. "As you are the scion of a notable family," he said to his daughter, "you are special enough—clothes and accessories, none of this will matter." The valiant girl had tears in her eyes, but she never spoke again about a new outfit. The rebbetzin scratched at her neck as she recalled the sobs from her children too hungry to sleep. How much more of this desperation could she withstand? From where would help come?

The rebbe did, in fact, own one possession of great value: the tefillin of the holy Baal Shem Tov he'd inherited from his father of blessed memory. The rebbetzin had pleaded with Reb Mordkhe to sell the precious phylacteries or at least offer them as security for a loan with which to buy some food. The rebbe had exclaimed, "You ask me to part with the tefillin of the holy Baal Shem Tov? And for what? Carrots? A glass of milk? Heaven forbid." And so, standing in the kitchen, the rebbetzin dropped her head into her hands and quietly entreated God to provide a few coins for the purchase of a meal for the upcoming holiday.

She was still absorbed in her prayers when she heard a knock on the door. A well-dressed stranger clutching a small blue box stepped inside. "Could I please see the rebbe?" he asked. The rebbetzin pointed to the tzaddik's room and watched the visitor march into the study and shut the door. Here was the answer to her supplication and so quickly, too: for surely the gentleman had come to ask the tzaddik for his blessing and would leave a few kopecks in appreciation. For the first time in so many months her tear-stained eyes shone with hope.

The rebbetzin waited impatiently for the guest to reemerge, the ten minutes an eternity. At last he reappeared, smiling and hurrying to the front door, stopping momentarily to wish her a festive holiday. He no longer carried the blue box but a small black package. A flicker of dread brushed through the rebbetzin's body. Regaining her optimism she hurried to her husband's study to collect the donation. There was still time to buy food for the holiday.

Reb Mordkhe was standing in the middle room looking more radiant than she'd seen him in weeks.

"Look, look," he exclaimed, and brought her to where an esrog lay unwrapped on the shelf. "A true beauty." He picked up the citron and delicately placed it on his desk. "Note the rich yellow color, not a blemish to be found, not the slightest puncture. Have you ever seen an esrog so perfectly proportioned, like a tower, wide at the bottom, narrower at the top and with a ring in the middle? Magnificent. So you see, the Master of the Universe did not abandon me after all. The holiday is to begin in a few hours, and He sends someone to sell me an esrog so I can perform the mitzvah with all the necessary zeal."

The rebbetzin's heart froze when she heard the word *sell*. "Sell implies buy," she said. "We don't have a kopeck in the house."

The tzaddik replied, "True, but thank Heaven this man was willing to accept the tefillin of the Baal Shem Tov in lieu of money. I bartered the tefillin for the esrog."

The rebbetzin's entire body convulsed in a surging fury. She ground her teeth and shouted, "We don't have money to buy medicine for our children. The soles of their shoes are thin as wafers. Tonight is Succos, and we can't afford a fresh vegetable. When I ask you to sell the tefillin to feed the family, you refuse to even consider the matter. And now...now you go and exchange the cherished tefillin for an esrog!"

The tzaddik cast a look at the esrog on the table and couldn't contain his delight with his transaction. Seeing his joy, the rebbetzin could restrain her rage no longer and hurled the esrog with all her might across the room. "The tefillin for an esrog but not food for the children?" she shrieked.

The rebbe's elation evaporated in horror as the esrog crashed against the far wall. With frightful apprehension, he rushed to where it lay on the ground. His hands quivered as he picked up the fruit and stared at the damage. The Chernobyl Tzaddik turned pale; it

26

....

A man is what he is, not what he used to be.

—Yiddish proverb

"Elisha?"

"Yes."

"Avrumy."

"Avrumy!" Why would his brother call him? "Is everything okay with Tateh and Mommy?"

"They're fine," Avrumy said. "But…"

Elisha listened to the news and slowly hung up the phone.

He picked it up again and called Katrina. She was surprised to hear his voice. He'd been there only an hour before.

"My uncle died. Uncle Shaya."

"I'm sorry."

"The funeral is tomorrow morning in Brooklyn. 8 a.m."

"You'd better get some sleep."

"I'm not going."

"What do you mean you're not going? You have to go."

"I can't."

"Why not?"

"I can't face all these people. After all this time. Not all at once."

"'Leish, this is your uncle Shaya's funeral. How could you not be there? You of all people?"

"I just can't do it."

She couldn't believe what he was saying. "I'd even go along if I didn't think it would be a distraction. It would only make things worse."

"That it would. But it's a moot point. 'Cause I'm not…"

"It's not right," Katrina said.

Elisha greeted daybreak with his second coffee of the morning. He'd been up all night and waited a half hour for the luncheonette to open. But now it was time to go. He glanced at the mirror and almost didn't recognize himself in the black suit. He straightened his collar and tightened his tie. The day already felt surreal.

It took Elisha nearly twenty minutes to walk the four blocks from the train station to the funeral home. He steadied himself as he entered the chapel. Should he enter? All night he'd pictured Uncle Shaya smiling at him, calm and unhurried. How could he not?

Every seat was already taken. Just as well. He preferred standing where he was, in the rear, against the wall.

A stream of Chassidic rebbes was eulogizing Uncle Shaya, extolling his Torah scholarship and piety. But Elisha's attention was drawn to the familiar faces in the crowd: cousins he hadn't seen in years, old friends of the family. The entire shteibl seemed to be in attendance. In the women's section, his grandmother sat motionlessly, one hand gripping the arm of his aunt Malka, the other holding the arm of Elisha's mother. His sister Deena, shorn of her childlike playfulness, sat in the row behind them. He heard his father called to the podium.

His father began to speak in a voice so low, so shattered no one beyond five rows could hear him. "Shaya, Shaya, Shaya," he wailed.

Did anyone in the room know as Elisha did how these two men adored one another? How deep was their mutual respect?

"I never saw a tear in my brother-in-law's eyes," his father said, his voice broken, but loud enough now to clear the length of the room. "I asked Reb Shaya about this once. And he told me that in the concentration camps people worried not that they'd never again be able to laugh if they survived, but that they'd never again cry. And Reb Shaya couldn't. The Kotsker Rebbe said, 'What is the greatest human crisis? When a person has a reason to cry, wants to cry, but cannot cry.' Shaya lived in permanent crisis."

Elisha's father paused for what seemed an interminable length but continued. "I must tell you all, however, there was also so much joy in Reb Shaya, peace be on his soul. The Psalmist says, 'They who sow with tears, with joy shall reap.' Our Chassidic sages teach us to punctuate the comma so the verse reads, 'They who sow with tears, with joy, shall reap.' A life is whole when it is made of both tears and joy. This was Shaya's life."

They carried the casket down the street to the waiting cars, the immediate family directly behind, the other mourners following. Elisha's father began to hum a melody that soon spread throughout the crowd. It was the threnody Uncle Shaya sang when he led services in the shteibl each year on the anniversary of his father's death. Uncle Shaya had heard his father sing the tune as he led a group of his Chassidim to the gas chamber. Elisha found his mother, kissed her on the cheek, and greeted his grandmother and Aunt Malka. He bid them be strong; in Elisha's branch of Chassidism, women did not go to the cemetery for the burial of the dead.

He sat quietly during the entire ride to the cemetery, looking out the car window at the passing exit signs of the New Jersey highway. It was still morning.

His father was standing at the open grave site when Elisha walked up to wait his turn for the shovel. They nodded at each other, and Elisha brushed away the tear that rushed his eye. He poured wet earth into the open grave then stood to the side and watched the wooden casket disappear under the fresh mound. He shuddered as Uncle Shaya's son Yankel recited the kaddish; the boy would celebrate his bar mitzvah next month as an orphan.

Elisha walked a few steps away and lowered his head. He had a kaddish for his uncle as well. A kaddish for a man whose disobedience Elisha sometimes confused as his own. A kaddish for the one who taught him stupidity and fear were far worse than inconsistency. A kaddish for his uncle he never did understand, but who thankfully understood him.

Elisha looked up and saw his father leaning on a nearby stone, swaying slowly with the wind. Elisha took in a long breath, then another, and walked toward him.

"Tateh."

"Elisha'le."

"Can I speak with you?"

"Of course." His father signaled to others to go on without him. He'd find his way home on his own.

Elisha had rehearsed his words the entire night before. How he was sorry for the pain he caused, but there was no other way. How he loved them but also needed his independence. But nothing now came. Not a word. Not a sound.

Elisha looked into his father's eyes and broke into uncontrollable sobs. He put his arms around his father's chest and his head on his shoulder. He cried as if the dam of his soul had burst.

"Tateh, Tateh, I'm trying to get it right. To be as honest as I can. I'm exhausted from trying. It's all so complicated."

"Don't I know?" his father said, tenderly stroking the back of his son's neck. "You're way ahead of me. When I was twenty-two, I thought I understood everything. Come, let's walk."

Arm in arm, father and son weaved through the cemetery, the silent graves respectfully granting them their privacy.

Elisha's father stopped in front of a headstone. Sheindel Rosengarten, the name said. Born in 1897, died in 1953. Who was she?

His father said he'd rented lodging in her apartment for a few months when he first arrived in America. A wonderful woman. "I began writing a book in that room," he said. "Under a pseudonym, of course."

"What was it about?"

"About a young man growing up in the shtetl. The possibilities that came his way. The ones he took, the ones he rejected. It wasn't very good. I tore it up and threw the pieces into a trash can."

"That's terrible. You should've kept it."

"But why? Do you know that in his last years the Kotsker Rebbe would summarize his year's thoughts on a single page then burn the paper together with his unleavened bread the day before Passover. Once, only once, did he permit his dearest student, the Rebbe of Ger, to read what he wrote."

"And what did it say?"

"That's what all the Chassidim begged the Gerer Rebbe to reveal. But all the rebbe would say was, 'My teacher wrote what he wrote.'"

Elisha laughed, delighting in the whimsy of Chassidic lore, a part of the tradition so few recognized. He laughed at the thought of Kafka hearing that story and deciding to destroy his own work as well. But he laughed mostly with the joy of hearing his father's sweet, vintage anecdotes as they walked alone, together.

Elisha told his father about his studies in anthropology, his frustration with the small-mindedness of its most celebrated professors, his awe of the brilliant few. His father told him he'd almost completed the book he'd been working on for years, the one he *would* publish, a collection of responses to queries sent to him dealing with contemporary Jewish law. They talked politics. His father now better appreciated the younger generation's complaint about the war, but still disagreed with their methods of protest. They talked about family: Zaidy's terminal illness, Avrumy's developing maturity, his sister's talent for impersonating relatives and her teachers.

The conversation hovered over, skirted near, and finally landed on Elisha's relationship with Katrina.

"I can't approve," his father said. "You understand that."

"I do," Elisha said.

"She visited me. As you probably know."

"Yes. I was upset with her."

"You shouldn't be. She did it for you. She's a wonderful young lady."

Elisha told his father how much he'd learned from her, sparing his father the physical details. He said he was torn up by the thought of her leaving. He didn't want to lose her. He wasn't sure what he'd do. Perhaps he'd apply to school in England. And that Katrina—of her own accord—was studying Judaism.

"It's been so rich," Elisha said. "Intoxicating, sometimes. But it's easy to fool yourself. I know feelings change when people are that far away from one another."

"That might happen," his father agreed. "But often the best things in one's life are like that. Bittersweet."

They walked on, without words, without direction, for many minutes, neither father nor son wanting to take leave of the other. Eventually they found themselves at the taxi stand at the gate of the cemetery. It was time to go home.

Elisha's father said, "Did I ever tell you about this urge I had as a boy to look at the Kohanim during the blessing?"

"You, Tateh?"

"Everyone must have that desire, though I suspect mine was stronger than most. I have this streak of curiosity, as I bet you've noticed."

"Did you peek?"

"No, I didn't. Perhaps if I had, other mischief might have followed. You break through one fence, why not another?"

"I did peek," Elisha said.

"Oh, I know. It was on the holiday of Succos."

"How did—"

"I watched you. From under my talis."

"But you never said anything."

"Why should I have said anything? Part of me was proud of you. Of your curiosity. I still am."

"You are?" Elisha asked, but his broad smile said he knew it was true.

His father put his hand on Elisha's shoulder. "We missed you at the Seder," he said.

Elisha looked away at the ground.

"There was a seat waiting at the table for you."

"I know."

"Always. Always." Then his father grinned. "You can come as the wise son."

"I'll come," Elisha said. "I'll be visiting. Often. Wise or foolish."

"We'll take what we can get," his father said, and grinned again. "But would it kill you to get a haircut?"

Elisha kissed his father's face. He let his cheek linger against his father's flowing beard.

Nowhere in the universe felt as safe.

Acknowledgments

Several years ago, I was rummaging in the closet of my childhood home in Boro Park and came upon a box filled with typewritten Chassidic stories. These were the tales my father wrote and read on the Yiddish radio station WEVD back in the 1950s and 1960s. The program was called *Chassidim Dertzaylin,* which translates to something like Chassidim Recount or Chassidim Retell. Since my father's death fifteen years ago, I'd wanted to translate these tales from the Yiddish and rework them for a broader non-Chassidic audience.

This book began as a collection of some of those Chassidic stories to which I added my own counter-stories from the modern world along with a loosely drawn protagonist toggling between the two worlds to provide the narrative's thin spine. But this did not a novel make. I was lucky, however, to have a Starbucks on my corner and a neighbor, the wonderful writer Tova Mirvis, who, like me, turned the coffee shop into an office for several hours a day. Tova insisted that I'd find a genuine novel lurking if I pressed these stories into the service of a larger narrative (rather than the other way around); I resisted, she prodded…and whatever novelistic success this book achieves traces to her early encouragement and advice.

My deep appreciation goes, as well, to my incisive, indefatigable agent, Carol Mann, who rallied behind a first novel and landed the book on the desk of Hillel Black at

Sourcebooks. With his long-honed editorial experience and fresh vigor, Hillel badgered, cajoled, advised, and taught me to "operate without anesthesia," in ridding the text of anything that stood in the way of the story. I'm indebted beyond words to his supererogatory attention to both detail and the larger picture as well as to his overall literary wisdom. My profound thanks, too, to the ever-helpful, ever-keen Ted Carmichael and Stephen O'Rear and the other pioneering staff at Sourcebooks.

Friends read and commented on earlier parts of this long-simmering book, among them, Rabbi Irwin Kula, Joshua Neustein, Nancy Schwartz-Weinstock, and Peter Silverman. Thank you all. My mother—may she live to 120—continues to regale me with the intricate histories of our Chassidic dynasties and her insights resonate throughout the text. I'm so grateful, as well, to my daughter Ariana who read the entire draft with her incisive, filmic eye and offered terrific suggestions, and to my son Amitai for unsheathing his honest and helpful responses to the stories I retold no doubt too often. And, as always, my abiding appreciation to my wife Yocheved who lived with me and this book with her usual majestic patience and intelligence and provided her usual extraordinary critical reading of the manuscript. What a gift to have her at my side.

The book is dedicated to my father, of blessed memory. It gives me comfort to know that he would see below the surface story line to the underlying celebration of the Chassidic spirit that propels this book and its author. Some might find this novel an odd way to continue his legacy, but I'm convinced he would not be among them.

And, finally, I need to emphasize that this is a work of fiction. It is not my story nor are its characters stand-ins for real individuals. On the other hand, what is more real to us than our own fictional worlds?

Reading Group Guide

How do you think Uncle Shaya, who reconciles the religious and the secular in a very unique and individual way, influences Elisha's behavior and growth throughout the novel? Does Elisha completely follow Uncle Shaya's path, and, if not, how is Elisha's faith different than his uncle's?

Shaya demonstrates his unique faith when he finds Elisha with a copy of *Tropic of Cancer*. What do you think of his reaction, and his assertion that "even a holy body is still a body"?

Elisha's family believes that Manhattan is a seductive world of alien values. Nevertheless, Elisha embraces what his community calls a "forbidden territory." Have you ever dared to trespass into a world alone, with no support from family or friends? How do you think this journey changed Elisha?

How does the tradition of Chassidic storytelling illuminate the relationship between Elisha and his father?

Throughout the novel, Elisha is torn between his rich heritage and his desire to cast off the weight of hundreds of years of tradition. Have you ever ignored or gone against a family tradition? How did this feel? Do you think Elisha completely loses touch with his family's ancestral faith when he chooses to move out?

Katrina displays an avid curiosity to learn about the conventions and responsibilities of Chassidism. Do you think she is inquisitive simply because she wants to know Elisha better? Or does the Chassidic faith resonate with her in a deeper and more personal way?

Elisha's family and community have a very different, much more reverent and all-encompassing faith than mainstream America. Do you think Elisha's choice to not adhere to his faith with the same strictness and obedience as his family reflects a larger societal drift from religion? Do you think religion's influence on our everyday lives is shrinking or growing in America?

Do you think Shaya's unique approach to Judaism influences Elisha to reconnect with his father? Or does Shaya's premature death signal the dangers of his unorthodox opinions and warn Elisha of the dangers of straying too far from his original faith?

A loving parent holds his child's happiness as a foremost priority. But a loving parent also intervenes when that child strays in a dangerous direction. Elisha's father lovingly attempts to protect his son and reinvigorate his connection to Chassidism. Do you think Elisha's father's attempts to guide his son are overbearing, or that he deals with his son's changing beliefs as a thoughtful parent should? Do you think Elisha's father is asking too much when he lets Elisha know he does not want him to marry outside the faith?

Oftentimes it appears that a change in scenery helps Elisha resolve his own internal conflicts. Have you ever found that taking a vacation or going on an unplanned journey helps you think through your own ideas and attitudes?

Why do you think Katrina patiently respects Elisha's sexual development over the course of many months yet severs her fidelity towards him the same moment he finally finds peace with his decision to love her?

Uncle Shaya explains, "Freedom in America is in its own way a major threat to the Jewish people. Not that we don't appreciate it or want it otherwise. But it's a danger." What do you think he means? Do you agree?

For Elisha, when one "fixes" a story, one owns it. Do you ever purposefully embellish stories you tell for your audience? Do you think embellishing a supposedly "true" story is always simply a lie, or can it serve a positive purpose?

About the Author

photo by Dennis DiChiaro

Joshua Halberstam has published on a wide variety of topics, including philosophy, education, culture, and religion. His previous books include *Everyday Ethics: Inspired Solutions to Everyday Dilemmas*; *Work: Making a Living and Making a Life*; and *Schmoozing: The Private Conversations of American Jews*. He studied at the Rabbinical Academy of America and received his PhD in philosophy from New York University. He has taught at NYU and TC-Columbia University and currently teaches at BCC of the City University of New York.

Mr. Halberstam is a descendant of prominent Chassidic dynasties from both his mother's and father's side—his grandfather was among the first Chassidic Rebbes in New York. This is his first novel.

A SEAT AT THE TABLE

A NOVEL OF FORBIDDEN CHOICES

JOSHUA HALBERSTAM

SOURCEBOOKS LANDMARK™
AN IMPRINT OF SOURCEBOOKS, INC.®
NAPERVILLE, ILLINOIS

Copyright © 2009 by Joshua Halberstam
Cover and internal design © 2009 by Sourcebooks, Inc.
Cover design by Stewart Williams
Cover illustration by Stewart Williams

Sourcebooks and the colophon are registered trademarks of Sourcebooks, Inc.

Published by Sourcebooks Landmark, an imprint of Sourcebooks, Inc.
P.O. Box 4410, Naperville, Illinois 60567-4410
(630) 961-3900
Fax: (630) 961-2168
www.sourcebooks.com

Library of Congress Cataloging-in-Publication Data

Halberstam, Joshua
   A seat at the table : a novel of forbidden choices / Joshua Halberstam.
       p. cm.
   I. Title.
   PS3608.A54564S43 2009
   813'.6--dc22

                                    2008026344

              Printed and bound in the United States of America
                     CHG 10 9 8 7 6 5 4 3 2 1